THEIR CONFESSION

The Black Door Trilogy, Book Three

By S. Valentine

THEIR CONFESSION

Limitless Publishing, LLC
Kailua, HI 96734
www.limitlesspublishing.com

Formatting: Limitless Publishing

ISBN-13: 978-1-64034-063-3
ISBN-10: 1-64034-063-7

Dedication

To the readers.

Author's Note

Please note that safe sex is practised by all persons throughout this novel, unless otherwise stated.

Chapter One

Gabi

Present day

Gabi had a feeling things were about to change for the worst, and soon. She picked up her glass and drained the last of her champagne. She hadn't visited The Black Door club in months. Shifting on the leather couch, she took in her surroundings. It had been completely refurbished. The décor, which used to be red, was now all black, from the marble tables and sofas, to the carpet. The room was bathed in a fluorescent violet light, which reflected off the mirrored walls. Rather than it being glamorous and elegant with chandeliers and red interior, it now had a cool, modern vibe. It was the perfect place for a liberated and sexually adventurous crowd to mingle.

As she observed the twenty-something-year-old women on the dance floor, wearing the skimpiest clothes she'd ever seen, and flirtatiously flicking back their hair, she swallowed. Men, with hunger on their faces, and nothing but pleasure on their minds, scanned the room, like predators on their prey. Everywhere she looked, she was surrounded by beauty, by adventurous people eager to satisfy and be pleasured. Nothing was off limits. No one was out of reach.

When she had first approached the club, especially the gentlemen's club downstairs, she had been filled with warmth. Memories of how she and Darion first met had flashed in her mind. The second she had seen him up close, she had been physically attracted to him. His mysterious, seductive aura had drawn her in.

Now as she watched him standing near the bar, a glass of whisky in hand, deep in conversation with the new owner, butterflies formed in her stomach. The butterflies weren't from desire, longing, and the need to be close to him. They were from a feeling of unease. She wasn't stupid. He was hiding something.

When he turned his head, she saw the flash of fear cross his face. As usual, he provided her with a slow, saccharine smile, complete with a dangerous twinkle in his eye. He downed the last of his drink, excused himself from his companion, and made his way toward her. Every single woman he passed stopped what they were doing to admire him. Gabi didn't miss the small grins on their faces, the way they nudged the person next to them, stopped talking, or held their drinks in mid-air. Gabi was used to the attention Darion received.

As much as the club brought back some pleasant memories, it also reminded her of the bad times, the evenings when Darion wanted to explore the playrooms. He had introduced Gabi to the world of swinging, and wanted nothing more than to reveal her kinky side, make her lose her inhibitions and become the woman he thought he craved. But Gabi wasn't that woman. She would never be that woman. Surrounded by voyeurs, exhibitionists, fetishists, sadomasochists, masochists, and whatever else she was unfamiliar with, she'd felt way out of her depth. The curious side of her had her succumbing to the playrooms, until her identity was stripped and she no longer recognised herself.

She had expected Darion to seek someone new, someone with the same desires he had when she'd admitted she couldn't participate in the rooms again. Instead, he'd declared his love and shocked her by stating he wanted to turn his back on that lifestyle and sell the club.

A small part of her knew he missed this once fun, spontaneous life. Had he returned to it secretly and betrayed her? An acidic feeling persisted in her stomach, and her throat ached with the urge to vomit. When Darion gracefully lowered himself next to her, and placed a hand on her knee, her spine stiffened. His usually confident demeanour, his care-free attitude had been replaced by fiddling hands, eyes that constantly flittered around the room, and a tongue that kept licking lips to moisten them. Gabi knew a scared man when she saw one. Or was it a guilty man?

"Are you sure you're okay?" she asked for what seemed like the tenth time that evening.

"Yes, Gabi."

His hand slid higher up her thigh, causing her to close her eyes for a split second. Lust took over her, as heat spread through her body, making her heart race frantically. Darion was now so close she could feel the warmth of his breath on her lips, could smell the scent of whisky, and feel the heat radiating from him. His lips met hers. She was reluctant to respond at first. As his full mouth became possessive, greedy, and his tongue slipped in, she knew she'd lost the battle. As usual, she could never resist temptation when it came to Darion Milano.

His hands cupped her face, and the kiss became deeper. Gabi sunk into the sofa further, and as she massaged his tongue with firm, leisurely licks, she wrapped her arms around him. It was as if no one else in the room existed but them. She melted into his touch, wishing they could kiss for hours without being disturbed. She was content when he cradled her in his big, protective arms, and giddy when he placed a kiss against her temple. She felt loved when he whispered those three words in her ear.

Then her perfect little bubble burst. She was certain Darion's body tensed before he shifted slightly away. Daring to glance over her shoulder, there she was. Gina. Gabi didn't get a chance to say hello, as Darion shot to his feet, and welcomed her with a tight smile. Then the rest of the party arrived: Lexi, Marnie, Wendy, Tiana, Lennie, Travis, and other people that had once worked with Darion— one big happy reunion.

Gabi plastered on a grin and greeted them all. It was only when the crowd, except for Gina, went to the bar to order drinks, that she sensed the animosity between Gina and Darion. The tension in the air was so thick you could cut it with a knife. Gina slumped on the seat farthest away. Neither seemed about to strike up conversation.

Gabi observed them suspiciously. Shouldn't Darion be happy to see Gina? After all, he hadn't seen her for months. Normally so flirty with one another, playful and touchy feely, they seemed strained and made polite chit chat. Perhaps there were still unresolved issues between them, unfinished business. Maybe Gina still held a torch for Darion.

"So, Gina, how have you been?"

"As good as can be given the circumstances."

Oh. "Is your mom okay?"

"She's fine."

"And London?"

"Busy." She blew her blonde hair out of her face.

Gabi crossed one leg over the other and reached for her drink. Had she done something to offend Gina? Taking a long swig of her drink, she placed her glass on the table, and lifted the champagne bottle. "Want some?"

"I thought you'd never ask."

Gabi filled the glass in Gina's outstretched hand. She couldn't help but notice it was shaking slightly. Gina gulped back the drink, and held her glass out for a refill. Gabi topped it up. Gina's eyes, usually full of life and confidence, were glazed over, and she appeared sad. Lost. Helpless.

"Is Gina okay?" she whispered, leaning into Darion's ear.

"She's obviously just had one too many." Darion seemed disinterested as he averted his gaze.

Gabi bit her lip in confusion. Since when had Darion stopped caring for Gina? When an uncomfortable silence loomed upon them, Gabi couldn't hold her tongue any longer.

"Well, this is awkward."

"What do you mean?" Darion asked, staring at her incredulously.

"Correct me if I'm wrong, but you haven't seen one another in months, and yet you have nothing to talk about."

When Gina snorted, followed by a smirk, Gabi's eyes widened. "Gina, have you got something to say?"

She shrugged a shoulder. "No, but I'm sure Darion has."

"What's going on?"

"Nothing is going on. Enjoy the evening." Darion leant back in his seat, and took a sip of his whisky. His intense stare was on the bar, as if mentally pleading Lexi, Marnie, and the others to intervene.

"Don't patronise me, Darion." She turned to Gina again. "What's wrong? You can tell me anything. Maybe I can help." They weren't the best of friends, but neither were they enemies.

Gina's eyes welled up with tears, and within minutes, she was sobbing hysterically. Gabi clasped a hand to her chest, completely taken aback. She couldn't remember ever seeing Gina's vulnerable side before. It must have been serious. Darion rubbed his palms up and down his face, clearly uncomfortable, and let out an exasperated sigh.

"Gina, not here. We discussed this," he said firmly.

"You discussed what?" Gabi spluttered, turning to face him. "You didn't tell me you'd been in contact with her."

Why would he hide that fact? *Oh God. Please no.* Her chest tightened. Her breathing suspended for a second as she became lost for words. She prayed Darion and Gina hadn't been having an affair. Surely he wouldn't do that to her. Not after everything they had been through. But what if they had? What if Darion wanted to break things off with Gina? Or what if he wanted to end his relationship with her *for* Gina?

"Gina, what's going on?" she managed to ask when she'd gathered her wits. Out of the corner of her eye, she could see Lexi, Marnie, Tiana, Eva, and Wendy were now collecting their drinks. They would soon be on the way over. "Gina?" she repeated.

Gina eventually stopped crying and wiped her face. She smoothed her blonde locks down, and looked at Darion. "I knew you wouldn't tell her," she said, her voice shaky with emotion.

Darion turned to Gabi. For the first time she could see his expression was full of lies, deceit, panic, and fear. He wasn't the man she knew. It was as if he were a stranger sitting before her.

Gabi's limbs trembled slightly, as she became fearful of what she was about to be told. The last confession of Darion's was that he led the life of a swinger. She couldn't take another confession. She had a feeling it was much worse. The unsettling feeling in her gut made her believe this was something of an entirely different nature.

"Gabi..." Darion began. She saw his Adam's apple dip as he swallowed. His eyes were now glistening, whether with tears or from the light, she had no idea. "I'm so sorry."

Gabi abruptly pushed herself to her feet. *No. No. No.*

"Me and Gina..." As his lips moved, Gabi failed to hear the words coming out. It was as if time had frozen, and she was momentarily paralysed, having lost her ability to hear, to move, to speak, to understand. She blinked rapidly. She needed to hear it again. She *had* to hear it again. Although, deep down, she knew she didn't want to hear the confession at all.

Chapter Two

Gabi

Two months earlier

"Darion!" Gabi slapped his hand away, preventing him from groping her breast. "Behave."

"Never," he said, a slow mischievous smile forming on his face.

"You promised you'd help me choose a dress for Thursday."

"No. I promised I'd watch you get *undressed* a dozen times."

She shook her head, slightly amused. "Swap this for a size ten." She shoved a dress at him, and yanked the curtain shut, blocking his view of her in the changing room. She heard the sound of footsteps as he left the room.

Gabi swiveled around and looked down at the pile of clothes at her feet. One of her colleagues had secured a new job, and so the majority of the staff at Millers & Co Publishers were going for drinks on

Thursday night. She was actually looking forward to it. Usually, Gabi declined staff outings, always making up excuses. Outside of an office environment, she was unsure of what to talk to her colleagues about. Mallory, however, had pleaded with her to join in the celebration. Mallory was no stranger to a good night out, or one to turn down a shot of tequila and a dance floor.

"Size ten." Darion handed her a dress.

"Thanks."

"Gabi." He poked his head around the curtain. His devilish eyes gleamed at her, a wicked smile surfacing on his face. "Let me come inside."

"No way. I come to this shop all of the time. I'm not risking it, Darion."

Her words were muffled as he pressed his lips firmly against hers. His tongue massaged her own, sucking, licking, and circling the tip around it greedily, with such urgency. The coldness of the mirror spread through her buttocks as she was pressed against it. Groaning into her mouth, Darion's hands were in her hair, and then fondling her breasts. She closed her lids, and her head rolled back, a soft sigh escaping her lips. Her nipples tingled and hardened as he caressed them through the flimsy material of her bra. Heat flooded her pelvic region when he ground his erection against her. Grabbing hold of his fit, firm ass, she pulled him into her and claimed his lips again.

"You…need…to…get…out," she said in between kisses.

"Do I?" He pulled back, his absence making the needy ache in her body increase. His brows rose as

10

if challenging her. Darion was such a tease.

"Yes."

She hated having to turn him away, but unlike Darion, she wasn't as much of a risk-taker. If they were caught, and god forbid she bump into anyone she knew, she'd never live it down.

Just to ensure he didn't think she was boring, *vanilla,* she added, "We can pop in Ann Summers when I'm finished here."

Darion snagged his lower lip between his teeth, his irises raw and blazing, full of lust and longing. "Oh, Gabi." He chuckled softly. "You're gonna wish you never said that."

"Why?" She shrugged a shoulder. "There's nothing in there *too* raunchy."

"You obviously weren't looking properly," Darion responded in his low, seductive voice.

When he left the changing rooms, she remained rooted to the spot for a moment. She tried to imagine in her head the items Ann Summers sold. So it did vibrators, whips, X-rated DVDs, sexy lingerie. She could handle that. She caught sight of her face in the mirror, and noticed her features were screwed up in confusion. What else did it sell? *Shit.* Knowing Darion and his sexually adventurous side, he'd probably dig out something she'd never even seen, used, or knew what to do with. Shaking her head with a laugh, she was a little excited at what he'd suggest. Darion, as always, was full of surprises, and nothing about him was ever *ordinary.*

Slipping the black dress over her head, she smoothed it down and confronted her reflection. It clung to the curves of her breasts and hips, and complemented her slender figure. Falling just above the knee, and revealing a bit of cleavage, it was classy but sexy at the same time. She decided she'd buy it. Tearing it off, she quickly got dressed in her black pencil skirt and white blouse. She slipped on her black Louboutin heels, with red soles as bright as her lipstick. It was time to reward Darion for being a good sport and allowing her to drag him around shops.

***

Darion

Darion blew smoke from the side of his mouth and watched couples strolling by hand in hand, laden with shopping bags. Smiles were plastered on their faces and they appeared like they didn't have a care in the world. Balancing his weight against the wall, he took another drag on the cigarette, hoping the nicotine rush would rid the empty ache in his heart. How he wanted to be like those types of people with nothing but love for one another.

Of course he wanted the excitement, spontaneity, and unpredictability some relationships could bring, but he also wanted to feel secure, settled. A few nights ago at The Black Door, he'd told Gabi he loved her. He realised he was no longer hung up on his ex-wife Eva, and doubted whether he'd really loved her at all. It must have just been lust—the strong kind, for it didn't compare to the feelings he had for Gabi. He didn't know why he was hooked, but he couldn't shake it off, nor did he want to. She made him want to be a better person. He had made a promise to sell the club he'd owned and enjoyed for years, and to turn his back on the lifestyle he'd become accustomed to—swinging.

An old friend of his, Carl Johnson, was buying The Black Door. He'd given Darion his word that none of his employees would be out of a job. It suited him just fine.

Darion had been looking forward to a new chapter in his life until he'd been the recipient of news that could change it forever. Before he could replay everything in his mind, Gabi appeared. Taking a final pull of his cigarette, he strolled toward a metal bin, and stubbed it out.

"You happy with your dress?"

She nodded.

They walked alongside one another in comfortable silence for a moment.

"Do you want to go for food?"

"Whatever you fancy, Gabi." He shoved his hands in his jean pockets. "First, we have another shop to visit." He jerked his head in the direction of an adult shop.

"Yeah, because that's one shop you don't mind being in." She playfully pushed him on the shoulder.

"Believe me, anything we get from that shop," he began, "the pleasure will be all yours."

"I'm sure we can find something for you too. After all, you'll need something to fill the void of the playrooms."

"In that case, we may need to buy the whole shop." Darion meant it as a joke, but seeing Gabi's mouth drop open, he pulled her into a tight hug, crushing her against him. "Don't worry," he said, staring down at her. "You're enough for me, Gabi."

She tucked a strand of hair behind her ear. "How can I be enough?"

"I told you, I lacked something with women in the past. I don't lack anything with you." He meant it from the bottom of his heart. "They say sex feels better when you're in love, and it's so fucking true."

"I can't see how you'll go from having wild, risky sex with several different women fulfilling your every desire, to having ordinary sex with just me." The insecurity and worry in her eyes seemed to mirror his own.

Manufacturing a small smile, he said, "I only need you, and believe me, darlin', there will never be anything ordinary about our sex life." He flicked his tongue over her bottom lip teasingly.

Gabi ducked her head with a giggle, and he was sure she was a little more secure. She hooked her arm in his, and together they made their way to the shop with the magnificent window display. Sexy lingerie and fantasy outfits hung from mannequins, not to mention the huge posters of women who could give Victoria Secret models a run for their money. Darion knew what was beyond that window. At the club, they'd had to stock up on orders constantly in respect of toys. Why not pleasure *most* of the erogenous zones? If Gabi thought sex between them would be ordinary, then she had another think coming. Didn't she know him by now?

He couldn't refrain from leaning forward and

kissing her on the forehead. From afar, and to an outsider, he knew they looked like those couples—happy, in love, carefree.

Beneath the surface was the biggest obstacle their relationship would ever face. Darion was unsure of whether it would strengthen their bond, or shatter it completely. He was afraid it would be the latter.

Chapter Three

Gabi

Gabi couldn't stop the smile on her face, even though it strained her cheeks. Swaying her chair from side to side, she glanced at the cerulean sky. She hadn't seen it so clear in a while. She could feel the sun beaming down, warming her face. The weather reflected her mood—nice and bright.

Yesterday with Darion had been more than pleasant. After they'd finished shopping and stocked up on a box of kinky goodies, they had enjoyed food at his favourite restaurant. Tucked away in the hills, it was peaceful and beautiful, surrounded by the leafy nature. She couldn't believe the change in her relationship with Darion. She was ecstatic he was selling The Black Door.

It was like a big weight had been lifted off her shoulders. She didn't need to worry about what he was up to at the club anymore, whether his ex-wife Eva, or Gina had got their claws into him, like she'd often thought. She didn't need to stress herself out, wondering if he'd given in to the tempting playrooms, enjoying them without her. At that moment in time, everything was good.

Turning from the window, she tapped her foot on the floor repeatedly. It wasn't too good, was it? She silently prayed nothing would come along and ruin what they had.

Their relationship had already been through hell and back. Firstly there had been Darion's confession of leading the life of a swinger, which had shocked her to the core, then there had been her confession about making the worst mistake of her life—kissing her ex-fiancé Lawrence when she'd been feeling lost, shut out, and distant from Darion. Gabi was unsure she could handle any more surprises.

"Hey, Miss Woods." Mallory's voice startled her as she entered the room.

The coffee aroma instantly filled Gabi's nostrils, and her mouth watered. It was just what she needed. When Mallory handed her the warm cup, Gabi thirstily took a long swig.

"How's your afternoon going?" She dropped onto the chair at the opposite side of the desk.

"Busy. What about yours?"

"I haven't got much done." She propped her legs on the desk. "There's a new man on our floor. Gabi, he's pretty fucking hot." Mallory threw her head back with a laugh. "His name is Ben."

Gabi shook her head in amusement. Mallory had been with her partner Steve for years; however she didn't shy away from appreciating a bit of eye-candy. As loyal as they came, she would never act

17

upon it and betray Steve.

"I'm so glad you sorted things out with Darion, by the way."

"Yeah. Me too."

"Take that, Lawrence, you soul-destroying asshole," she said as if he could hear.

"It was my fault too, Mal."

"Gabi. You were drunk. Your head was all over the place. Lawrence took advantage." She folded her arms across her chest. "Besides, it was cruel of him to threaten you like that. You should have been able to tell Darion when the time suited you. You could have lost him."

"I won't be making that mistake again."

"You might when you see Ben." She winked.

"About Thursday night…" Gabi sighed heavily, leaning back in her chair. "I don't even know Lloyd all that well. Are you sure he'll want me there?"

"Gabi. It's a works do. Everyone and anyone will be there. Lloyd barely knows me. I'm only going because I find it impossible to refuse a free bar."

Gabi couldn't help but laugh. "Okay, I'm sure it will be fun."

"It will." Mallory lifted her cup to her lips and began drinking her coffee. Only when she finished it all, did she set it on the table. "Are things okay with you and Darion anyway?"

"For now, yes."

"Good."

"How did I forget to tell you?" She shot up in her chair, suddenly remembering. "He's selling The Black Door, Mal. Can you believe it?"

"Wow. Looks like a leopard can change its spots."

"He believes it will all happen quite quickly. Eva has agreed to sell her share too, as she needs the money. I reckon she's back for Darion as well."

"I bet."

"His friend is buying the club, but Darion's letting him take over it now, whilst the sale is going through. He must have had enough of it, Mal, with Eva being there, and the stress of Gina leaving."

"Well, that's brilliant news. What are Darion's plans now?"

She shrugged a shoulder. "I don't know. I can't quite picture him in an office, can you?"

"I could, but I doubt the women would get much work done." She beamed.

"I'm sure Darion will think of something."

Mallory stood up and smoothed down her blonde hair, which had grown out of the bob, and now fell to her shoulders. Like Gabi, she took care of her appearance, and had regular facials, manicures and pedicures. She also had a wardrobe to rival Olivia Palermo's.

"Okay. I better get back to perving over Ben. I mean work," she teased.

"Yeah. Don't work yourself too hard, whatever you do." Gabi fixed her with a look.

When Mallory left her office, she dug through her handbag and retrieved her mobile phone. Touching the screen so it lit up, she checked if she had any missed calls or messages. She didn't. She wondered how Darion's meeting was going with his friend, Carl Johnson. She hoped he didn't have second thoughts about selling The Black Door.

Chapter Four

Darion

Darion picked up his glass of Coke and gulped it back. Setting it on the table, he reached into his pocket for his cigarettes. He offered one to Carl, who was sitting opposite him, and Eva, who was sitting to his right. Carl took a cigarette, placed it into his mouth, and lit it.

"So, does your wife know what sort of club you're buying?" Darion asked. He lit his cigarette and took a drag before blowing the smoke from the corner of his mouth.

"Yes, she does," Carl responded. "My wife doesn't get involved in my business affairs." He paused for a moment. "I take it yours does?"

Darion was certain he saw a hint of a smirk curl Eva's lips.

"Gabi has never asked me to sell the club. I wanna sell it."

"Eva, any second thoughts on your half?" Carl turned his attention to Eva.

"I'd rather not sell, but I could do with the money."

Carl nodded. "I'll have my solicitors draw up the documents. Darion, do you still want to turn the club over to me immediately, pending the sale process?"

He reclined in his chair, taking another puff on his fag. "That works for me."

"Looking for a manager?" Eva asked, flicking back her silky, black waves.

"Seeing as you're already familiar with the place, why not?"

Darion didn't miss the way Carl's gaze swept over Eva, his eyes twinkling in admiration. Maybe there was another perk to selling the club—Eva not being on his case.

Darion twisted his body around in his chair to survey the club once more. He would miss it. He would miss seeing Lexi, Marnie, Wendy, Tiana, Lennie, Travis, and his other staff regularly. Although he'd promised to stay in touch, he knew sometimes everyday-life prevented meetings from happening as much as one would like.

"Will you be changing much about the place?"

"Oh absolutely." Carl's attention flittered around the room. "I love what you've done with the décor and everything, but I need to put my mark on it." He grinned.

Darion nodded and memories flooded his mind of when he'd first purchased The Black Door. He'd been like a little kid in a candy store, so excited, and unsure of what to do first. How the years had flown.

"So, the dancers want to keep their jobs?" Carl

asked, stubbing out his fag.

"As far as I'm aware." Darion flicked his cigarette into the ashtray.

"Great," Eva muttered.

Carl's brow rose. "Anything I should know?"

"The dancers have a slight problem with authority."

"They don't," Darion cut in with a head shake.

"They do," Eva continued, propping her elbows on the table and toying with the rim of her glass. "But if I'm managing the place, I'll ensure they follow the rules."

"Eva." Darion leant closer to her and flashed a menacing smile. "Don't you dare upset those girls." His tone came out a stern warning, as he intended. Hadn't she already caused enough trouble?

"They're not *your* girls anymore."

His spine stiffened and he unbuttoned his collar, feeling hot all of a sudden. Not being able to protect the girls and ensure they were okay worried him. He knew Eva hadn't really taken a liking to them, and although Eva was a hard worker, she was a bitch with a power trip.

"Shall I give you pair some privacy?" Carl asked, clearing his throat with a cough.

"No, it's fine." He pushed himself to his feet. He'd rather swallow glass than be alone with her. He couldn't wait to see the back of Eva.

"Well, whenever you want to clear your office, let me know. I'll be here all week," Carl informed him.

"Thanks."

"I can't fucking wait to start this new chapter in

my life, Daz." Carl rubbed his hands together, the glee visible on his face.

Darion wished he could say he was excited about the new chapter in his life, but a certain phone call kept swirling round in his mind, like the buzzing of a mosquito that wouldn't go away. He was pleased however, to be at a comfortable stage financially, and could start a new business should he want to.

Digging into his pocket, he retrieved the key to the club. Dropping it on the table, he pushed it toward Carl.

"Enjoy."

"Oh. I have every intention. Don't you worry about that, my friend."

Carl stood and held out his hand. Darion shook it firmly.

"Do you want to see the upstairs for the last time, before I refurbish the whole place?"

With a shake of his head, Darion said, "I've seen enough of this club to have memories to last me a lifetime."

"I agree," Eva said, with a giggle.

"It's all yours." He picked up his jacket.

"No celebratory drink?"

"Call me when the place is back open. You're shutting for a month, right?"

Carl nodded. "I'll send you an invitation to the grand opening."

With a nod of his head to Eva, Darion made his way toward the exit. He heard the clacking of Eva's heels on the floor. When he stepped outside into the fresh air, breathing it in, the sun beaming on his face, he smiled for a second, forgetting about all of his troubles.

"Darion." Eva placed a hand on his arm.

He edged away. "What do you want, Eva?"

"I'm gonna miss you."

"It's a small town. Unfortunately, we'll be unable to avoid bumping into one another."

"I hope you know what you're doing, selling this place."

He lifted his head to take in the sign that read, **'The Black Door.'** The light to the upstairs was switched off, and Darion already missed the red glow that cast on the street below. In his early twenties, he had been so excited about opening the gentlemen's club. Many amazing parties had been held there, and many nights of pure pleasure had occurred in the playrooms. He was ready for a change. Wasn't he?

"It's time to move on."

"I hope I didn't have anything to do with your decision. If you wanted me gone that badly, I would have left."

"My decision has nothing to do with you." He turned on his heel.

"What will you do now?"

He shrugged a shoulder. "I need to weigh up my options."

He slowly sauntered toward his black Audi, gripping the keys in his hand. Opening the door, he climbed in, and remained still for a moment. Looking back toward the club, an unfamiliar empty ache lingered in his heart. He didn't know what the future held. He'd be lying if he said he wasn't afraid. Dropping his head back so it hit the headrest, he let out a long, heartfelt sigh. He sensed Eva's presence still, could feel her eyes burning holes into him. Turning his head, he noticed the expression on her face, which could only be described as sadness. Heartbreak. Pain. *Welcome to my world,* he thought.

Jamming his key into the ignition, the engine roared loudly. "Damage" by Kosheen blasted from the speakers. Putting the car in gear, he pressed his foot on the accelerator, and sped off. The tyres screeched on the tarmac, leaving behind smoke. He drove away from his old life, from his club, from his ex-wife, and from everything he had ever known.

Chapter Five

Gabi

When Thursday evening made an appearance, Gabi was in a lively, modern bar not far from work. Lloyd was already drunk and Gabi was unable to remember most of the names of her colleagues. She sipped her cocktail and returned her attention to the receptionist, Julie, droning on about staff policies. She almost kissed Mallory when she saved her, and dragged her toward the dance floor.

"That woman cannot be married." Gabi laughed. "Seriously, I was feeling great until she dragged me down into the depths of hell!"

"Why do you think I avoid the reception area like the plague?" Mallory began swaying her hips and arms to the beat of the music. "She's the type of woman who would win the lottery and complain about spending the pound on the ticket."

Gabi burst into hysterics. "Oh, Mal. How Lawrence didn't like you baffles me to this day." She hiccupped.

"Lawrence only likes people with sticks up their arses, who like fishing, golf, watching horse races, and talking about politics."

"So true." She paused. "Hang on. What does that say about me?"

"That you were young and naïve, and thought an older man would do you good."

"Darion's not much younger than Lawrence."

"Darion acts his age. He doesn't act eighty, Gab. In fact, my granddad is eighty, and he's more fun than Lawrence."

"Yeah, well, he's a thing of the past now."

"Thank God."

Gabi continued to dance. She glanced over her shoulder at the table where they had been sitting. The men from the office were laughing loudly at something, whilst the women sat rigid in their seats, obviously too uptight to dance.

"I need the toilet," Mallory shouted down her ear.

"Mal. I'm drunk, not deaf." She took a step back.

They huddled their way through the bustling crowd. Once in the bathroom, Gabi stood before the mirror and fiddled with the black dress that clung to her body. Satisfied she looked reasonably decent, except for her nude lips, she added a coat of lip-gloss.

She was just about to call Mallory when her mobile rang. Rummaging in her clutch bag, she took it out and glanced at the screen. Darion. She hadn't heard from him all day. Assuming he'd been busy, she hadn't followed her text message with another.

"Hi," she answered cheerily.

"Hi, darlin'," his low, sultry voice filled the line. It played havoc with her hormones. God, he aroused her with his voice alone. She heard a faint blowing sound and knew he was smoking. Her mind tortured her with an image of a half-naked Darion lying across his sofa, relaxing, the television or stereo on in the background.

"What are you up to?" she asked.

"Just listening to a bit of music."

She half smiled.

"How's your night going?"

"Good," she responded.

"You missing me yet?"

"Always."

The line was silent for a moment, and Gabi waited with bated breath for him to bring up the club. Had he agreed to the sale? She slid onto the counter as her stomach somersaulted. She wanted to ask him, but she was afraid of the answer. She prayed he was prepared to turn his back on his past, and start a future with her, nobody else in the picture. All she wanted was Darion Milano to herself for once, finally.

"I can meet you tomorrow night," he said, which was all of the confirmation she needed. He obviously no longer had work at The Black Door.

Mallory exited the cubicle and paraded to the mirror. Gabi watched as she soaped and washed her hands.

"Okay."

"Bye," he said before adding, "don't have too much fun without me." His tone was playful.

The words filled Gabi with warmth, as she knew he was referring to other men, for her to behave. Not like she'd misbehave anyway. Darion showing his jealous side made her feel loved. Usually he got off on feeling jealous, wanted her to dance with other men, work herself up until he was with her. Now it seemed he didn't like sharing her at all. Deliriously happy and full of energy, she couldn't wait to get back on the dance floor.

"Come on, Mal," she said once she'd ended the call. "I can hear my fave song playing."

She and Mallory took up the dance floor until their feet swelled and their limbs ached. They then retired to the table to find the women from work had left. Lloyd and a few others were still present, and now, extremely drunk. They were eyeing up women at the next table, and making perverted comments. Gabi knew they were all married men, having spotted the bands on their fingers. Now the swinging lifestyle sort of made sense to her. Instead of these men cheating on their wives, lying and being deceitful about it, why hadn't they partnered with someone who agreed to an open relationship, who had no problem in sharing them? At least Darion and Eva had been on the same page when married, and wanted the same thing—no restrictions.

"Shall we go to another bar?" Mallory asked, draining the last of her drink. "I can get us into the VIP section at Havana." She winked.

"Sounds good." Gabi picked up her bag.

They said their goodbyes to the men, wished Lloyd every success for the future, and ambled

30

outside. Taxis were constantly driving back and forth on the busy street of bars, so it didn't take them long to hail one down.

When they were eventually sitting in the plush VIP area of Havana, cocktails before them, Gabi examined her surroundings. The crowd seemed well-dressed, well-spoken, and rich. Usually Gabi didn't particularly care for pretentious places, but everyone seemed friendly enough, dancing, giggling, and smiling. On arrival she noticed the drink prices were extortionate. However, she and Mallory had been offered anything they wanted for free.

"How do you manage to get into VIP everywhere?" She took a large sip of her fancily decorated drink. She gasped in contentment. It was delicious.

"Steve works with a man who is related to the owner of this bar. And as he knows all of the other owners, we've only got to text him when we're in the area."

"Nice." Gabi nodded. "I like it in here."

House music was playing, and the large dance floor just beyond the VIP section was packed with swaying bodies.

"It feels a little different without Suzie, doesn't it?"

"Yeah, it does," Gabi agreed. Suzie was their close friend, and if she hadn't been pregnant, she definitely would have joined them on the night out.

Mallory shuffled on her seat, making herself more comfortable. "Speaking of which, we need to go and visit her soon. You know how she gets being cooped up all day."

"I'm up for that. We could go to Starbucks in the week," she suggested.

"I'll call her tomorrow. Wednesday work for you?"

Gabi nodded, downing half of her drink and setting it on the side.

"So, Miss Woods..." Mallory's face lit up in mischief. "Gossip time."

Gabi folded her arms across her chest, smiling smugly. "Would you believe for once, I actually don't have any gossip? I think my life may actually be *normal* for once."

"Sweetie, you don't get to have a normal life with a boyfriend like yours."

"What do you mean?" Her mouth dropped. "Mal, he's done with all of that stuff now."

"Yeah. But what will he replace it with? What fantasy comes next?"

"Thanks a lot, Mal. I had actually thought about that, but knowing you think it too worries me."

"I'm not trying to unsettle you, but Darion is clearly a man who easily gets bored sexually. Just keep him on his toes." She winked. "Now he's no longer fulfilled by that lifestyle, come up with something fresh. Kink it up a bit." She grinned slowly. "*And* it's more fun for you."

"How?" Her mind whizzed through a million things she could do to ensure their relationship remained exciting, but she'd already experienced a lot with Darion sexually. "What is there left for me to do?"

"What have you tried?"

"Sexy lingerie, sex in public places, light bondage...Mal, I even kissed other men and women. I'm not prepared to push boundaries further. I can't do it."

"Honey, you don't need to involve other people in your sex life for it to be exciting. Me and Steve try new things all of the time. Just the two of us."

"Like what?" Her relationship with Lawrence had been so boring, and the sex simple. She'd never had to constantly come up with ideas to please him. Missionary, lights off was more than enough for him.

"Role play, dress up, toys, watch some saucy movies...the list is endless."

"Do you think it's necessary?"

"Gab, just because he's turned his back on swinging doesn't mean Darion is no longer a sexual deviant, and you can slack between the sheets. The way to a man's heart is a full stomach and empty balls."

Gabi keeled over as she burst into hysterics. "Oh, Mal. Since when did you become the sexpert?"

"Since I've been with Steve for like forever, and we went through a rough patch that almost destroyed us."

"What?" Gabi straightened her posture, giving her friend her full attention. "You never told me this."

"Yeah." She lifted her glass to her lips and downed the last of it. "It became so bad we were only having sex like once a month. Sex just didn't feel fun anymore. It was like a chore, something we had to do, not because we wanted to do it."

Gabi shook her head. "You and Steve seem like the perfect couple."

"Even the most perfect couples can go through a dry patch. Steve was close to leaving me. There was no intimacy, nothing. We may as well have just been roommates."

"How did you fix it?"

"By trying new things. By keeping the passion alive. The only reason I'm telling you is because now you've finally got Darion all to yourself, I don't want to see you hurt and losing him. Just don't ever stop making an effort in your relationship."

"Hmmm," Gabi mumbled, speech eluding her.

The cogs of her mind were going into overdrive. She knew Mallory was right. Darion wasn't like ordinary men who were happy with getting their leg over. He constantly sought new thrills. Although he stated he'd be satisfied with *just her* and that sex would never be ordinary, what did he have in mind? How had she thought it'd be plain-sailing, that he'd give up swinging and just settle for whatever she had to offer, which judging by Mallory's ideas, now seemed bland? She slumped in her seat, her mood turning sour. Perhaps there were other surprises in store, and maybe The Black Door hadn't even been the worst of it.

Chapter Six

Friday evening, Gabi was lying on her bed with a book in her hands, when a tingling sensation raced up her leg. Placing her book down, she slowly rolled over. Green, smouldering eyes burned into hers. She hadn't even heard him enter her apartment. Kneeling on the bed, Darion stripped his shirt off in one swift movement. Gabi swallowed, excitement building in her stomach in the form of butterflies.

His hands ran up her legs, sliding under her blue silk nightie. As it moved over her stomach, and then her breasts, Gabi inhaled air. Darion whipped it over her head, and tossed it to the floor.

"Good day?" she asked.

"It's about to get better," he said in a low, husky tone.

Positioning himself between her legs, he lay on her. He didn't waste any time in claiming her lips. Gabi wriggled as the button of his jeans brushed against her clit. An achy need loomed in her stomach. She frantically searched for the button, and unclasped it. Every part of her wanted his rough touch. Darion assisted in removing his jeans and boxers, as impatient as she was. When his naked body collided with hers, she moaned. She could already feel the heat emanating from him.

She stroked her hands down the length of his spine, settling on his ass, and pulling him into her. When he thrust in deeply without warning, she cried out. She was pleased he was rock-hard and ready, with no need for foreplay.

His stare was intense. She marvelled at his perfect features, his gleaming eyes, his devilish grin. His hands came up and gripped the sides of her throat. She loved his aggressiveness, how much he needed her. As he bucked his hips, sliding in and out of her in a slow, teasing rhythm, she could see the strain and pleasure now etched across his face.

"You feel so good," he murmured against her nipple. It hardened and tingled, and she grimaced as he swirled his tongue around it. Her breathing became laboured and short, as he knew how to tease her sensitive parts.

She arched her back, pushing her groin upwards, wanting him harder and faster. Heat swept sinuously through her veins, her whole body throbbing with pleasure. Darion took a breast in his mouth, his suction hard. His tongue lapped away greedily.

"Ah…"

She mumbled incoherently, unable to form a sentence as lust assailed her. He worked his full length in and out of her repeatedly. When his face was before hers, she opened her mouth to allow his tongue to roam in. He kissed gently and then more powerfully.

Throwing her head back in despair, she concentrated on controlling her climax, not wanting it to end.

"Gabi..." he grimaced, the cords of his neck taut. His body was drenched in sweat as he slammed into her forcefully and urgently. "Fuuuck..."

Grabbing hold of her hips, he rolled over so he was on his back. Straddling him, she traced her palms over his firm chest. The sight of his delicious body caused her internal muscles to tighten around him. Lifting herself up, she gently lowered back onto him. Her head rolled back on a satisfied groan. Continuing to rock backwards and forwards, she loved every pleasured grunt that escaped his mouth.

"Faster, darlin'," his voice was hoarse. "Harder...that's it."

As commanded, she picked up her pace. Her buttocks slapped against his thighs loudly. It was so good it was almost unbearable. The length and width of his cock fit her snugly. He thrust upwards, filling her as deep as possible. Gabi squeezed her eyelids shut in pure ecstasy.

She bit down painfully on her lip as he gripped her waist, taking control. He bucked upwards, his slams even faster. Her body shivered in delight as the pressure began to build.

Her toes curled, her lungs heaving. His hands caressed her heavy, tender breasts, massaging them, his fingertips tweaking her nipples.

"I'm close," she panted, knowing he was too. She could feel him swelling and pulsating inside her.

"Not yet."

With their bodies still intact, he shuffled over and opened the bedside drawer. She heard the buzzing sound of the bullet-shaped vibrator. When it met her clit, she writhed fervently. Her hands balled into fists. It was too much. Her whole body tingled and trembled. With the fast vibrations shooting between her legs, and Darion's relentless thrusting, she screamed out.

"Now!" she whimpered.

She shattered around him on a loud cry, riding him as she orgasmed in sharp, intense waves. Darion followed, clamping her to him, pushing into her a few final times. Throbbing inside her, he shuddered and grunted before his body went limp.

She collapsed on him, her heart racing wildly, her body soaked in sweat, and her muscles aching. They lay in a shattered heap, trying to catch their breath. Darion fidgeted and the buzzing sound of the toy stopped.

Exhaling on a satisfied sigh, she knew she could rest in his arms forever. When she gained some energy, she began stroking his bicep gently. His fingers were in her hair, the circular motions making her sleepy.

As silence hung in the air, she wondered if Darion had given much thought to their future. They had met one another's families, but what was next? Did he want the same things she did: marriage, children? She'd tried to bring up the conversation in the past, however, he'd dodged it. She'd hate to feel she was wasting her time chasing things he didn't want.

"Darion." She built up the courage to ask. "Would you ever get married again, or has Eva put you off?"

"Eva put me off a lot of things. Now, she doesn't have that power."

"So you would get married again?"

"Why not?"

"What about a family, and a nice, big house?" she teased.

"Are you hinting something, Gabriella Woods?"

"No. I just want to know if you ever think about those things."

"I want all of those things with you," his tone was serious.

"Do you think we could have all of that?"

"Why couldn't we?"

She shrugged a shoulder. "Sometimes I don't think we're compatible."

"What do you mean?"

"Sexually."

"Gabi." He softly chuckled. "Were you not present just then? Didn't you feel what I did?"

"Yeah, I did…but I don't think it's enough for you, Darion."

"Why?" Lines creased his forehead. "Because I owned an adult club?"

Gabi sat up and hugged her knees to her chest. "I'm probably the most boring woman you've ever bedded." Insecurity stabbed away at her, making her feel like she could never compete with his past lovers, that their relationship wouldn't last.

"That's not true." He shot her a fierce stare.

"I bet your sex life has been crazy with all of them."

He hesitated and she knew she was spot on. "Not all."

"How did you lose your virginity?" she challenged him, hoping he'd at least experienced normal, *vanilla* sex with at least one person.

He traced his finger along his bottom lip whilst deep in thought. "It was an older woman. A stripper."

"See?" Gabi huffed.

"It's a good thing. She taught me a lot. Everyone I have ever been with has made me the man I am today." He knelt over her and yanked her down the bed, so she was lying flat on her back. "Do you think I'd be this enthusiastic to please if I hadn't experienced some great lovers?"

She remained silent, feeling her stomach somersault, envy and sadness overwhelming her.

"Would you rather me be inexperienced, clumsy, a terrible fuck, who'd had less partners?" His pupils flashed dangerously, and a slow, seductive smirk surfaced on his face. He pushed her legs open and ducked his head.

Gabi gripped the bed sheets when his tongue swirled around her clit, causing her breathing and heartbeat to increase. Sucking her gently, she wriggled in excitement, unable to control her fidgeting limbs. And then he stopped.

"I didn't quite hear your answer," he said, his voice low and husky. "Would you want me to be any different?"

Gabi hated to admit it, but no, she wouldn't. She

loved Darion for the way he was. She shook her head. Her lids closed on a soft sigh when he resumed to sucking, licking and nibbling between her legs. As he brought her immense pleasure, his past, the club, his ex-lovers started to fade away. She had Darion Milano now, and surely the future was worth looking forward to.

***

Darion

Darion could hear the running water of the shower and Gabi softly humming to herself. He jumped out of bed in search for his boxers. As he was pulling them on, his mobile bleeped. He snatched it from the side to read it, but it was too late. The screen went black as the battery died. Twisting around, he scanned the bedroom for an iPhone charger. Gabi had the same mobile. When he failed to find one in the bedroom, living room, and kitchen, he began opening and closing draws next to her bed. He shook his head in amusement as he came across the crap she collected: make-up to last her a lifetime, tons of creams, nail polishes, Yankee Candles, notepads, and a black velvet box.

Bile rose in Darion's throat as he guessed what it was. He hoped he was wrong. His hands trembled as he picked it up, suddenly feeling sick with jealousy. The lid creaked as he opened it. His breathing suspended for a moment. There it was, a white gold band with a huge square diamond in the middle sparkling up at him—her engagement ring.

Shoving it back in the drawer, his face heated as the blood rushed to it in rage. Why the fuck did she still have her engagement ring from Lawrence, whom she not only split up with months ago, but also kissed and cheated on him with? He fell back on the bed. His brain ached with information overload. Gabi had previously told Darion she had kissed Lawrence behind his back because she had been feeling insecure, lost, and unloved by him as he hadn't declared his feelings enough, and she hadn't known where they were headed. Perhaps she had kissed Lawrence because she'd been having second thoughts, and still loved him. Why else would she keep the ring?

Was she having second thoughts about *their* relationship? Maybe that was why she had brought up the compatibility bullshit. Maybe she wanted out of it. If she still had feelings for Lawrence, then he needed to know. He rubbed his palms up and down his face with a long, exasperated sigh. He had given up everything for Gabi.

You're not so innocent yourself, his brain reminded him. Could Gabi be lying and hiding a big, dark secret just as he was?

Chapter Seven

Gabi

Gabi turned her head to the sound of giggling. Darion was standing at the bar ordering drinks. She picked up her menu and tried to distract herself from the woman who was clearly flirting with him. Yes, so Darion was hot with his tall, broad physique, luminous green eyes, sleek dark hair, and dazzling smile. She got it. He was stunning to look at, and the sound of his seductive voice made women delirious with lust. She noticed Darion duck his head with a chuckle and was relieved he never *ever* flirted back. He politely accepted a stroke to the ego and moved on.

"White wine," he said, placing two glasses on the table. His was a beer.

"Thanks."

A waitress approached them and took their orders. Gabi waited for her to leave before she took hold of Darion's hand. He was sitting at her side of the table, as he always did, rather than opposite. She shuffled closer and nuzzled his neck, inhaling his cologne. He turned his head and pressed his lips against hers firmly. She parted her lips to allow his tongue to sweep in and massage her own. Her lids closed in pure pleasure, as she got lost in the kiss. As Darion's hand stroked tenderly up her leg, leaving tingles in its wake, her insatiable need for him increased. Then he pulled back on a long, drawn out moan.

"I love you," she said breathlessly and bravely, hoping he was now comfortable to express his feelings. Their relationship had reached the next level. They had met one another's families, and she had made it clear he never had to hold back on his feelings. She would never betray him again, nor would she leave him.

A dark hunger passed over Darion's face, and he slowly licked his lips. "I love you too." Holding her face in his hands, he dotingly planted a kiss on her forehead.

Gabi melted at his touch. Her heart was so full of love she felt it would explode. If she had to spice things up a tad and keep her man on his toes then so she would.

"I've got a surprise for you," she whispered in his ear with a little giggle.

"What is it?"

"If I told you then it wouldn't be a surprise," she teased.

They were interrupted when the waitress brought over their food. Gabi hungrily dug into her starter, a tomato and ricotta bruschetta. Darion had taken her to a new fancy Italian restaurant in town. It was a small, intimate place with soft music playing, and candles glowing on the tables. There were only a few other couples present, fully engrossed in one another and also enjoying their meals.

"Thanks for bringing me here." She placed down her fork and picked up her wine.

"You're welcome."

Taking a sip, she stared at Darion inquisitively when his mobile bleeped and he showed no intention of checking it. "Don't mind me." She smiled warmly.

Darion retrieved his mobile from his pocket, glanced at the screen, and then put it away. As he continued eating, she noticed his face was devoid of emotion.

"Is everything okay?"

"Yeah. It's Carl. He has a couple of questions about the club."

"Oh." Curiosity niggled away at her about his recent visit. Had Eva been there? How did he feel about selling it? "How were things at the club?" She casually swept a strand of blonde hair out of her face, and began eating.

"Good." Darion swallowed his food. "Carl can't wait to get it up and running."

"So we've seen the last of Eva then." Her tone came as a little too excited.

"Unfortunately not."

Gabi held her fork in mid-air, waiting for him to continue.

"She'll still be managing the place. Carl's agreed to take the dancers on too."

Gabi's shoulders dropped as she deflated. *Was*

there no getting rid of Darion's past? She sucked in a lungful of air, and was just about to blow it out in annoyance when she caught Darion's expression. He was focused on the window, his clenched jaw twitching and his free hand tapping on the table. He was just as displeased about the news as she was.

"Oh well," she said cheerily, feigning happiness. "You're out of that place and on to something new."

He nodded. "I'm certainly on to something new," he said. She didn't miss the icy tone of his voice.

"Mr. Milano, your main courses." Oblivious to her, a waitress had approached and was placing hot plates of food before them.

"Thank you."

Gabi leant back slightly so the waitress could collect the empty plates of their starters.

"Can I get you some more wine?" she asked.

"You can bring a bottle over if you like." Gabi beamed.

"Celebrating something?" Darion asked with a lift of his brow.

"Yes." She planted a chaste kiss on his lips. "You."

"Aren't I the lucky man?"

"Yes, Mr. Milano, you certainly are, because I'm going to ensure you're the happiest man alive."

"Sounds like you've got your work cut out for you."

"I'll enjoy every challenging bit of it." She ran a hand through his hair and stared straight into his eyes, which were filled with love and longing. His features softened and he appeared relaxed. That was what she liked to see—Darion happy. He'd been neglected by his parents, cheated on by his ex-wife and other ex-girlfriends. He'd never been praised for anything he'd achieved in his entire life, and it seemed he'd gone without a lot of things growing up. Gabi wanted him to know things would be different. He was a little damaged and secretly insecure. She made a promise to herself she'd make everything just right.

"I'm so proud of you," she told him. "It's not easy turning your back on something you loved, your business. But I know things will only get better from here."

Darion bowed his head, as if uncomfortable at taking a compliment.

"Let's eat." He grinned. "Our food will get cold."

It was midnight when they fell into Gabi's double bed. She was tipsy and her stomach was completely full. Usually they'd watch television or a movie, however Darion was exhausted too. Stripping her clothes off, Gabi dived under the covers. She wrapped her body around Darion's smooth, firm nakedness and closed her eyes on a soft sigh. She could hear the pounding of his heartbeat against her ear. As she stroked his chest slowly, working her hand in circles, the pace of his heart slowed down. Minutes later his gentle snores filled the air and she drifted into a peaceful sleep not long after.

***

Darion

Darion spun around, his eyes searching frantically for an escape. He ran his hands along the walls and floor, yet they were smooth, without a single dent. Lifting his head, he spotted a small window in the ceiling. He stretched his arms above him and jumped, but then scolded himself for being ridiculous. It was way too high. The room was completely bare with nothing to use to make an exit. His chest expanded as his breathing became heavy. His stomach churned. Feeling a hot flush spread through his body, and getting light-headed, he tore off his top. It seemed as if the walls were closing in on him. He was trapped and there was nothing he could do about it.

He screamed out for help, but the only sound he heard was his echoes. The silence after that was eerie and unsettling. The loss of control made his heartbeat increase. As his breaths became shallow, he feared he'd have a heart attack.

The walls were definitely closing in on him, making the space he was in even smaller. As his freedom slowly began slipping away, he slid down to the floor. Burying his head in his hands, he squeezed his lids shut. There was nothing he could do.

Darion jolted upright. His whole body was shaking and drenched with sweat. He clutched his chest and gasped for air. It was pitch black and his eyes failed to make sense of his surroundings. Shooting to his feet, he crossed the room, his arms outstretched. He felt before him until metal came into contact with his hand. A door handle. He pulled it open, and was relieved to see it was lighter beyond the door. As familiar objects came into focus, he remembered he was in Gabi's apartment. He'd obviously had another nightmare, although it had seemed more like a panic attack.

Heading for the kitchen, he needed something to ease his dry, scratchy throat. At the sink, he filled a glass with water, and drained it back hurriedly. When he finished, he leant against the counter, trying to steady the pace of his heart and breathing.

Glancing at the clock on the wall, he noticed it was early hours of the morning. It was still dark outside. Gently placing the glass in the sink, he then made his way back toward the bedroom. Gabi was still sound asleep and he didn't want to disturb her. She didn't flinch when he crept in beside her. He desperately wanted to wrap his arms around her petite body, seek comfort in her. Instead he remained lying on his back, his stare fixed firmly on the ceiling.

An hour of trying to block out worrying thoughts, and trying his hardest to sleep, he was finally able to drift off.

Chapter Eight

Gabi

Gabi woke with a smile, luxuriating in the soft, warm bed covers. The sun was beaming through the small gap in the white curtains, flooding the whole room with light. She stretched before rolling onto her side and meeting a sleeping Darion. He was breathing gently, his bare, smooth chest rising and falling slowly. She had a desperate urge to press her lips against his, to wake him up and take full advantage of his delicious body. However she managed to control herself and let him sleep.

Climbing out of bed, she scooped up her nightie and slipped it on. She quietly tiptoed out of the room and closed the door behind her. It was Sunday morning and she wondered what to do with her day. She was full of energy, her mood at an all-time high. As she made a coffee, she contemplated giving the apartment a spring clean, although in all fairness it was pretty immaculate. Gabi had tons of stuff: books, ornaments, souvenirs she had collected on family holidays when younger, an endless supply of clothes, shoes, and make-up, although everything had its perfect place.

Cradling her hot cup, she strolled into the living room and peered out of the window. She spotted a young child running before her garden. The blonde-haired little girl giggled and babbled away. A woman who must have been her mother scooped her into her arms, and spun around, causing the girl to laugh loudly. Gabi couldn't wait for the day when she had children. She already had boy and girl names stored in her brain from the times she had heard them on TV, or read them in a book, and liked them. Then there were the outfits, little matching clothes and shoes. Feeling warmth spread through her body, she couldn't help but shake her head in amusement. The idea of someday having a tiny little person to love, and to love her in return, filled her with joy.

Settling on the sofa, she grabbed the television remote and scrolled through the shows she had stored in her favourites. She didn't know whether she was in the mood for Blair and Serena, or Carrie, Samantha, Charlotte and Miranda.

"Gabi."

She inhaled sharply, almost spilling her coffee. With a low giggle, she sipped some of the liquid, placed it on the table, and looked up. Darion was leant casually against the doorframe, wearing nothing but black jeans, which hung low on his waist. Ground rules needed to be set. Darion Milano could not parade around the apartment with his impressive biceps, washboard stomach, and tight abs, and not expect Gabi to instantly become aroused. He raked a hand through his brown, sexily dishevelled hair, and sat beside her. Gabi scooted closer, taking hold of his hand. It was weird Darion not having plans to visit the club come Monday morning.

She was on cloud nine. Maybe they could have a normal relationship after all: security, stability, but with all of the fun parts included. Had she really tamed the bad-boy beast? Was he really *all* hers? She hoped so.

"What are you smiling at?" Darion asked, with a lift of his brow.

"Nothing." She chewed her lower lip. "Do you fancy doing anything today?"

"Yes. You."

She laughed. "Darion, I know there is more in that pretty little head of yours than just sex."

"There is," he began, stroking her fingers gently. "But it gets clouded by the sex."

Gabi tried to keep a straight face. Darion had a way of being funny, but doing so in a cool and collected manner. She leant forward and pressed her lips against his.

"Fancy breakfast?"

"I'm not hungry." He stood up and peered out of the window. "I don't know what to do with myself. The club was a big part of my life."

"I know," Gabi soothed.

She stepped toward him and wrapped her arms around his waist. She got a whiff of his cologne and his natural, clean smell. As she pressed her head against his chest, she could feel the heat radiating from him.

"Have you decided what you'll do instead?"

"I might check out some bars in the centre. See if anything is up for rent."

"What, like a normal bar?"

He smiled softly, and smoothed her hair back with his hands. "A normal bar, Gabi."

"A cocktail bar would be nice," she hinted with a laugh.

"Then I definitely would be surrounded by nothing but women." He planted a kiss on her lips. "You know, I've always wanted to own a nightclub."

"Westhaven is short on clubs. It only has the one, doesn't it?"

"Sky Bar, yeah." He was silent for a moment and Gabi knew the cogs in his brain were going into overdrive. Darion had always been an ambitious man. "I think it's about time there was a new bar type club in town." A slow, lazy smile surfaced on his face, his luminous green eyes shimmering.

"Well, whatever you decide to do, you have my full support." Gabi clasped hold of his hand and squeezed it.

He nodded and rubbed his neck, as if to alleviate some sort of discomfort. Gabi linked her hands together, stunned by the rejection. She hated that an uncomfortable silence hung in the air. What was going on? She turned her back on him to hide her confused expression. Something was on his mind and she had a feeling it had nothing to do with the club. She made a mental note to find out what it was pronto.

***

Monday morning came quicker than Gabi had hoped. She hated how the weekends always seemed to fly by. Tapping away on her computer, she responded to a few queries, and then shimmied to the kitchen. As it was a colleague's birthday, the counter was lined with delicious smelling cupcakes. Unable to resist, Gabi picked one up. She groaned in delight as the cream sponge went down her throat. After she'd finished it, and drained back a glass of water, she went to print out some documents. She spotted Mallory chatting and giggling away, the phone balanced in the crook of her neck. It was obviously a personal call.

Gabi waited patiently as pages began to pour out. She scanned the rest of the floor. Everyone was fixated on their computer screens. There was a lively buzz about the place, though. People were gossiping at the same time as working. Smoothing down her grey knee-length dress, which matched her stilettos, she snatched up the papers, and returned to her office.

She read five pages of a manuscript before she became restless. Her hand hovered over her mobile as she contemplated ringing Darion. Deciding against it, she kicked off her heels and tucked her feet up underneath her. If he was distressed about something, then surely he'd tell her.

Chapter Nine

Darion

Darion switched off the television. He remained lying on the sofa for a moment, staring at the ceiling. He had already watched a few episodes of *Dexter,* showered, cleaned the apartment, and now had nothing to do. Visiting the club didn't seem appealing. He wasn't ready to face the changes Carl had made yet. Not being able to recognise The Black Door anymore affected him more than he'd thought it would.

Visiting his parents definitely wasn't an option either. He considered calling Lennie and Travis to see if they fancied a beer and a game of cards, then decided against it. If he so much as touched a glass of whisky, he knew he'd never stop. Plus, with gambling, he'd probably end up losing a load of money. He needed a distraction though, that much was certain. He needed to rein in his worrying thoughts about the changes his future would bring.

Rolling onto his side, he closed his lids. After

five minutes of controlling his breathing, trying to block everything out, he sat up. It was no use.

Dragging himself to the kitchen, he decided to cook up a beef lasagna. His stomach hadn't stopped rumbling for the past hour and he now actually had time to cook. Opening and closing cupboards, he took out everything he needed and set it on the counter. He used to eat out regularly or order in, but ever since Darion had begun a relationship with Gabi, he'd ensured his cupboards and fridge were stocked up. He wanted her to be comfortable when she stayed at his apartment, and to have everything she would need. He was impressed he was doing quite well without having Gina around to help out. Little by little his bachelor pad was becoming a proper home.

He'd just grabbed hold of a pan when his mobile rang. Glancing down, he noticed his knuckles were turning white. His heartbeat increased, and his throat suddenly became dry. *Relax,* he told himself, loosening the pan. *It's probably Gabi.* He strode into the living room and picked up his mobile. His spine went rigid. It was the same number that ended in 369. Squeezing his eyes shut, he inhaled deeply. He knew he should answer it. He knew he had to face the situation head on, but he couldn't. He was afraid. He pressed the reject button, and collapsed onto the sofa. A sharp ache shot through his heart as he became overwhelmed with guilt. Life really did have a way of throwing a spanner in the works. He knew he couldn't ignore it forever.

Having lost his appetite, he grabbed his jacket and decided to go for a drive. The apartment was stuffy and he needed fresh air, desperately. He didn't bother taking his mobile with him. He wanted to be away from everything and everyone.

***

Gabi

"Hey, Kalli." Gabi waved at her friend as she entered the room.

"Hi, Gabi." She beamed. "How's it going?"

"Great, thanks. You?"

"Same."

Gabi pulled bottled water out of her bag, unscrewed the lid, and downed a quarter. She took in the empty hall. Only a handful of people were present, including the dance tutor who was setting up the stereo. She was early. Before she had left work, she had changed into black leggings, a matching crop-top, and trainers. She had been looking forward to the lesson all day. She always left The Royal Dance Academy feeling invigorated.

When more people poured into the room, Gabi stuffed her bottle in her bag, and positioned herself next to Kalli, who was stretching her limbs.

"Okay, everyone ready?" the tutor asked with a clap of her hands.

A 'yes' echoed around the room, and then the music began.

"Okay, let's jog on the spot for a moment...get those muscles nice and ready."

Gabi mirrored the tutor and jogged on the spot. Stealing a quick glance out of the window, she could see clouds had gathered in the now orangey coloured sky, and the sun was setting. She wondered what Darion had done with his day. She had tried to ring him earlier, but hadn't received an answer. She hoped he was okay. She knew it would take time for the loss of his club to set in. It was all he had known for a long time. Gabi couldn't even imagine not working at Miller & Co Publishers. She had been there for so long she didn't even know where she'd start if it came to new employment. All of those nerve-wracking job interviews, and then being up against people who may have more experience and qualifications. She groaned inwardly. At least Darion had always been his own boss, and had no plans of ever changing that. She had been relieved when he'd informed her his intentions were to run *normal* bars—no gentlemen's clubs with naked women, and no adult clubs with kinky stuff going on.

An hour and a half later, when the lesson had finished and Gabi had showered, she set off for the car park. She had just gotten comfortable in her seat when her mobile rang. Rummaging through her handbag, she dug out her mobile phone.

"Gabi."

"Darion, hi."

"Sorry I didn't answer your call. I left my phone at home."

"It's okay. So, did you do much today?"

"I stopped off at Dion's to see how she and Odelia are doing."

"That's nice."

"I should probably visit more often."

"I think she'd like that." Gabi strapped her seatbelt across her body. "Are you doing anything tonight?"

"I'm gonna get an early one."

She chewed her bottom lip. *No explanation, short answers. It seems that Darion's back to his usual closed-off self,* she thought. "Well, if you need anything, let me know."

"I will. See ya, Gabi."

"Bye."

She ended the call. With a heartfelt sigh, she rested her head on her arms, which were draped across the steering wheel. She hoped Darion was selling the club because he wanted to, and not because he was feeling pressured that it was what she wanted. As much as it pained her to admit it, she didn't want to take away something that meant so much to him and for him to be miserable. She'd rather walk away from him than ruin what he was passionate about. She silently prayed he'd soon find a new bar to rent, or buy, and his spirits would lift.

Pulling out of the car park, her mood dampened when specs of rain began hitting the windscreen. Flicking on the window wipers, she pressed her foot firmly on the accelerator. She wanted nothing more than to sit in the warmth of her apartment with a book or magazine and a nice, hot cup of tea.

Chapter Ten

Darion

"Have you heard anything from Gina?" Darion took a bite of his cheesecake. He stared at Lexi questioningly.

"Not for a while. The last I heard she told me her mom was on the road to recovery." She held her spoon in mid-air. "I take it you haven't heard from her?"

"Briefly." He placed his spoon down. "She still with Johnny?"

Lexi shook her head, took a final bite of her cheesecake, and stood up. "He left her."

"Any particular reason?"

"He was too jealous, possessive, controlling...Gina was always going to be too much for him to handle, Daz."

Lexi swilled her bowl under the hot water before dropping it into the sink. Turning around to face him, she scooped up her red hair and tied it into a messy top knot on her head. "So, how is everything with you, being on the straight and narrow?"

"I'm bored shitless, Lex," he confessed. "I need to get working again before I drive myself insane."

"Me too." She groaned. "What is Carl playing at? Surely it can't take a fucking month to decorate the club."

"Carl likes to ensure everything is perfect." Darion reached for his cigarettes. When he had hold of the box, he offered Lexi one. She accepted without hesitation.

"How is everything going with Gabi?" Lexi popped the fag in her mouth.

"Good."

"I'm real proud of you, Daz. Gabi is so good for you."

"I think so too." He lit the cigarette, took a slow, long pull on it, and then blew out smoke.

"I cannot believe Carl is hiring Eva!" she screeched. "Thanks for that. You could have intervened somewhere, on behalf of all of us that hate her."

"She's not my problem anymore."

"Too right, she's ours," she huffed. "Come on, let's sit in here." She indicated for Darion to follow her into the living room.

Darion stepped over a pile of clothes and shoes, removed a handbag from the sofa, and sat down. "At least the month off will give you more time to get this place sorted."

"Cheeky." She shook her head with a laugh and tucked her feet under her bum.

"Come and work for me."

"Darion, as much as I would love your company

61

every day, I make way more money dancing than I ever would pulling pints." She blew smoke rings at him. "Open another gentlemen's club and I will."

He shook his head. "I'm out of that game now."

"Yeah, because you're getting old." She giggled.

"Or wise."

"I'm gonna miss seeing your ugly mug every day." She stubbed her cigarette in the ashtray.

"You know where I live."

"Are you sure I'm allowed in the king's castle? The place where you rarely ever took women?"

"I took some there."

"Only the very special ones like Gina and Gabi." He knew from her sparkling eyes she was teasing him.

"You've been to my place before."

"No, I haven't."

"Well…now you have an invitation."

"Don't I feel lucky?"

Darion rose to his feet and leant down. Staring at Lexi, he doused his cigarette in the ashtray and smiled. "You should."

"You're such an arrogant asshole." She chucked a pillow at him.

"Arrogance and confidence are two different things."

"Darion." She shot him a look. "I know you, remember? I see behind that bad-boy persona."

He held a finger to his lips. "Shh. Don't tell anyone."

"Your secret is safe with me."

Taking his car keys out of the pocket of his jeans, he told Lexi he was heading home. He was surprised when she jumped up and threw her arms around him. It took him a second to accept the hug and then he reluctantly hooked his arms around her. Burying his head in her hair, he closed his eyes. He wanted to open up to Lexi, confide in her so badly about his problems, but he knew he couldn't. Not yet anyway.

"Call me soon." She disentangled herself. "Don't you dare forget about me."

"That won't happen."

"It does happen. I've seen it happen a hundred times. Now we won't be working together, you'll be moving on, the calls will become less frequent, and then I won't hear from you at all."

"Relax, Lex." He ran his thumb across her cheek. "I'll call you soon."

Once he was in the warmth and comfort of his car, he took out his mobile and scanned through his call list. Clicking on the number that ended in 369, he waited with bated breath for an answer. When it rang out, he ended the call, relief sweeping over him.

Switching on the stereo, he blasted "Me, I'm Not" by Nine Inch Nails as loud as the stereo would play it. The Audi cruised smoothly along the roads. Nodding his head to the tune, he sped up, and soon he was racing past buildings until they were too blurry to make out. The adrenaline rush was just what he needed.

Chapter Eleven

Gabi

Gabi spritzed some perfume on her neck, and then fastened the cord on her black Mac coat. It just skimmed her behind and revealed her long, slender legs. She was wearing her best pink La Perla underwear set, and the highest black stilettos she had. She felt girly, sexy. She expected to, given the price of the set and shoes. *The things you do for love,* she thought, adding another coat of pink lipstick which matched her nails. Scrutinising her reflection one final time, she dropped on the bed and waited patiently for Darion. He was showering, but she knew it wouldn't take him long to throw on some clothes, and give his hair a quick towel-dry.

As she was skimming through the images in her mobile, smiling to herself, Darion's mobile bleeped. Glancing toward the en-suite bathroom, she could hear the running water of the shower. Shuffling toward the bedside table, she picked it up. It was a text message from a number not listed in his contacts, ending in 369. She swallowed, feeling a hot flush spread up her chest, and a piercing pain shoot through her gut.

07844***369: Call me please x

Why would Darion not have the number stored? Who was messaging him with a kiss at the end? With trembling fingers, she quickly checked the call log. There were several calls from the same number that had been unanswered, displayed as 'missed.' Whoever it was, they were obviously desperately trying to get hold of him, and it appeared Darion was avoiding them. She placed the mobile down and stared at the wall before her, lost in thought. When she heard the creaking of the bathroom door, followed by Darion's footsteps, she looked up. He was naked except for a teeny white towel around his waist. Water droplets glistened on his body, and his dark, chin-length hair was swept back, soaking wet. Desire coursed through her blood and she ached for his touch, forgetting about the text message instantly. He was way too distracting and tempting.

His eyes, full of salacious longing, landed on her. As if he could read her mind, he dropped the towel. She couldn't control the pounding of her heart. Catching sight of his firm, tanned arse in the mirror and muscular thighs, she wanted to grab hold of him, and yank him onto her, cancel the evening's plans, and spend it in bed.

"Let's stay in," she suggested.

"As much as I'd love nothing more than to fuck your brains out, darlin'…" He sprayed himself with aftershave, "I promised Carl we'd meet him and his wife for drinks."

"You're such a tease." She shook her head.

The bed dipped as he crawled across it toward her. He seized her face in his hands and kissed her hard. Gabi was lowered onto the bed. His tongue found hers, and they wrestled together hungrily, passionately and possessively. Their moans collided, and Gabi grabbed a fistful of his hair, pulling him in closer. She forgot everything but the feel, taste and smell of him. She fancied him *so* much. The raw passion between them was almost tangible. When he drew back to place kisses on her neck, the tension coiled in her stomach, a throb of desire pulsing between her legs.

"Let's…stay…in." she murmured, the neediness in her voice clear. "Please."

Darion knelt back on the heels of his feet. Her gaze dropped to his erection, and she had never wanted him more. A dangerous gleam appeared in his irises, and he said in a silky and provocative voice, "If we hold it off, it will feel better."

"I can't hold it off," she sulked, feeling the pit of her stomach burn and ache. She glanced at the clock. "We can be quick."

Darion pushed himself to his feet and began to dress. Gabi threw a cushion at him and cursed. He infuriated her at times. *Payback is a bitch,* she thought, remembering she had a surprise for him. The surprise she had forgotten to do until now.

When Darion was smartly dressed in navy jeans and a matching shirt, the top buttons undone and the sleeves casually rolled up, Gabi called a taxi. It didn't take long until they heard the bleep of the horn. Gabi sprinted to the car, protecting her blonde waves from the rain with her clutch bag. The night air was chilly and she was relieved she had worn her Mac.

When Darion provided the driver with the name of the bar, Gabi cuddled up to him. "So, am I allowed to discuss The Black Door with Carl's wife, should she ask me any questions?"

Darion nodded. "She knows all about it."

"Really?" She knew the shock must have been visible on her face. "Is she um…into that stuff then?" she whispered.

"No, Gabi. She's not a swinger. But she appreciates the fact Carl will make a lot of money, and business is just business."

Gabi straightened her posture. "Are you saying I didn't appreciate that fact? Because it wasn't just business with you, Darion, it was pleasure too."

"I'm not saying that. I just don't want you to judge her."

"I won't," she snapped, crossing her arms across her chest protectively. "Did I judge you? Am I still here?"

Darion roughly yanked her toward him and kissed her cheek. "I forgot to tell you how fuckin' beautiful you look."

"You don't even know what I'm wearing."

"I don't need to know. You always look beautiful."

***

Darion

Darion patted Carl on the back to greet him, and then leant down to peck his wife, Tara, on the cheek. He then introduced them to Gabi. She greeted them both before taking a step back and fiddling with her hair self-consciously. He snaked his hand around her waist, pulling her into him.

"You okay?" he asked, leaning down to her ear.

She nodded.

"What do you want to drink?"

"Um…wine will do."

"You'll be okay here with Carl and Tara, right?"

"Sure."

He wove through the vibrant crowd toward the bar. Feeling someone pinch his ass, he glanced back. A pretty brunette flashed him a smile, followed by a wink. He ducked his head with a chuckle. He continued to the bar, and when before it, he lifted his hand to get the attention of the barmaid. The blonde with silicone breasts sashayed toward him.

"What can I get you?" she purred.

"White wine and a whisky."

"Coming up."

Seconds later she handed him the drinks with a flirtatious grin. Darion handed her the money, and whilst waiting for his change, he surveyed the room. He noticed a group of men watching Gabi, mischievous grins plastered on their faces. Gabi was oblivious to it, talking to Tara. He clenched his teeth, making an effort to stay in control. He silently dared one of them to touch her. They knew she was taken, as he'd noticed their stares on her upon arrival, to which he'd shot them a murderous look. They were trying to wind him up, probably after a fight. He knew it. That and trying their luck with Gabi.

"So," the barmaid's voice dragged him back to her. "Are you single?" She handed him a note and some coins.

He looked her over slowly from head to toe. She was attractive. Her waist was decorated with tattoos and her belly-bar shimmered in the light. If he was single, he would have taken her home, no questions asked. But times had changed and he wasn't a bad boy anymore. Well, he was, but for one woman only. No one could tear him away from Gabi. She made him a better man. He felt loved and secure when he was with her. He usually got bored of women quite quickly, yet he adored Gabi's company. When they spent time apart, he crazily found himself missing her. He'd recently started to embrace the fact he was in love. He was no longer ashamed of his feelings, like Eva had so often made him feel. He just hoped what he had with Gabi was strong and that they could overcome anything. He'd made a lot of mistakes in his life, but some things just couldn't be taken back.

"Well?"

"Sorry." He shook his head. "I'm with someone."

"Aw." She pouted. "That's a shame. Well, enjoy your night." She gave him a little wave and turned on her heel.

Darion stuffed his change in his pocket, picked

up the drinks, and strolled back toward Gabi. As soon as he placed them on the table, he glanced at the group of men, who were still checking Gabi out. His jealousy was unfamiliar. Usually when his girlfriend was the centre of attention, he liked it, got competitive, and loved the fact they wanted something *he* had. Now it seemed different. It was just like the time in the playrooms when it came to partner swapping and he'd been unable to get aroused, to allow Gabi to get intimate with another man.

"Are you okay?" Gabi asked him.

He stepped to the side, inhaling deeply. The men still had their stares on Gabi and he knew from their sleazy expressions they were either badmouthing or talking crudely about her. He *hated* when people disrespected him. "Stay here with Tara. There's something I need to sort."

Gabi's gaze landed on the group of men, and obviously sensing the animosity between him and them, she blocked his view. "Darion, please don't do anything stupid."

"They're trying to piss me off," he said sternly. "They've been checking you out ever since we got here."

Gabi wrapped her arms around him and tiptoed to give him a kiss. "I'm all yours. You never need to worry."

Are you sure about that? he wanted to ask. The kiss with Lawrence and the engagement ring flashed in his mind. Was it only a matter of time before she ran back to Lawrence? Was Darion her temporary bit of fun, until she got bored and wanted the perfect little house, wedding, and family?

Turning back to the table, Darion spoke with Carl about the club whilst Gabi chatted with Tara. It was half an hour later when Gabi's hand caressed his behind.

"Guess what?" she whispered in his ear.

"What?" He stared at her inquisitively.

"Remember that surprise I told you about?"

"Yeah."

"I've got nothing on."

"What?" He took in the coat she was wearing. "You've got no clothes on under that coat?" He needed clarification.

"Just my underwear."

"Oh, Gabi," he groaned, sliding his hand under the back of her coat. Coming into contact with her bare skin, he became aroused. "We need to go somewhere now."

"No." She edged away. "If we hold it off, it will be better," she repeated his words from earlier.

"Don't tease me like this." He flicked his tongue over her bottom lip before kissing her.

"Daz, we're going to the bar. Want another drink?" Carl asked.

"No, I'm good."

When Carl and Tara walked hand in hand toward the bar, he yanked Gabi into him. Before she could bat his hand away, he tugged at the collar of her coat and peered inside. The urgency to have her became overwhelming. Her perfectly firm breasts were encased in a tiny pink bra. He couldn't see beyond that, but he desperately wanted to. Nibbling her earlobe, his jeans tightened around his zip as he grew hard.

"I want you…now." He took her ear between his teeth and tugged on it hard.

Gabi batted his hand away with a grin. "Later."

An hour passed of conversations about The Black Door and Tara's beauty salon. The whole time Darion was frustrated Gabi was next to him, in nothing but sexy lingerie. As she stroked his fingers, he tried his hardest to concentrate. He sighed in relief when Carl and Tara finally said their goodbyes, as they needed an early night for work.

"You ready?" Darion finished the last of his beer.

"Almost." Gabi hiccupped and giggled, and he knew she was tipsy.

"You've made me wait long enough."

She jumped, knocking into him, and he realised one of the men had pinched her behind. *What the fuck.* He cracked his knuckles, feeling his blood boil.

"Darion, no."

"Out the way," he ordered.

Throwing himself at the bald man, he grabbed him around the throat. The man tumbled backwards, landing on the table. Beers smashed to the floor, shards of glass flying everywhere. Darion curled his hand into a fist and punched him hard in the gut. The man spluttered, and then whacked Darion in the face.

"Darion, stop!" Gabi's screams met his ears.

Darion felt another hit to his jaw, so he forcefully punched the man in the cheek and then the forehead. He was just about to lash out again when he was hauled up. He yelled, before noticing it was the bouncer. He was being yanked toward the door.

"Get off," Darion spat, freeing himself. "I'm leaving anyway."

Out on the street, he smoothed down his clothes and noticed Gabi wobbling slightly in her heels. She reached for him, checking over his face and body, asking if he was okay. The worry was apparent in her eyes. When he reassured her he was fine, her features hardened and she shook her head disapprovingly.

"What was that about in there?" she shrieked.

"I'm sorry, Gabi, but that man crossed the line."

"You can't go around beating people up!"

"I can if they disrespect me...or you."

Gabi hastily turned on her heel. She tripped over the curb, to which he lunged forward to support her. He latched his lips onto hers before she could lecture him further. He kissed her fiercely, the sort of kiss he had wanted to give her all night.

***

Gabi

Gabi's mouth was still in contact with Darion's, and his tongue roamed deep inside. She was a little light-headed, whether it was her hormones going crazy from the full-on kiss, or the alcohol, she didn't know. Pushing him away slightly, she stepped back.

Although she was pleased at his possessiveness,

that he cared enough to protect her, she didn't condone violence. Darion needed to settle things without using his fists. Being a club owner in the past, she understood he'd dealt with a fair share of drunks, and aggravating customers, but there had to be a better tactic.

"You worry me sometimes."

He stared at her quizzically.

"You need to resolve things without fighting. What if something bad had happened in there?"

His lips quirked upwards as he confidently said, "It wouldn't have."

She shook her head. "Promise me you'll stop behaving like a lunatic."

"I promise." He yanked her toward him. "Next time, I will think before I act. Do you forgive me?"

She hesitated a moment before nodding. "Did you…get jealous in there?" she asked, studying him intently.

He brought his head up and his steely gaze levelled on hers. "I did," he confessed. "And I hated it."

Sliding her hands through his hair, she had an overwhelming urge to be as close to him as possible. As they kissed ferociously, she backed him down an alley.

"Where are you taking me?" The amusement was visible on his face.

She didn't know where. She wanted him and that was all that mattered. As she turned the corner, she was glad to see it was a deserted car park. She shoved Darion against the wall, making him chuckle.

"You're daring tonight."

"You bring that side out in me," she murmured, crashing her lips against his.

Darion's hands skimmed up her legs, diving under her coat until his fingers were between her legs. He groaned as he caressed her. Her skin tingled under the trail of his touch.

"I like this side of you."

"Good." She bit his lip. "You'll...be...seeing...a lot of more...of it," she said in between kisses.

A breeze cooled her skin when he whipped open her coat. He eased her breasts out of her bra, and began massaging them firmly. Gabi's nipples hardened, and her head fell back on a soft sigh. When he took one in his mouth, his tongue swirling around it, the muscles in her belly clenched. His hand was now down her thong, and the tips of his fingers stroked her throbbing clit.

"Oh, Darion..." she whimpered.

Grabbing fistfuls of his hair, she tugged on it roughly before lowering her head to kiss his forehead. Fully aroused, her body accepted his plunging fingers, and she sucked in air, feeling her heartbeat race. Although the night air was chilly, her body was now flooded with heat.

"You feel so good..."

He silenced her with a firm, fast kiss, his tongue claiming hers, making her breathless. His stubble scratching her skin didn't deter her from deepening it. When he eventually pulled back, she unzipped his jeans and released his erection. She trailed kisses along his neck, and grimaced when his fingers continued to thrust into her.

"Ah..." she cried out. He knew exactly which spot to hit. Her inner muscles tightened and ached, her body silently screaming for more.

She stroked up and down his length several times. When his face screwed up in pleasure and he was rock hard, she guided him into her. He withdrew his hand and forcefully jerked his hips forward. Gabi gasped as he filled her entirely, the impact both pleasurable and painful. He rocked his hips back and forth continuously, until she was loving every second of it. She gripped at his buttocks, pulling him in deeper.

"I can't believe you wore just this." A naughty glint shimmered in his pupils as he stroked the material of her bra. His stare travelled down her body, his mouth curling up into a smile. "You look incredible."

Gabi licked her lips, which were dry and swollen from all the kissing. Darion pummelled into her fast and hard. He now had a menacing snarl on his face, his eyes blazing as if he were possessed. Her body was being slammed against the brick wall, and although it hurt, she didn't want him to stop. She attacked his neck, her teeth clamping into his skin.

"Fuuuck!" Darion pulled back, his jaw clenched.

He gripped her hair roughly, dragging her head down to his and kissed her again. His tongue wrestled with hers, both of them unable to get enough of one another. Pleasured grunts escaped his lips.

As he continued to buck his hips upwards, sliding in and out of her in a hurried rhythm, delightful spasms shot through her body. They fit together so perfectly. The pleasure was almost unbearable. She bit her lip to muffle moans that were threatening to spill loudly. The last thing she wanted was to be caught. She knew she didn't have the patience to wait for a taxi home though, and she also didn't want the sizzling moment to pass.

Hooking her legs around his waist, she rocked into him, meeting each delicious thrust. Her core clenched, her loins heating, and she knew she was close. Darion's finger and thumb closed hard on her nipple as he tweaked it repeatedly. She groaned.

"You...sexy...bitch," his words were soft and close to her ear.

She searched his eyes, which appeared drunk but full of lust. He was so sexy, rough, and rugged, and she feared losing him. She *never* wanted to lose him.

"Hey!" An unfamiliar voice caused her to look up, her breathing suspending. She noticed a man appear from a door. "This is a private car park. Can't you read the sign?"

Gabi was relieved a car was blocking them from being seen.

"Ignore him," Darion groaned, showing no signs of stopping.

"If you don't get the fuck out, I'm calling the police."

"One second," Darion roared, plunging into her, his face strained. "I'm close," he told Gabi, panting.

"Did you hear me?" the man yelled even louder. "What are you doing over there? You better not be touching my car."

Gabi panicked, trying to free herself from

Darion. "Stop," she pleaded, although her body didn't want him to.

Tension coiled in her stomach, the ache getting heavier. She gripped onto Darion, clamping her lips shut to keep silent. She was seconds away from succumbing to the orgasm that was threatening to tear into her.

"Oh, Gabi...." Darion pounded into her faster. He glanced over his shoulder. "The man's on his way over...come....now."

"I can't," she cried, fear making her push away.

"Now, Gabi."

He pounded into her relentlessly making her focus again. Her breathing got quicker and her inner muscles tightened. Delightful vibrations rushed through her body, making her moan out and shudder.

"Ohhhhh..." She panted, her body exploding around him.

Darion throbbed and jerked inside her as he allowed his own climax to overtake him. Then he withdrew, setting her on her feet. She pulled her coat around herself, whilst he zipped up his jeans.

"Let's go," he demanded.

"Hey," the man screamed out, racing toward them.

Gabi was trying to fasten the only buttons she had left on her coat, as she ran to keep up with Darion. He was now dragging her along by the arm, and glancing over his shoulder every few seconds. When they turned the corner and the man was no longer in sight, they burst out laughing.

Gabi held her aching tummy, trying to stop

herself from collapsing on the floor. Happy tears streamed down her cheeks. Before she knew it, Darion swooped her up in his arms.

"Darion, no," she shrieked. "You'll drop me."

Just as she predicted, Darion's foot got wedged in the curb and they both tumbled to the ground with a painful thud.

"Owwww…"

She couldn't find the strength to move her limbs and so she remained lying on the ground. Darion linked his fingers in hers and she kept her focus on the pitch black sky. The twinkling stars were scattered about. The moon was perfectly round and bright, and when she faced Darion, she could see it reflecting in his eyes. He looked at her and they began laughing again at the scenario.

Regaining control, she rolled onto her side, wincing when a sharp pain shot up her spine. "We…need…to…get a taxi," she managed to form the words.

She was relieved when half an hour later, they were snuggled in her bed. Hooking an arm and leg around him, she rested her head on his chest. She was so exhausted she could no longer keep her eyes open. The last thing she remembered was Darion softly stroking her hair.

Chapter Twelve

Gabi woke on a loud groan. Her whole body ached and her head throbbed with a migraine. She peeked at the alarm clock from under the covers. It wasn't set to go off for another hour. She squeezed her lids shut and attempted to sleep a little longer. Darion's light snoring was the only sound in the room. The daylight poured through the gap in the curtains, but she wasn't yet ready to face it.

Sighing heavily, she sat up. She was unable to get back to sleep. Swinging her legs over the side of the bed, she bit her lip to hold in her moans. She felt like she'd been run over by a bus. It was only when she was before the bathroom mirror did she notice the bruises on her body. She rubbed her elbow as she inspected other areas on her body. The marks must have been a result of falling over with Darion. She couldn't help but laugh as last night's sexual antics invaded her mind.

By the time she showered, being careful not to get her hair wet, and dressed, Darion was awake. Propped up against the pillows, his tanned, firm chest was on show. He flashed her a dazzling smile.

"Last night was fun." He chuckled.

"Yeah, and not a night I'll be forgetting for a long time. I'm covered in bruises."

"Shame. I thought you were referring to something else." He winked.

"And that." A smile tugged at her lips.

Darion threw the covers aside and stood up. He was completely naked. He mumbled he was taking a shower and strolled out of the room. Gabi was unable to resist watching his ass in the process. She caught sight of her dreamy expression in the mirror and rolled her eyes. *Get a grip, Gabi.*

As she ran a brush through her waves, she stilled when Darion's mobile bleeped. She sprinted toward the bedside table and glanced at the screen.

*07844***369: Am I seeing you today? x*

Gabi had to hold on to the bedside table to prevent her weak legs from giving way. That horrible pain in her gut appeared again. It was the same pain, the same gut feeling she'd had when she'd thought Lawrence had been cheating on her. Who the hell was Darion meeting up with in secret? If it was a friend, then surely the number would be stored. She listened out for the running water of the shower, and deciding it was safe, she scanned through his mobile. The text message she'd seen previously from that number asking him to call had been deleted. She checked the call log. There were no missed calls from the number ending in 369. It was as if he had deleted them all yet kept the other call logs, such as her own, Lexi's, Dion's and Carl's.

She set the phone down and resumed brushing her hair. She was glad that when Darion returned, her back was facing him. She knew her expression would have revealed how worried she was. From the corner of her eye she noticed him check his phone.

"Fancy breakfast?" he asked, yanking on some boxer shorts.

Gabi had no appetite whatsoever, yet she needed the time to snoop again. "I'd love some pancakes." She beamed.

"Sure."

She silently prayed he didn't take his mobile with him. Her tense muscles relaxed when he left the room, his mobile still in the same place. Was the message still there? If he had deleted it then he was definitely hiding something. She lifted her head, trying to hear what he was doing in the other room. When she heard the opening of cupboards, she grabbed his mobile before she lost the courage. She clicked on his inbox. Her breath held tight in her throat. The text message had been deleted. *Oh my god.* She willed her heart to slow its racing beat. Tears sprang in her eyes and she hated how upset she was getting. Was Darion having an affair?

She sat on the bed and tried to remember any suspicious events. There had been times in the past when he hadn't wanted to meet up, the times he was late, and the calls he made in private, which he stated were all 'business-related.'

He'd informed her yesterday he had to meet an

estate agent regarding a bar to let. She hadn't even bothered to ask him when.

Slipping on her heels and grabbing her handbag, she strode into the kitchen and sat down. The pancake was ready and she knew she had to force it down. Her stomach churned when she took a bite.

"What are your plans today?" she asked in as nonchalant a tone as she could muster.

"Not much."

"When are you meeting the estate agent?"

"Friday."

They were silent as they ate their breakfast. When Darion had finished his, he placed the plate in the sink and leisurely approached her. Cupping her head in his hands, he planted a soft kiss on her lips.

"I hope you know how much I care about you," he said, the sincerity apparent in his eyes.

Gabi's spine stiffened. She wondered whether he was declaring his feelings because he was feeling guilty about something.

"I know you do," she responded. "And I hope you know I'd *never* hurt you again." She meant it. Kissing Lawrence was the worst thing she had ever done. Would Darion hurt her?

She studied his expression intently to see if a flicker of guilt flashed across his face, remorse, sadness, anything—yet it was devoid of emotion. Darion was good at pretending to be confident, and immune to any other feelings, especially ones that made him weak.

"I believe you, Gabi," he said softly.

"Right." She stood up. "I better get to work. Are you going home?"

"Yeah. Let me get dressed and I'll walk out with you."

Gabi stared at the wall before her for what seemed like an eternity. She had made up her mind. It was time to see what Darion was hiding.

When they were both outside ten minutes later, Gabi allowed Darion to kiss her, his tongue wrestling with hers, his hands wrapping around her waist. He kissed her like it was only them in the world, as if they weren't standing on the street with people walking past. Pulling back, she wiped her mouth.

"Have a good day, darlin'." He took hold of her hand and squeezed it.

"You too," she responded.

Gabi turned on her heel, the smile vanishing from her face. She unlocked her car door, climbed in and waited patiently. She watched as Darion got into his Audi. He pulled off hastily, leaving a trail of exhaust smoke behind him. He was obviously in a rush. She allowed a couple of cars to drive past, and then she started the engine, put the car in gear, and set off to follow him. She felt insane playing little Miss Detective, but she needed answers. There was no point in confronting him about the messages and calls. If he didn't mind her knowing about whatever it was, then he wouldn't have deleted everything.

As she turned several corners, keeping a close watch on his car, she became claustrophobic. She was afraid of what she would find. Winding down the window, she sucked in air. *Please don't break my heart, Darion,* she thought, knowing she couldn't handle it. If he was having an affair, it was obviously serious if he was in contact with the person regularly. It wasn't like her stupid one-off kiss with Lawrence. It would have been planned— the calls and text messages, the secret meetings. With a free hand, she rubbed her throbbing temple. *Shit!* The traffic lights turned red. Drumming her hands on the steering wheel, she craned her neck, trying to ensure she didn't lose sight of his car. When the lights changed to green, she floored the accelerator and caught up with him.

After fifteen minutes of tailing him, he turned a corner, and then she noticed his right indicator light flashing. He was pulling into a car park of a hospital. Confusion swept over her. She drove on by and headed for work.

What was Darion doing at a hospital? Her heart slammed against her chest with worry. Was a member of his family sick? But surely he wouldn't keep that from her. Was *he* sick? She felt faint at the thought. What if there was something wrong with Darion and he hadn't mentioned it so as not to worry her? Maybe the text message was from someone he trusted, someone he confided in to keep his secret. Darion was the sort of person to hide an illness should he have one. He rarely ever moaned or complained about anything. He kept everything bottled up, thinking that discussing feelings was weak.

Her head ached with confused thoughts, as she didn't know what course of action to take. She didn't want to admit she had checked his mobile and followed him like some crazy person. She knew waiting patiently until he opened up to her was probably the best idea. At least he wasn't having an affair. Well, it didn't appear that way. She wished Darion could open up to her, that whatever it was, he didn't have to face it alone.

***

Darion

Darion rubbed the tense muscles in the back of his neck as he neared the hospital. His hands were damp, his mouth bone-dry. He lifted his gaze to the grey coloured, depressing looking building, the place where bad news was often delivered. Was he ready for answers? Fearing his weak legs would buckle beneath him, he balanced against the wall for support. He couldn't do it. He wasn't ready. Removing his mobile from his pocket, he switched it off.

He paced to his car. Once inside he buried his head in his hands. He had never been so scared, so worried in his entire life. When his heartbeat and body temperature resumed to normal, he started the engine. He needed a strong drink. He needed something to take his mind off everything. A game of cards and some beers with Lennie and Travis had never seemed so tempting.

Chapter Thirteen

Gabi

The working day passed quickly, and afterwards, Gabi and Mallory headed to a salon to get their hair and nails done. Gabi didn't confide in her about the text messages she had found in Darion's mobile, or his hospital visit. She wouldn't have minded Mallory's opinion, or a reassuring speech to soothe her worries, should one come. However, she wanted to find out for certain what was going on before she made a big deal about it.

"How's dance class going these days?" Mallory asked, admiring her glittery, grey nails.

"Yeah. It's good." Gabi watched the lady stroke pink polish onto her nails.

"Have you seen Ben yet?" she asked, her eyes lighting up.

"I saw him by the elevator the other day." Gabi chuckled. "Mal, are you going through that dry patch with Steve again?" she teased.

"Nothing wrong with a bit of eye candy,

sweetie."

"I suppose not." She lifted her head to the mirror. Her blonde hair fell in soft waves down her shoulders. If only she was feeling as good on the inside as she did on the outside.

"It looks gorgeous, Gab."

"Thanks." She studied Mallory's hair, which was perfectly straight, and a darker blonde than she'd previously had it. "Yours looks stunning too."

Gabi rose to her feet when she was instructed to place her hands under the ultra-violet light. Sitting at the counter, she waited patiently for her nails to dry. When satisfied they were, both she and Mallory left the salon.

"Fancy going for a quick drink somewhere?"

"Sure, but it'll have to be coffee. I'm driving, remember?"

They settled at a table in the nearest coffee shop they could find. It was fairly busy with people in suits, having recently finished work, or youngsters transfixed on their mobiles or laptops. They spent the next hour discussing work, Suzie, Steve, and celebrity gossip. For the first time that day, Gabi had completely forgotten about all of her worries.

It was 9 p.m. when she strolled into her apartment. Hanging her coat and handbag in the hallway, her stomach rumbled, reminding her she hadn't eaten properly. She kicked off her heels and entered the kitchen. Nothing in the fridge looked appetizing. She wasn't up to cooking, so grabbed a container of cold pasta.

She took it, along with a fork, into the living room. She sat in silence as she ate it, no noise distractions from the television, no words of a book or magazine filling her mind, just complete silence. As she shovelled the pasta into her mouth, she studied her living room. Romance books lined her bookshelf, only a few of which had been read. Photographs sat in pretty silver frames of her family, and the special holidays she had been to abroad. Ornaments decorated shelves and stunning oil paintings hung from the walls. The place was neat as usual, and it looked homely. It was then she realised she had nothing in sight to remind her of Darion, or to even show she had a boyfriend.

Leaning back on the sofa, she searched her mind of whether she had any of her belongings in his apartment. She didn't. Well, except for a toothbrush and a few cosmetics. She made it her mission to capture and print some photographs of them for her place. Maybe even leave some at his 'bachelor pad,' and replace the ones he had of Eva in his bedside drawer.

Finishing the pasta, she threw the container in the bin, the fork in the sink, and trudged to the bathroom. A hot relaxing bath would do her the world of good. Once inside, she stripped off her clothes and stuffed them into the laundry basket.

Perched on the side of the tub, she waited for it to fill up halfway with hot water and then added cold. Climbing in, she gasped in delight as the warm water spread over her body, softening her tense muscles. She submerged her body in the bubbles, and rested her head against the tub. Closing her lids, she imagined she was at some fancy spa hotel in a Jacuzzi. She wouldn't have minded a short break somewhere. Perhaps she and Darion needed to get away from everything for a while. She decided then and there she would book somewhere special for her and Darion. Maybe it would strengthen their bond. Perhaps he would open up and tell her what was going on with him.

After she soaped and shaved everywhere, she climbed out of the tub. She was drying herself with a towel when she heard her mobile ringing.

"Hello," she said, as she slipped a robe on.

"Gabi," Darion's sultry voice filled the line, followed by a low blowing sound as if he was smoking.

"Hi." She padded over to the bed, and sat down. "How was your day?"

"Good."

She bit her lip in exasperation at his one word answers. "Did you do much?" she pried and waited with bated breath for his response, hoping he would come clean and tell her about his hospital visit.

"No...how did your day go?"

Ah, subject changer. "Work went well. Then I had my hair and nails done." She stroked her hair. It was silky soft. "Is everything okay with you?"

"Why wouldn't it be?"

"No reason." She rearranged the cushions and then lay down. "Oh," she said cheerily, suddenly remembering. "I've got a surprise for you."

"I love surprises." From the sound of his tone, she could just imagine the twinkle in his pupils and the mischievous grin on his face. "What is it?"

"You'll soon find out. Do you have anything planned for tonight?"

"I'm going to the club to get the last of my stuff."

"Okay. Well, I'll speak to you tomorrow."

When they said their goodbyes and Gabi ended the call, her shoulders sagged in disappointment. Why hadn't he confided in her about the hospital visit? Was he really going to the club or was he meeting someone? *The truth always comes out in the end,* she told herself.

Chapter Fourteen

Darion

Darion exited his Jeep and strolled toward The Black Door. As he took in the lonely-looking building, the lights off, and no music booming from the doors, a pain shot through his heart. Carl needed to get the business up and running. He hated seeing it closed. He wondered whether the locals and members were missing it as much as he was. He made a mental note in his head to arrange some bar viewings with the estate agent. He was going insane having nothing to take his mind off things. He needed to be around loud people, have chatter and rock music filling his ears, a business to motivate him.

Tossing his cigarette butt to the curb, he pushed on the door and was surprised to find it was open. He stepped inside and was instantly met with the fumes of paint. Black sofas and marble tables surrounded the room, protected by plastic covers. The shelves behind the bar were empty and there was nothing of his in sight. Carl was buying the club fully furnished, although it appeared he really did want to leave his mark on the place.

Sliding onto a new stool at the corner of the bar where he always used to sit, he sighed heavily. He hoped he'd done the right thing. Then he reassured himself that he had. He couldn't run that sort of business facing the new chapter in his life.

"It won't be the same without you."

He straightened when he heard her familiar silky voice. Eva swayed toward him, a smile tilting her lips. Grabbing a stool, she sat next to him.

"What are you doing here?"

"Carl asked me to open up. He said you needed to collect some things."

"Why didn't he come himself?"

"There was no point in him traipsing across town when I'm just around the corner."

"Any news on the opening?" He stroked the stubble on his jawline and knew he could have done with a decent shave.

"Soon." She flicked her hair back. "Don't worry, Daz, I'll make sure he takes care of this club."

He nodded.

"The girls too," she added quickly.

"You do that."

"How are things with you and Gabi?"

"Fine," he lied, the engagement ring torturing him again. He rubbed his palms up and down his face and inhaled deeply. He used to have photographs of Eva in his drawer when he believed he still had feelings for her. As soon as his feelings for Gabi had become clear, he'd tossed them out.

Surely Gabi wouldn't hold onto the ring unless there were feelings she was unsure of.

"I'm glad to hear that," Eva's voice broke his thoughts. "Fancy a drink?" She stood up and began rummaging behind the bar. "There must be something around here."

"No, Eva," he said sternly. "I'm here for one reason only, to get my stuff." Pushing himself to his feet, he strolled toward his office. When inside, he grabbed a cardboard box from the side and began opening cupboards and drawers and filling it. Then he took the pictures from the walls, smiling fondly at each one he came across.

"Will you visit much when it's back open?" Eva was leaning against the doorframe, her arms folded across her chest.

"I don't have any reason to visit."

When his mobile bleeped, he rummaged through his pocket. He hoped it was Gabi saying goodnight. Panic set in when he glanced at the screen. He went hot and then cold, like he had a fever and instantly needed to sit. Perching on the edge of the desk, he squeezed his lids shut for a second, trying to control the hammering of his heart.

07844***369: *You can't avoid this forever. x*

"What's the matter?" Eva asked.

"Nothing." He slid the mobile back into his pocket and grabbed hold of the box. He examined the room one final time until he was certain he had everything. Brushing past her, he strode toward the exit. He needed air. His stomach was churning, an acidic taste appearing in his throat. He felt like he would vomit.

"If you ever need to talk to anyone, I'm here, you know."

He glared over his shoulder. "We both know you'd be the last person I'd come to."

"Oh, Darion." She shook her head with a merciless laugh. "You seriously need to get over the past already."

"Easier said than done," he mumbled.

As he sprinted to his car, he could hear the sound of Eva's heels behind him. He clenched his teeth, unable to disguise his rage. Why couldn't she take the hint and leave him alone? Setting the box in the boot, he walked around the car and unlocked the door.

"You know, one day you might need my help," she yelled after him.

No one can help me, he thought. *No one at all.*

Chapter Fifteen

Gabi

Gabi was browsing through endless pictures of luxury spa hotels in London. A weekend of nothing but pure relaxation and pampering was just what she and Darion needed. Excitement built as she clicked on stunning indoor swimming pools, exquisite in-house restaurants, and modern suites.

Retrieving her debit card from her handbag, she tapped in her details. She ticked boxes for the penthouse suite, including breakfast, dinner, and use of the spa facilities. Situated in Mayfair, she decided they could even go sightseeing this time around. She hadn't splurged on expensive shoes, or treated herself in a while, and so shrugged off the fee, which was a tad pricey.

Grabbing her mobile, she located her parents' number. She could probably even pay them a visit. After a few rings, she received an answer.

"Hi, Mom."

"Gabi," her mom squealed in delight. "How are

you?"

"I'm good. How are you and Dad?"

"We're fine, honey. We're going to Italy on Friday."

"Sounds lovely." She grinned. "I was going to visit, but we'll arrange something some other time."

"That'd be nice."

"Is Samuel still there?"

"Yes, but not for too long."

"Okay. Well, tell him I said hello."

"I will do. How's Phil these days?"

Gabi chewed the end of her pen. She hadn't bumped into her boss for a while, now that she thought about it. She never had any reason to venture to the top floor where his office was. "I haven't seen him a while."

"Send my love when you do."

"Sure."

Mallory entered the room, holding two cups. The coffee aroma filled the air.

"Mom, I better go. Have a lovely time in Italy, and we'll catch up soon."

"Bye, darling. Take care."

Gabi set her mobile on the desk. Kicking her Valentino stilettos off, she tucked her feet up and made herself comfortable.

"Why do you look like the cat that got the cream?" Mallory gave her the cup.

"I've just booked a spa getaway for me and Darion." She beamed before taking a sip of her drink.

Mallory sat down. "When?"

"The weekend."

"Oooh. Dirty weekend, huh?" Mallory lifted her cup to her lips and blew over the steaming liquid.

"I was thinking more *romantic*." She raised a brow. "Although I could add a hint of dirty."

The girls laughed in unison before taking sips of their drinks.

"When do you go to the Maldives?"

"Two weeks."

"Have you bought everything you need?"

"Pretty much. Although I suppose one can never have enough clothes." Mallory took hold of the manuscript Gabi had been reading and cast her eyes on it. After a couple of seconds silence, she said, "Are you thinking of a shopping trip?"

"I'm free later if you are. I wouldn't mind a new dress."

"Sounds like a plan. How's Darion?"

"He's fine. And Steve?"

"He's good. We haven't had a holiday in so long, Gab. I cannot wait to be on the beach with a cocktail."

"Don't forget to take lots of photos."

"Oh believe me, I won't." Mallory placed the manuscript down. "I like the sound of this story."

"Yeah, I'm enjoying it. I think it will do really well."

Mallory downed the last of her coffee and rose to her feet. "I'll meet you by the elevators later."

"Sure."

When the door closed after her, Gabi sent Darion a text message.

Gabi: Pack your cases. We're going to London

on the weekend. x

Just as she tapped her computer keyboard to check for new emails, her mobile began buzzing, sliding all over her desk. Glancing down at the screen, she saw Darion's handsome face.

"Hi."

"Is this the surprise you were talking about?" The sound of his sultry voice sent a shiver down her spine.

"Yes, it is. You just wait and see the spa hotel I've booked. It's gorgeous."

"Send me the bill. I'll pay for it."

"I've already paid. It's my treat."

"I wish you wouldn't do that, Gabi."

"Relax."

"Well, in that case, I'm paying for everything else in London."

"Whatever." She giggled. "So, how's your day going?"

"I'll have a new bar to run next week."

She gasped. "That quick?"

"I'm only renting. But I need to do something before I go fucking crazy. I'll see how it goes for a few months, and then look at places to buy."

"Is it in Westhaven?"

"It's a couple of streets away from The Black Door."

"That's great news." *Not.*

"It's called Retox."

"Nice."

"Am I seeing you later?"

"I'm going shopping with Mallory, but I'll be

back about nine."

"I'll see you then."

"Bye."

Gabi slipped her shoes on and swung in her chair so she was facing the window. Dark clouds were gathering ominously overhead. The sun cast an orange glow over the busy street. Everyone appeared to be in some mad rush. It was probably the fear of predicted rain. Taking steps to get a clearer view, she placed her palm on the window pane. She screwed her face up when a woman with dark, sleek hair resembling Eva strode by. So Darion had a new bar. She groaned inwardly. She'd wished he was far away from his past, not within walking distance.

She twisted around when her office phone began ringing. Answering it, it was the last person she expected to hear from, especially after everything.

"Why are you calling me, Lawrence? I thought I told you never to contact me again."

"I was kind of hoping you'd contact me," he responded.

"Why would I do that?" she snapped. Was he deluded?

"I was hoping you'd finally seen the light of day and give me another chance. I guess you don't know about Darion's little secret yet."

She was unable to move or speak for a moment. What secret? Did Lawrence know about the text messages, calls, and meetings? If so, how? She hesitated for a moment before asking, "What do you mean?"

"You'll soon find out, I expect."

"Why are you playing games? Just tell me what you know."

"Goodbye, Gabi," he said. "When you find out, remember I'm here for you. I'm always willing to give things another go."

Before she could reply, the line went dead. Gabi sat there bewildered, staring at the phone in her hand. Lawrence knew something she didn't. She closed her eyes for a moment to compose herself. She contemplated calling Darion and demanding answers. But then again, maybe that was Lawrence's plan. He'd always been good at stirring up trouble. She decided not to confront Darion, and give Lawrence any satisfaction. Whatever Darion wasn't telling her, he'd confide in her eventually. Wouldn't he?

***

After a long day, Gabi collapsed on her bed with a yawn. There were several shopping bags on the floor but she didn't have the energy to put them away. She was sure she'd purchased everything she needed for the weekend break: a couple of new bikinis, a dress for the evening, and new make-up. Stripping her clothes off, she climbed under the covers and reached for the television remote. She flicked through the channels and settled on *Breaking Bad.* She needed to stay awake. Darion was on his way over.

It was half an hour later when the sound of the doorbell reverberated through the apartment. She slipped on her blue silk nightdress and trudged barefoot toward the door. Darion was leant against the frame, wearing black jeans and matching t-shirt, which clung to his impressive biceps. His hair was gelled back neatly, hanging down the nape of his neck. A cigarette was hanging from his mouth, the smoke obscuring her view for a second. He stepped forward and she noticed his gaze sweep over her appreciatively, his irises sparkling with interest.

"A dirty weekend is the best idea you've ever come up with." His lips wrapped around his cigarette and he slowly blew out smoke before flicking it to the grass.

Gabi closed the door when he entered, and led him toward the bedroom. "I was thinking more romantic."

"We'll see about that." He laughed a dirty sounding laugh. "I've been thinking about you all day."

Before she knew it, he shoved her onto the bed, and lay on top of her. His lips curled into a devilish smile as he slipped down the strap of her nightdress, freeing her breast. Gabi's cheeks grew warm as she became coy at his intense scrutiny. His gaze didn't leave hers when he swirled his fingertip around her nipple. It stiffened and tingled instantly. His face hovered over hers, making her stomach clench in anticipation. She knew he was about to kiss her. Every time he kissed her, it may as well have been the first ever kiss, for it filled her with excitement.

His lips captured hers, sucking on them gently. Gabi mirrored his actions until his tongue slipped in. She wrestled with it, her hands delving into his hair. It was slow, soft, and comforting. Drunk on endorphins, her only desire was to be close to him.

She hoped whatever obstacle was standing in their way could be overcome. She hoped it was all just a misunderstanding; which was why Darion hadn't mentioned anything. All she wanted from him was stability, commitment, and love.

"I love your body," he murmured, his soft, seductive tone hypnotising her.

She arched her back and curled up her toes when he sealed his mouth over her breast. His warm, wet tongue circling her nipple sent shivers down her spine. When his suction got fast and greedy, his hand massaging her other breast, she writhed impatiently. He rubbed his erection against her, causing her body to burn in pleasure.

"Ah, Darion..." She thrust her chest upwards, the licking and nibbling driving her insane.

"Mmm..." he groaned. "I could worship this body for hours."

Gabi frantically yanked his t-shirt over his head, revealing his smooth, solid chest. When he removed her nightdress and their bare skin collided, she closed her eyes, sighing in delight.

"Let's watch a movie," he suggested on a wicked smile, climbing to his feet. He grabbed the TV remote and began scrolling through the channels. He settled on an X-rated movie. Moaning and groaning filled the air, and Gabi was unable to turn her attention away from the big screen before her. A handsome tattooed man was pleasuring two women at the same time. He used his tongue to tease the blonde, and a vibrator to tease the brunette. Gabi focused on their flawless bodies, how they writhed in pleasure, the sounds they made as they exposed themselves completely.

"You like watching other people, don't you, baby?" Darion asked softly, as he slowly unzipped his jeans.

"Sometimes," she responded. Gabi had observed many intimate scenes at The Black Door, and they had, in fact, aroused her.

She turned to study Darion for a moment. His predatory stare was fierce on her. His tongue darted out and he licked his lips before a smug smile appeared. He wriggled out of his jeans, his erection springing free. Gabi took in every inch of his perfect nakedness. Desire coursed through her blood, the raw passion between them as strong as ever.

"Do you want me?" he asked softly, challenging her with a lift of his brow.

Gabi nodded, although he already knew the answer. She could never resist.

"How about we make use of our Ann Summer purchases?"

He slid to his knees and ducked under the bed. He returned with the pink box of kinky goodies. Some of the stuff Darion had chosen, and she had no idea what they were for. She recognised the vibrators, all in different colours, shapes and sizes, butt plugs, cock rings, jiggle balls, beads, blindfolds, masks, whips, paddles, and lubricants.

His hand curled around something before she got a chance to see it. The bed dipped as he crawled toward her. She gripped hold of the covers when his tongue met her leg. It trailed upwards at a leisurely pace. She watched curiously as he worked his way toward her thigh. Then he glanced up at her, a raw animalistic hunger showing. He didn't need to seek permission. He had an open invitation to do anything he wanted. As if knowing this, he chuckled lightly.

He bowed his head, lapping slowly at her throbbing clit. Gabi wriggled in frustration, grabbing fistfuls of his hair, wanting and needing more. His warm, wide tongue sent her senses reeling. He slid his hands under her buttocks to lift her closer.

"Ah...don't...stop..." she murmured.

His fingers plunged in, causing her pelvis to throb and burn. She rocked her hips and his tongue movements got faster. As always, he knew exactly what he was doing with that skilled tongue of his. She could easily orgasm from oral sex alone.

Fixated on the TV again, she gasped when lubricant was spread between her legs. Darion ordered her to relax. Something cold prodded into her anus and her sex. It was the gold double stimulation vibrator. She cursed loudly, but still Darion slowly pushed further. The toy began vibrating, causing her to throw her head back in despair. As Darion increased the speed, she bit her hand to suppress her moans. It was unfamiliar, especially *there*. Darion slowly eased it in more. Gabi waited for the pain to subside. When it finally got all the way in and her body accepted it, it was pleasurable.

"Darion!" she hissed, clenching her eyes shut as the vibrations got even faster.

"Open your eyes," he commanded, indicating for her to watch the movie.

She did as instructed. The thick vibrator sliding in and out of her back passage and her sex simultaneously made her tremble violently. She wasn't sure she could handle it. Then Darion's free hand began circling her clit too. Her body was full and overstimulated in every possible pleasurable way, except for her nipples. She tweaked them repeatedly, thrusting her hips upwards, wanting more. Needing more.

"Faster..." she whimpered.

Darion followed her orders, and leant closer, watching the toy moving in and out of her. "You're soaking wet," he whispered, pleased.

The man in the movie was now pounding into the blonde incessantly, his head buried between the brunette's legs. The cries became louder, further turning Gabi on. Darion increased the speed of the vibrator again, making her thrash about, close to sobbing. It was way too intense.

It was clear he was loving every moment. Continuing to control the vibrator, his other hand now slid up and down his shaft. When his grip got firmer, and his movements faster, pleasured grunts spilled from his mouth. He matched the rhythm of his pumping to the plunging of the toy. They were both in pure ecstasy.

"Get here," Gabi pleaded. Her insatiable need for him to be inside her grew.

She shuffled sideways on the bed so he could enjoy the movie also. The removal of the toy was worth it when Darion guided his cock to her drenched entrance. Nothing was as good as the real thing. He rubbed up and down a few times, making her stomach tighten. Teasing her with the tip, he licked his lips slowly, his dark, hungry stare on her.

She waited in anticipation for his next move. She never knew whether he'd enter her teasingly slow, or forcefully fast. He was gentle when he made love to her, and dominating when he fucked her. She liked both equally.

Slowly easing himself in, his thumb met her clit again. He circled it, sending delightful tremors rushing through her body. Sliding in deeper, she cried out when he completely filled her. As he worked his hips back and forth, her muscles clenched, tightening around him.

"Oh…yes…" she murmured weakly. "Don't stop…"

He continued to plunge into her at a steady, controlled pace, his thumb still massaging her throbbing clit. Their eyes were transfixed on the movie, which heightened the excitement. It was unbelievably erotic.

"Did you like the vibrator?" Darion asked between grunts, still watching the threesome before him.

"Yes," she replied breathlessly.

His top lip curled back over his teeth wickedly, and he picked up the rhythm. He lifted her legs over his shoulders, and she winced as he filled her even deeper. As he rammed into her fiercely, the pressure began to build. Her trembling intensified.

"You ready?" he asked, grinding into her deeper, building up speed.

107

"Almost…"

He pounded in and out. In and out. Each slam sent her closer to the climax she desperately craved. She cocked her head to the side, and almost came on the spot. She could see his fit, firm ass in the mirror behind him. The muscles in his cheeks clenched as he pounded back and forth. His smooth back and strong shoulders were a delight to take in.

She bucked her hips upwards, moving with him in sync. She reached down and massaged her clit, fast, circular movements. She loved the sounds of his appreciative grunts at each and every thrust.

"You're fucking beautiful," he hissed through clenched teeth, his features contorting.

"Now, Darion…" she groaned.

They focused on the movie again as they climaxed together. Their bodies shuddered violently, their moans filling the air. They continued to rock until they were fully satisfied. Gabi's weak legs dropped from his shoulders, and Darion fell onto her.

She wiped the sheen of sweat from her forehead and squeezed her lids shut. Her whole body was sore and aching. She could think of nothing better than having a warm shower, and falling into a deep, peaceful sleep with him.

Chapter Sixteen

Darion

Darion stepped into the hospital. He got an instant whiff of disinfectant. It made his stomach churn with the need to release vomit. The floor squeaked with each step he took, and whimpering sounds met his ears. Everywhere he looked he saw bad news: the upset expressions on people's faces, the cautionary signs on the walls to check your body for lumps, the images showing the effects of smoking. He hated hospitals. Most of all, he hated going for news. He'd tried to avoid attending, but he knew it was only a matter of time before he had to face the music.

Please don't let it be bad, he prayed. *Please let everything be okay.* When he was before the receptionist, he provided his name and informed her he was a little late for an appointment. He waited patiently whilst she tapped away on her computer. Looking over the rim of her glasses, she provided him with directions to room 401.

Darion inhaled air. At that moment in time, there was only one person he needed to be concerned about. He had made a mistake once, he wasn't about to make any more. He brushed his hands through his hair and paused outside the room. Tapping lightly on the door, he took a step back. A nurse answered.

"Mr. Milano?" she asked.

He nodded.

"Come in. We didn't know whether to expect you."

"Better late than never," another voice came from inside the room.

As he entered, it took all of his willpower to lift his eyes from the ground and look up. It was as if his brain and heart had stopped functioning properly, for he didn't know what to think or feel.

"Mr. Milano, please sit," the nurse instructed with a friendly beam.

He slowly sank onto the plastic chair.

"It's not all bad news," she reassured him. "Oh, before I forget, here is a clinic which will take a sample for testing for you. Summer Row Clinic." She slid a leaflet toward him. "If you ring that number, you will get an appointment fairly quickly."

"How long will it take until I get the results?"

"Five to ten days is the usual waiting period." The nurse glanced down at the papers on her desk. "So, let's discuss the news you came to hear today."

He apologised when his mobile started ringing. Checking the caller ID, it displayed it was Gabi.

"Mr. Milano, your mobile should have been

switched off when you entered the hospital."

"Sorry," he said again, with a cough, his throat having become dry.

Switching the mobile off, he slid it back into his pocket. He listened to what the nurse had to say for the next half hour. Afterwards, feeling physically and mentally exhausted, he called the clinic. He was relieved when they told him they had a free slot that day due to a cancellation. A part of him didn't want to go, whereas another part of him wanted it over and done with.

"I'll be there," he said before ending the call.

He made it his mission to ensure he had the best time with Gabi in London, for when the results came through, it could change everything.

***

Gabi

Friday evening, Gabi was unable to contain her excitement. Her lesson at the Dance Academy and the week at Miller & Co had flown by. She was in desperate need of an indoor heated pool and a massage. Although Darion had seemed a bit on edge the last time she had seen him, and had something on his mind, she could see he was still looking forward to their getaway. She hadn't noticed any more strange incoming texts or calls on his mobile, although she still planned to get to the bottom of it.

Stuffing cosmetics into her oversized Louis Vuitton bag, she leant on it to close the zip. She had packed way too many things. As she dragged the bag down the hallway, she mentally checked off everything in her head she needed to take with her: night dresses, clothes, cosmetics, shoes for the day and night and the box of kinky goodies.

Glancing at her watch, she exited the apartment and locked up. She was expecting the taxi to pull up any minute. She was lost without her mobile phone. It was switched off and in her bedside drawer. Darion suggested they leave their mobiles at home, and have the sort of break where they could relax, with no one being able to contact them. She wouldn't have minded the idea if she didn't think he was running from something.

A few minutes later, she heard the honk of the taxi horn. Grinning, she headed toward it. Inside, she relaxed against the cool leather seat, and appreciated the music from the stereo. She realised she hadn't been away with Darion before.

She linked her fingers together and caught sight of her smiling face in the car window. The journey was peaceful and pleasant. The rows of houses soon changed to green landscapes, and soon they were in Westhaven. When the taxi came to a halt outside Darion's apartment, she remembered she had no mobile to call him.

"Can you wait a moment whilst I go get him?" she asked the driver.

"Sure."

Leaving the taxi at the curb, she rushed into Darion's apartment block and took the stairs rather than the elevator. Once outside his door, she could hear the sound of rock music playing at a low volume. She pressed the doorbell and waited.

"Hi," she said as he opened the door. "You ready? The taxi's outside."

"Almost." He stepped aside to allow her to enter.

As he vanished into his bedroom, Gabi did a quick scan over the place. It was tidy as usual. Still modern. Still resembled a bachelor pad. None of her belongings were there, and there was nothing to indicate he was in a relationship.

Stepping into the kitchen area, she perched on a stool. She could hear Darion rummaging in the bedroom. She noticed a stack of opened mail on the counter, right next to her elbow. Her brow furrowed at a shiny invitation titled 'The Black Door Grand Opening.' Lifting it up, she read it quickly. The club was reopening in two weeks' time. She wondered why Darion hadn't mentioned it. He never missed a good celebration at the club. Surely he would want to be reunited with his old employees, Lexi, Marnie, Gina, Wendy, Tiana, Lennie, Travis, and others she hadn't remembered the names of. Turning it over, her eyes widened when she saw a small key was attached. In neat, swirly handwriting a message displayed:

Daz, the playrooms are yours and only yours for the last time. Enjoy! Carl.

"Ready?" She jumped at the sound of Darion's voice.

"Um...yes."

He took in the invitation and she noticed his throat dip as he swallowed. When he averted his

113

gaze for a second, and shoved his hands in the back pockets of his jeans, she was certain he was uncomfortable.

"So, are we going to the grand opening?" She flashed him her biggest smile in a bid to appear casual, and not in the least bit suspicious of why he hadn't mentioned it, or invited her.

"I was gonna give it a miss." He turned on his heel and strolled into the living room.

"Why would you miss it? Don't you want to see what Carl has done with the club? Or see any of the girls?"

"I'll go another time." He slung his bag over his shoulder and grabbed his keys.

Gabi's muscles stiffened. Why was he avoiding the opening, the reunion? That sickening feeling swirled in her stomach again, her gut telling her something wasn't right.

"I'd like to go."

"Gabi, you hated the club, everything it represented, and you weren't particularly fond of the girls." He stepped out of the apartment and with a wave of his hand, indicated for her to do the same.

"That's a lie. I got on with Lexi really well. I didn't mind Marnie either." She fiddled with her nails. "And Gina was okay if you got her in a good mood."

"The Black Door's in the past. Let's leave it there."

As they descended the stairs, Gabi sighed heavily. She didn't know how much longer she could pretend everything was fine between them. A part of her wanted to explode and confront him about the mystery caller, the hospital visit, Lawrence's call, and him avoiding the club. Another part of her felt like waiting until after the weekend. It had been a while since they had been in their perfect little bubble and shut the world out.

Once they were both seated in the taxi, Darion reached for her hand. Reluctantly, she let him hold it. She planned to stare out of the window for most of the journey, but Darion yanked her into him.

"Did you forget to give me something?" His wickedly gleaming eyes were fierce on her.

"I don't know. Did I?"

His gaze fell to her lips. She inhaled air, knowing it would soon be knocked out of her lungs when he went for her. As predicted, he gripped hold of her head and slammed her face into his on a hard, animalistic kiss. His tongue circled hers fast and greedily. She eventually reciprocated, kissing, licking and sucking. Her moans were muffled as he deepened the kiss. *Why can't I get enough of this man?* she screamed inwardly. He had the ability to vanish her bad moods with a kiss alone. Feeling a needy ache between her legs, she slid her hand up his shirt. She stroked his solid, perfect chest and wished they were alone so she could have him.

"Gabi," he grunted in her ear, before tugging it with his teeth. "You drive me crazy.'

Feeling daring and extremely frustrated, Gabi took hold of his hand. Parting her legs slightly, she moved it upwards. She spotted Darion's brow rise in surprise. His devilish side had definitely rubbed off on her. She wanted to ensure she kept things fun and interesting with him. He loved the thrill of doing something forbidden, and the risk of getting caught.

"Here?" he checked with her.

"Here," she murmured.

"You're full of surprises lately," he whispered in her ear on a slow, naughty grin.

She moved her underwear aside, and thrust his hand further between her legs. The circling motion of his fingertips on her clit sent a hot ball of fire in the pit of her stomach. Her body strained toward his, needing him. When he massaged her tenderly, she bit her lip to suppress her moans. She wanted to roll her head back, close her eyes and really enjoy it. The sensible part of her made her keep her eyes firmly fixed on the driver.

"Does this feel good?" His hot breath was back in her ear.

"Yes," she murmured.

A finger languidly slid in, causing her to squirm on the seat. It slid out slowly, and back in again. Gabi's internal muscles throbbed and ached. It was heavenly. Lost in sensations, he possessed her with his touch.

His mouth settled on hers, and she licked his tongue slowly, swirling the tip around, before sucking it. Pulling back, she glanced down at her lap. Darion pushed into her with two dominant fingers. As he penetrated her deeply, the excitement built at the naughtiness of the situation. It was difficult trying to keep still and silent, and she was thankful music was playing, and other cars kept the driver busy.

"You're so wet..." Darion was back in her ear,

nibbling and licking it.

Gabi pushed her hips forwards and backwards, wanting more of him. How she wished they were alone so she could undress him, and have him properly.

Plunging into her deeper and faster, Gabi clawed the leather seat, her orgasm getting closer. Her pelvic region was burning and aching, greedy for release. Darion was gauging her reaction, watching every squirm, listening to her every moan. Delightful spasms shook through her body as she was close.

"Don't you dare stop…" she whispered, even though she noticed the driver glance in the rear-view mirror.

As Darion pummelled in and out. She took a breath, and then another. Every muscle in her body tightened. He slid into her a few final times, deep and slow. Her fists clenched, her toes curled. She clamped her lips together to trap her cries. Shuddering, she came in a violent rush, spasms of pleasure rippling through her. The release was every bit as good as she knew it would be.

Her body went limp and she sank against the seat. Darion withdrew, a smug expression forming on his face.

Braving a glance at the driver, Gabi noticed he seemed none the wiser. With a little giggle, she pressed her mouth against Darion's.

Pulling back, darkness clouded his eyes, and in a serious tone he said, "That was exciting."

"Yes," she agreed. "It was."

The weekend was only just beginning.

Chapter Seventeen

When the taxi came to a halt, Gabi stepped into the cool night air. As she took in the people around her, it appeared they were enjoying the early evening. People strolled past holding hands, shopping bags, or mobile phones. Lifting her head she studied the grand hotel. Rows of windows cast lights onto balconies that held tables and chairs. Some guests were outdoors dining and others enjoying a drink.

When Darion had settled the taxi fare, she pushed her way through the plush reception area. Her shoes slid slightly on the white marble floor. There was a seating area to her left, doors to a restaurant on her right, and a main circular desk before her. The gold and white colour scheme from the carpets, drapes, and portraits throughout were elegant. It didn't take them long to check in with the friendly receptionist, and soon they were in the elevator heading for the penthouse suite. Minutes later, they were unlocking the door, anxious to get inside.

"Wow." Gabi's eyes widened as she took a step forward.

The place was huge. The living room area was modern, everything black or charcoal grey. A large television hung from the wall, an L shaped sofa sat on a grey, fluffy rug, and several tables throughout held vases of fresh smelling flowers.

Dropping her bag, she glanced at the dining area, where there was a glass table surrounded by eight grey padded seats. Above that was a chandelier.

She rushed to check out the balcony. The sight of London below with its lit-up buildings was breathtaking. She bit down a grin. Over the weekend, they would be exploring as much as possible together, creating memories.

"You chose well." Darion came up behind her and snaked his arms around her waist.

"How about we take advantage of the mini bar and have a drink out here?" She turned to face him, and pressed her lips against his.

Tucking a strand of hair out of her face, Darion's thumb traced down her cheek before he nodded.

Gabi re-entered the penthouse and slid open the grey doors to the bedroom. As curious as ever, she wanted a full tour of the place first. Slipping off her heels, her feet sank into the soft carpet. A laugh escaped her lips. It certainly didn't disappoint. A king-size bed was before a red wall. Two matching lamps sat on tables either side. It was also decorated with mirrors, statues and flowers.

Then she noticed the door to the en-suite bathroom. She gasped when she saw the huge tub in the centre of the grey tiled room. There was a television built into the wall, and opposite was a bowl sink and toilet. *I could certainly get used to this place,* she thought, running her hand across one of the soft hanging towels.

"Fancy ordering food?" Darion asked, over a menu he was holding when she returned to the balcony.

She dropped onto a cushioned chair, and picked up a glass of champagne, of which Darion had poured. "Sure."

Taking a sip, she groaned inwardly as the cool, crisp liquid went down her throat. Darion read out the menu to which she chose a chicken salad. As he retired to the living room to make the call, she sighed in contentment. Although they weren't too far from home, she felt a million miles away from everyone, and the niggling problems that had been eating away at her.

***

The next morning passed quickly. Gabi and Darion had enjoyed breakfast on the balcony, a selection of different foods and drinks. After a bus journey, they were now standing on the Tower Bridge admiring the River Thames. Tourists surrounded them, their cameras flashing continuously. Remembering she needed something of Darion to add to her apartment, she took out her digital camera. He was focused on the water. His long sleeved black top clung to his broad chest. Standing tall and confident, his hands were hidden in the pockets of his black jeans. His hair was blowing ever so slightly in the breeze. She couldn't help but feel smug. Darion could easily have been a model. She snapped away, ensuring she also got a headshot. When he turned to look at her, he gave her a wink.

"Perving at me, are you?" A devilish smile crossed his face. "Let's get one of us together."

Handing him the camera, she snuggled up close to him. Darion held it before them and snapped away.

"I love this one," she gushed when she swiped through the images on the screen.

"Come on; let's go on the London Eye."

"And then we'll check out the Tower Of London," she said cheerfully, interlacing her fingers with his.

Although Gabi had seen most of the sights before, she knew Darion hadn't. It took them a few hours until she was satisfied she'd shown him enough: Big Ben, Buckingham Palace, Hyde Park, and The Shard.

When they returned to the hotel, exhausted, the spa facilities were just what they needed. Gabi, bikini-clad, and Darion in his swimming shorts, charged straight for the sauna. She was pleased they had it all to themselves.

"This is so nice," she sighed dreamily.

Sat on the wooden bench, the smell of wood filled her nostrils, and the heat in the enclosed space relaxed every muscle in her body. She shuffled on the bench and lay down until she was comfortable. Glancing down, Darion lay on the bench underneath, his head where her feet were.

"I could literally fall to sleep," she murmured.

"Me too," Darion responded.

They remained still and silent for a few minutes. It was warm, peaceful, and perfect. Closing her lids, Gabi inhaled and exhaled softly. She prayed they wouldn't be disturbed. She liked it being just she and Darion. When they'd passed the heated indoor pool earlier, she'd noticed there had only been a few people in the water. The steam room hadn't been that busy either.

Gabi was almost certain she'd drifted off when tingles ran up her leg. She scratched the itch with her foot. Then she felt it again. Inspecting her leg, she spotted Darion sitting up, a dark hunger on his face. He ran his hand up her leg and she felt the same tingles again.

"Sit up," he commanded lightly.

"Why?"

"Do it."

Reluctantly, she sat up, to which he parted her legs, and knelt between them. She sighed gently when he began massaging her thighs firmly. Maybe Darion was giving her his own little spa treatment. As he worked away the tension in her muscles, hard spasms of pleasure rippled through her.

"You look amazing in that bikini," he said, his pupils alight with mischief.

"You don't look so bad yourself." She greedily examined his perfect, tanned body.

He planted kisses up her thigh, causing her to wriggle. It tickled. Then he began swirling circles on her skin with his tongue. Gabi wiped her forehead as she became hot and flustered. She couldn't decide whether it was because of Darion or the sudden stuffiness in the sauna.

"Darion, are you serious right now?" She moaned when he moved her bikini bottoms aside and leisurely licked between her legs. "Someone might come in."

"And if they do, I'll stop."

He continued to arouse her with his tongue. He circled her with the tip, causing a moan to spill from her lips. Gabi clenched her fists, her nails digging into her palms. *What does this man do to me?* she screamed inside. No matter how much she tried to resist him; he wore down her defences with his seductive, charming ways. She whimpered when he spread her legs further and applied firm, slow licks to her clit. She could feel his rough stubble grazing against her.

"Hmmm...Gabi," he grunted, biting her roughly.

Threading her fingers into his hair, she pulled him in closer. As she rocked her hips, she stole a glance over his shoulder. The coast was clear. When his fingers assisted his tongue, she shuddered in delight. The muscles in his shoulder flexed as he pounded away, hitting her sensitive spot.

"Darion..." she cried out, wiping her damp hair back.

He continued to pummel in and out of her, now fast and deep, whilst his tongue lapped at her clit. Her inner muscles throbbed and ached. Then he withdrew.

"What are you doing?" she sulked, the absence of pleasure now torturous.

He pulled her down from the bench. Before she

could speak, he backed her against the wall roughly. His lips were on hers, his tongue sliding in, and invading her mouth. Desperate for air, she pulled back, and inhaled deeply. The sauna was warming up. Her bottoms were moved to the side again, and Darion plunged his erection in deep, not giving her time to prepare for his thickness and length.

"Ah…Darion…I don't know if I can handle this," she pleaded.

"I won't be long," he promised, finding her mouth again and kissing her savagely.

He bucked his hips forwards and backwards, wrenching a cry from her throat. His features were strained, his heavy breathing audible as he took her to her limits. He was rough and impatient, his fingers digging into her hips.

"Fuck…" he grunted. "So good."

He seized her face in his hands, his eyes darkened, wild with need. A menacing smile taunted his face, and he slammed into her hard, aggressively, possessively.

"I love you," his voice was stern, reassuring, "I hope you know that."

Gripping onto her hair tightly, he pulled her face into his as he pounded into her mercilessly. It was just the way Darion showed how much he cared, by his actions. Gabi was delirious with lust.

"I love you too."

"You…sexy…fucking…bitch," he said with each slam.

She couldn't help but laugh. "And you're a dirty, kinky bastard, Mr. Milano."

"Always." His expression was as serious as ever.

"You ain't seen nothing yet, Miss Woods."

She squeezed her lids shut. *Fuck!* How much kinkier could he get? Could it get any better? Moving in and out of her endlessly, she wasn't sure how much more she could take. The intensity shot through her, making her whimper. The width, length, and speed of his rhythm was beginning to make her legs weak. She clung onto his shoulders for support. Her inner muscles throbbed and clenched around him.

"I'm close…" she panted.

A part of her needed to escape, to suck in fresh air. She was burning up. Sweat dripped from both of their bodies, causing them to slide against one another. She couldn't control the erratic beating of her heart. The other side of her made her stay put, to wait for the orgasm that was seconds away from tearing into her.

"Me too." He threw his head back, clenching his teeth.

He slammed into her so fast she was being slammed against the wood. She grabbed his buttocks, and forced him into her deeper, rocking her hips to meet his thrusts.

"I can't breathe…" her tone was quiet and weak. Her head was spinning.

"Almost there."

As he pounded into her a few final times, she exploded. Wave after wave of pleasure rippled through her, and she feared she'd faint from the intensity. Crying out and shuddering, she allowed the climax to completely take over her. Darion's teeth were clamped into her shoulder to suppress his loud groans. Then he came and she could feel him throbbing and jerking, emptying into her.

"Fuuuuckkk..." he roared.

Fully satisfied, he collapsed onto the bench, his head dropping in his hands as he gasped for air. Gabi tried to steady her heartbeat and deepen her shallow breaths. She couldn't. She became claustrophobic in the small space. Smoothing her hair back, she silently prayed the showers were free of people. She stepped out of the sauna and inhaled deeply. The cool air hit her like a sharp slap in the face, but it was nice.

Darion pushed her towards the showers. Once under the cold water, she groaned inwardly. It was heavenly. She thought she'd explode from the heat in the sauna. She knew her face must have been red as a tomato. As the water rained down on her, Darion in the shower nearby, she couldn't help but giggle. That was some session. As usual, Darion had given her a mind-blowing fuck.

Stealing a glance at him, she saw a smug grin on his face. It had obviously been just as good for him too. He slicked his hair back with water, and she watched as droplets fell down his smooth chest. *Could he be any sexier?* She could easily allow him to ravage her again.

When she built up the courage, she lifted her head to survey the swimming pool. A couple of giggling girls were watching Darion. The pool was busier than when she'd first arrived. As a man caught her stare, she turned away quickly, hoping nobody guessed what she and Darion had been doing in the sauna.

The doors to the steam room burst open and a man and a woman fled out, gasping for air. Their faces were as red as hers, and so her shoulders relaxed. It couldn't be that obvious what she and Darion had been doing then.

"I'm gonna have a dip before we have our treatments." Darion brushed his lips against hers.

"Okay. I'll be in the Jacuzzi."

He charged toward the pool and smoothly dived into the water. He swam underneath it and eventually resurfaced in front of the girls. Rolling her eyes in amusement, Gabi stepped into the warm, bubbling water of the Jacuzzi. She submerged her entire body and closed her lids. It was perfection. She shut out the noise from the talking couple beside her, and allowed the bubbles to soothe her muscles.

The last time she had been in a Jacuzzi was at The Black Door with Darion and Audrina. She'd been trying out the playrooms. She remembered how jealous she'd been when he'd kissed Audrina passionately. She thought now the club was sold, and Darion wasn't leading the lifestyle of a swinger, that she'd feel more secure. How could she have believed that being with Darion could be anything other than unpredictable and crazy? He was still a complex man, a puzzle she wanted to solve. A man she wanted a future with. A man she wanted all to herself. However, although he had declared his love for her, it seemed she didn't have *all* of him. There were always obstacles in the way.

Chapter Eighteen

"That massage was so good I almost fell asleep," Darion said, wrapping his lips around his fork and chewing a piece of steak.

"Same here," Gabi agreed.

Their treatments had been so relaxing. They had both received a full body massage and a facial. Gabi could still smell the sweet lotions they had applied to her skin, which was smoother than ever.

"How's your food?"

"Delicious."

They were sat in the hotel's restaurant, eating and drinking wine. The tables were adorned with white and gold cloths, fancy silver cutlery, and a vase of white flowers in the centre. Laughter and chatter filled the air, and the atmosphere was relaxed.

Gabi placed her fork down when she'd finished her meal, and took hold of Darion's hand.

"I had a nice day today."

"Me too." He reached for his glass and took a long swig.

Gabi withdrew her hand and sat back in her chair. She'd noticed whenever Darion wasn't busy, his mind seemed somewhere else. Although he tried to reassure her he was fine, she knew by his rigid posture, wandering eyes, and fidgeting hands that he was far from it. Usually calm and collected, he definitely wasn't himself.

She wished she knew what was going on. Darion avoiding The Black Door especially didn't make sense. Was it Eva he didn't want to see? Had he been lying when he said he had never loved her? Was he having second thoughts?

Tucking a strand of hair behind her ear, Gabi decided to be straight with him. "Have you had any more thoughts on the opening party?"

His grip tightened on his fork, and his jaw clenched. "I'm not gonna have any more thoughts. I already told you I'm not going."

"I thought you would have been over the moon about seeing everyone."

"Gabi," he leant toward her, his tone low, "drop it."

"Is it because Eva will be there?"

His face didn't flicker with worry. His eyes were devoid of emotion. Eva obviously wasn't the issue. Normally, talking about Eva sparked a reaction in him. "You hated the place. Why are you so desperate to go?"

She paused for a moment before saying, "I feel like you're hiding something from me."

"What do you mean?" He placed his cutlery down and shoved a hand through his hair.

Straightening her posture, she looked him

squarely in the eye. "Have you got something to tell me, Darion?"

"No, why?" His finger traced across his bottom lip and he wouldn't look at her for longer than a couple of seconds.

Gabi's blood boiled. There was more to it, she knew there was. Leaning into him, she said as confidently as she could, "Look me in the eye and tell me you've nothing to share."

Ducking his head for a moment, he chewed his lip, the muscles in his neck taut. Then his steely gaze levelled to hers. "I've nothing to tell you." He appeared so sincere she almost believed he was innocent with nothing to hide. Or maybe he was a convincing liar. "What's brought all this on?"

Gabi rubbed her aching temples. She opened her mouth to question him about the calls and texts, and then decided against it. She needed time. If the texts were from Eva, or another woman, he didn't have his mobile with him, making it easier for him to lie about whatever she asked. She needed to be clever about it. If she revealed she was onto him, then he could be extra careful with his mobile. No way did she want that. Lawrence had made a fool of her once, she wasn't about to let it happen again.

"Gabi," Darion said softly, taking hold of her hands. "Why are you being like this?"

"I just find it strange why you don't want to go to the club."

"If you really want to go to the opening, then we'll go."

"Let's go then." She wasn't backing down.

He nodded. "Is that all this was about?"

"Yes," she lied and blinked back tears. "And I'm just scared of losing you sometimes." It was the truth. If she didn't care about him so much, the situation she was in wouldn't make her act so insane.

"I'm scared of losing you sometimes too." She saw sadness and fear flash in his eyes.

"Why would you lose me?"

He rubbed his brow as if to ward off a headache. "I found your engagement ring."

She swallowed.

"Why do you still have it?"

"You think I still love Lawrence?" Gabi shook her head, taken aback. "You think I kissed him because I still love him? Is that what you really think of me?"

"Why else would you have the ring?"

"I'd completely forgotten about the ring until yesterday when I found it. I asked Mallory to return it to Lawrence before we came here." She sighed resignedly. "I can't believe you think I'd be with you, whilst unsure if I loved someone else. I told you why I kissed Lawrence. You obviously didn't believe me."

A waitress interrupted them, asking if they wanted the dessert menu. Gabi declined. She had well and truly lost her appetite.

***

Darion

Darion hated lying to Gabi, although technically

131

he hadn't lied. She had asked him if he had anything to tell her. He didn't. He wouldn't receive the hospital results for another week at least. There was no point in worrying her until he got the results.

Unbuttoning his shirt, he stared absentmindedly at the television, which was playing a chick-flick. They hadn't been back in the room long, and Gabi had vanished straight to the bathroom. Tossing his shirt to the floor, he dropped on the bed and lay down. If only he hadn't refused going to the opening party, then Gabi wouldn't have been suspicious about him hiding something. She was probably getting her knickers in a twist thinking he was avoiding Eva, or something. What else could it be?

Clambering to his feet, he rummaged in his pocket for his cigarettes. Opening the box, he took one out and strolled toward the mini bar in the living room. He poured himself a large glass of whisky, and took it to the balcony. All he could hear was the sound of traffic below. Peering at the other balconies, he saw they were deserted. He hadn't planned for his night to be sitting alone, torturing himself with 'what ifs.' What if the results weren't good news? What if he lost Gabi? What if he'd made a complete mess of his life?

Stuffing the cigarette in his mouth and lighting it, he perched on the outdoor sofa. He took a long drag and blew out the smoke. He needed to make it up to Gabi. He should never have doubted her feelings for him. Her love for Lawrence had disappeared long before she met him, which is why she had gotten involved with him in the first place.

Taking a few more puffs, he then stubbed the cigarette in the ashtray, and ambled toward the bathroom.

"Gabi." He tapped gently on the door.

"Yeah?"

Pushing the door open, he found her lying in the huge tub, eyes closed, surrounded by bubbles. Settling on the toilet lid, he watched her for a moment, marvelled at her perfect body, firm breasts, smooth stomach, and slender legs. His fingers ached with the need to reach out and touch her. He groaned inwardly, feeling himself getting aroused.

"Are you okay?" she asked, before opening her eyes.

He nodded.

"I'll be out in a minute," she said drily, as if wanting him gone.

"Gabi," he said softly, lowering to the floor, and crawling toward her. "I'm sorry I jumped to conclusions about the ring." When she didn't speak, he continued. "I got jealous, and it's jealousy I'm not familiar with." He took hold of her chin and turned her face to him. "This relationship stuff is fucking hard."

"I know," she agreed, closing her lids again.

Unable to resist, Darion placed his fingertips on her breast, and stroked circles around her nipple. It stiffened under his touch. His mouth watered with the need to taste it. Seeing Gabi wriggling slightly, her lips parting, he took it as a sign she wouldn't refuse him. Leaning over her, he sealed his mouth over her breast, and sucked gently. Her low moans made his cock throb, wanting her desperately. Swirling his tongue around her areola, his hand sunk under the water. He massaged between her legs, causing her breathing and groans to get louder.

"Do you want me to join you?"

She looked at him, her brown eyes filled with lust and hunger for him. She casually shrugged a shoulder.

He stripped off his jeans and boxers, and stepped into the depths of the warm, bubbly water. Sitting at the opposite end of Gabi, he leant forward to capture her mouth in a kiss. He massaged her breasts tenderly, before finding her clit again. Her body relaxed, her head rolling back on a sigh. They'd never had sex in the tub before. He wanted to ensure they tried almost *everything* once.

Chapter Nineteen

Gabi

The next week and a half passed fairly quickly. Darion had been spending most of his time at the new bar, Retox, decorating it, and interviewing potential employees. Gabi had barely seen him. She'd kept herself busy with work, dance class, and spending time with Suzie and Mallory. It was Thursday evening and come Saturday, Mallory would be flying to the Maldives. It was also the grand opening to The Black Door.

Gabi had showered, dried her hair, and was in bed for ten minutes when the doorbell rang. Placing the book she was reading on the side, she scurried to answer it. Darion was leant against the wall. Noticing her, he sauntered toward her at a leisurely pace. He was dressed casually in navy jeans and a matching t-shirt, the collar buttons of which were undone, displaying some of his smooth chest. She noticed he had two-day old stubble, which made him look rough and rugged, just the way she liked

135

him.

"Hey, darlin'." He grinned, his pupils glinting dangerously.

"Hi." Her heartbeat got faster, and she scolded herself for still feeling coy around him at times. He openly admired her with his insatiable stare, taking her in from head to toe.

"Have you missed me?" He leant forward and flicked his tongue on her bottom lip, and let out a dirty sounding laugh.

"I have, actually," she confessed.

His hands reached out as he fondled her breasts over the flimsy material of her nightdress.

"Stop, my neighbours might see," she scolded him, slapping his hands away.

"So what?"

Shaking her head on a giggle, she led him to the kitchen. Switching on the kettle, she was about to make coffee when he pulled her into a hug. He squeezed her so hard it hurt. She snaked her arms around his waist with a smile. It seemed he had really missed her.

"Coffee?"

He shook his head. "Juice will do."

Flicking the kettle off, she poured two glasses of orange juice and followed him into the bedroom. He kicked off his shoes and peeled off his clothes so he was naked, except for his black Armanis. Gabi bit her lip, remaining rooted to the spot as she perved over him. His new employees would be all over him, tongues hanging out, she knew it. Well, at least they weren't dancers, and would be dressed. It would certainly make a change from seeing Lexi,

Marnie, Gina, Wendy, and the others parading around with their boobs out.

"Come to bed," Darion commanded, his top lip curling back over his teeth wickedly.

She placed a glass of juice on the table at his side of the bed, and then sashayed to her side, setting the other glass on the table there. Climbing under the covers, she didn't get a chance to make herself comfortable as Darion attacked her with his lips. Their teeth clashed as they kissed urgently, their tongues wrestling. She felt the stirrings of lust as his hands roamed over her body. His mouth was working down her neck, and a warm sensation blossomed between her trembling thighs.

"Impatient, are we?" She pulled back on a giggle and wiped her mouth.

"When it comes to you...always." He leant over and drained back half of his drink. "What's on?" He nodded toward the television.

"Oh. It's a girly show. Sex And The City. I doubt you'd like it." She grabbed the remote to change it.

"Anything to do with sex, I more than like." He winked.

Gabi shrugged a shoulder, dropping the remote. "It does show a lot of boobs."

"Then I'm all for it." He flashed her a saccharine smile.

"Perv." She nudged him playfully.

"Well, you're not showing me yours."

"I can hold a decent conversation, you know," she teased.

"A dirty conversation?" He nuzzled her neck.

"I should let you miss me more often."

Taking the hint, Darion fluffed up his cushion and leant back, fixated on the show. She snuggled up to him, resting her head on his chest.

"So the opening is on Saturday," she said, stroking his bare chest in circular motions.

"I forgot about that."

Gabi was certain his heartbeat sounded faster. "I called Lexi to see if she was going. It will be nice to see her."

"And is she going?"

"Yeah."

"Who else is going?"

Gabi sat up to read his expression. Was he asking out of curiosity or because he was worried? She couldn't tell. "Um..." She paused to rethink the conversation in her head. "Lexi thinks everyone's going." When Darion didn't speak she asked, "Are you worried about something?"

"No." He rubbed at his stubble. "I'm just not overly enthusiastic about seeing my ex-wife."

"Eva doesn't have a problem with you now, does she?"

"Eva will always have a problem with me." His tongue darted out as he wet his lips. "How about we put a movie on?"

Gabi agreed, although she knew he was putting an end to the discussion. Flicking through the channels, she settled on a romantic comedy. She yanked the covers up, draped an arm and a leg over Darion, and nestled in the crook of his neck. Inhaling his masculine cologne, she half smiled. Choosing a movie over him took a lot of willpower.

She liked snuggling up to him though.

An hour later, she heard Darion's gentle snores. Sitting up, she studied him whilst he slept. He was so handsome. She couldn't resist and so stroked his cheek. She loved him more than anything in the world. She was about to lean down and kiss his face when his mobile bleeped. She stilled. She prayed Darion didn't wake. When he didn't, she quickly leant over to catch sight of the text before she missed it. It was from the number ending in 369 again.

07844***369: We need to talk. x

Gabi sunk back onto the mattress, her mind going into overdrive. Who would text him so late, and what would they need to talk about? Did this person know he had a girlfriend? If they did, then it was clear they didn't care if he got caught out. It seemed they called and messaged him whenever they felt like it. Or perhaps they didn't know he had a girlfriend, and this was their way of finding out whether he did or not.

As she surveyed Darion again, she saw his features weren't relaxed from a pleasant dream. As usual, his face was scrunched up, and now he was grunting as if he was having a nightmare.

The Black Door opening party couldn't come quick enough, and if all was not revealed there, then Gabi decided she would confront Darion once and for all.

Chapter Twenty

Darion

Darion was sat in Retox, drinking a glass of whisky. Men were in and out delivering black sofas and tables. They were positioned against two walls, facing the lit up blue bar which stood at the back of the room. Black stools lined the bar, and beyond it were blue shelves containing spirits and liquor. With its low lighting, it was modern and glamorous, just as he'd wanted. On the fourth wall, floor to ceiling windows looked out onto the street. He'd already noticed curious faces peer in.

He knew it'd take him a while to get used to not seeing a main stage, podiums, and stripper poles. However, he supposed it meant less to worry about. The dancers had been difficult to please at times.

"Hey, Daz!"

He swivelled around on his stool to come face to face with Lexi. Peeling her coat off, she placed it on the side, along with her handbag.

"Oh my god," she squealed. "It looks amazing in

here."

He set his glass down and took a silver tin of cigars from his pocket. It had been a while since he'd smoked one. Now it was a special occasion, he believed it was very much deserved.

"Want one?"

She jumped onto the stool next to him with a smile. "Yeah. Why not?"

He handed her a cigar, and lit it once she put it in her mouth. "So, what have you been up to, Lex?"

"Not much. Getting prepared for the opening. I can't wait to get back to work."

"I take it Carl's all set, then?"

"Yep. How can he not be? He's got Eva the control freak up his ass."

Darion chuckled. "I'm glad she's not my problem anymore."

"If she even dares to boss me around, I'm quitting, and coming to work here."

"I wish you would." He took a puff of the cigar and exhaled slowly. "So, everyone will be at the opening?"

"Yeah, they will. Oh, and Gina's back." She clapped her hands excitedly. "She called me to say that she'd be there."

"Did she say anything else?"

"No, why?"

"Just wondering,"

"So." She leant closer. "Have you sorted staff yet?"

He nodded. "Got a few bar staff, a doorman, and a DJ."

"Ooh. Check you out." She nudged him. "I'm so

coming here on my nights off."

"I can't wait to open the doors, Lex. I've got a feeling this will be so much smoother to run than the strip club and playrooms were."

She blew out smoke. "How's Gabi? Has she been keeping up with your wicked ways?"

"She's fine...and so far, so good." Darion stepped behind the bar and selected two glasses. "What will you have?"

"Orange juice and vodka will do me."

Darion poured Lexi a drink, handed it to her, and headed to the sound system. Fiddling with the buttons on the remote, "I'm Only Joking" by Kongos blasted from the speakers. Returning to his stool and whisky, he nodded his head along to the music. He realised for the first time in a long while he felt completely chilled out. Working on the bar definitely took his mind off things.

"So, give me a tour then." Lexi stood up.

"Follow me."

A door behind the bar led to a corridor, of which met his office, the stock room, and staff toilets. He showed Lexi each room, which were all modern and fully decorated in black and grey. Back in the bar area, he briefly showed her the bathrooms and the small VIP area.

"Very fancy." She whistled. "I'm so proud of you, Daz."

He focused on the floor on an uncomfortable laugh.

"Hey." She slapped his arm playfully. "Don't be so modest. So, will your aunt be coming to check it out? I know you're close."

He nodded. "I haven't seen her in fucking ages." He smoothed his hair back. "She's always busy with the kids, so contact got less frequent."

"Well, make sure you call her. I know she'd be happy for you."

As they resumed their position at the bar, Darion's mobile vibrated in his pocket. His spine stiffened. He had a feeling who it was. He took the mobile out, and stared at the screen long and hard. It wasn't her number ending in 369. It was a number he didn't recognise. He excused himself and retreated to his office. Inside he shut the door to block out the music.

"Hello?" he asked, hating that his voice was shaky with emotion.

"Hello, is this Mr. Darion Milano?"

"Speaking."

"Hi, Mr. Milano. It's Miss Reid from Summer Row Clinic. I took your sample for—"

"Yes," he cut her off, wanting to get it over and done with.

"I tried to reach you a few days ago, but your mobile was switched off...anyway, we sent your results by post. I'm just calling to see whether you received them."

Shit! He hadn't checked his post in days. He'd assumed he would receive the results over the phone. "I haven't checked my post yet. If I haven't received them, I'll get back to you."

"Okay. Have a nice day."

"Bye."

His stomach churned, and he felt like he'd spew his guts up. He needed to get home to see if the results were there. It was time to find out where his life was headed. Taking a deep breath, he calmly strolled back to the bar, and manufactured a smile.

"Everything okay?" Lexi asked, the concern apparent on her face.

He nodded. "Fancy another drink?"

"I never say no to a drink." She laughed.

As Darion refilled their glasses, he wondered whether to go home afterwards, or to stay at the bar and get completely trashed.

***

Gabi

Gabi smoothed down her red dress, which complemented her figure. It matched her lipstick and nails. Her blonde hair cascaded down her back in loose waves, with one side secured with grips. Slipping into her high, black platforms, she then spritzed on some perfume.

She'd be lying if she said she wasn't sick with nerves. She kept thinking she'd bring up her dinner. Her hands wouldn't stop shaking, and her heart was beating at an erratic pace. *Get a grip, Gabi.* It was she who had pushed Darion to go to the opening party at The Black Door.

Grabbing her black clutch bag, she made her way into the living room and waited for Darion to show up. He was already ten minutes late. A part of her wished he'd changed his mind, whilst the other part of her still wanted to go, and needed answers. Whether she'd get them or not, she had no idea.

Another ten minutes passed, so she attempted to call him. Her eyes widened in surprise when she reached his voicemail. She poured herself a glass of wine to calm her nerves. He'd show up. Surely he wouldn't stand her up. Taking a sip, she leant back on the sofa. She silently prayed her relationship with Darion wasn't in trouble, that he hadn't betrayed her in some way, that there was some plausible reason for everything.

When she'd finished her wine, she heard the honking of a horn outside. Pulling the curtain back, she spotted Darion's Audi. She breathed a sigh of relief. Setting the glass on the side, she picked up her bag, and waltzed outside.

"Hi, you," she greeted him cheerily once she was in the car.

"Hey."

She got an instant whiff of his aftershave. Surveying him, she could see he'd made an extra effort on his appearance, like he always did when it came to parties at The Black Door. He was wearing his favourite black Armani shirt, unbuttoned at the collar, with the sleeves rolled up. It matched the colour of his jeans. His dark hair was slicked back, hanging neatly down the nape of his neck. She noticed he'd shaved, as his stubble was fainter than the last time she had seen him. She wished she could dive on his lap, and have her wicked way with him. He was so handsome she couldn't help but feel smug again.

"You look handsome," she told him, stroking his hand that was gripping the gearstick.

"You look good too."

"Everything okay?"

He nodded.

As he sped off down the road, she immediately sensed he was nervous. And as she knew he would, he blasted rock music to shut out any conversation.

Chapter Twenty-One

Present Day

Forty minutes later, Gabi was standing outside The Black Door staring up at the familiar window to the upstairs. Now instead of a red glow on the pavement below, it was violet. It looked less intimidating. Linking her fingers through Darion's, she allowed him to lead the way. They entered the gentlemen's club first, which was downstairs. She gasped at the décor. It was so modern, and had a young vibe to it. After she'd stopped gawping at the place, she slid onto a stool at the bar, next to Darion.

"Hey, Darion. Hey, Gabi," Jasmine greeted them with a huge smile. "Long time, no see. How are you both?"

"We're good." Gabi beamed. "How are you?"

"I'm great." She flicked back her ash blonde hair. "You like what they've done with the place?"

147

"It's amazing," Gabi responded, examining the room once more.

Darion nodded in agreement, and popped a cigarette in his mouth.

"Um…" Jasmine shifted on the spot awkwardly. "Carl said no one is to smoke in here."

"Did someone say my name?"

Gabi twisted around to see Carl and Tara heading toward them.

"Darion." Carl patted him on the back. "So glad you made it…hi, Gabi."

She waved.

"You remember Tara, right?"

"Hi, Tara," she greeted her with a wave.

Darion rose to his feet to plant a kiss on Tara's cheek. "So what's this I hear about no smoking?" he joked, about to put his cigarette away.

"We're not all rule breakers like you, Daz." Carl laughed. "But go ahead and have a cheeky one."

With a chuckle, Darion stuffed the cigarette back in his mouth and lit it.

"Jasmine, can you get these pair a drink?"

"Sure. What can I get ya?" she asked, thrusting her ample chest out.

Gabi turned her head and bit down a grin. She was so glad Darion didn't own the club anymore. She caught sight of some new dancers, half-naked, twirling around the poles, and another on the stage, teasing the audience.

"What do you think of the club?" she asked Tara, who took up residence on the stool next to her.

"It'll take a while to get used to." She giggled. "I'll be working here with Carl, helping manage the place, so I needn't worry about anything, really."

"Oh. I thought you had a job."

"I did, but I hated it." She leant in closer to Gabi and said quietly, "Besides, I think I'll need to keep an eye on these Barbie dolls."

Gabi threw her head back on a laugh. "Have you met Eva yet?"

"Is that the lady with all of those dreadful tattoos?"

Gabi nodded. "She's Darion's ex-wife."

Shock etched on her face. "She's going to be a handful, I can tell."

Gabi studied Tara. She was pretty, with immaculate nails and designer clothes. She seemed pure and naïve, a bit like Gabi had been when she'd first visited The Black Door. Back then she had no idea she was entering a world miles away from her own, that it would open her eyes to new things, and change her identity. She'd been sitting in the exact same spot when she'd met Darion.

She smiled fondly at the memory. The club wasn't all bad. Everywhere she looked, her mind was filled with a memory: the private booth where Darion had pleasured her with his tongue, his office where she'd been sprawled on his desk, the staff bathrooms where she'd been shoved up the cubicle door and ravaged, the public bathroom where she'd been perched on the counter. That was downstairs alone. Upstairs in the playrooms, she had experienced even more with him. The hot tub, the dungeon suite, the rotating beds, the partner-swapping rooms, light bondage, fancy dress, girl-on-girl action, kissing other men. And Eva had the nerve to say she was *vanilla*. She certainly didn't feel it.

Her mind was also invaded with the bad memories, the time when Darion had confessed he owned not just a gentlemen's club, but a swingers club, then there was the time when Eva had returned to Westhaven, having interrupted them in the playrooms. Plus, the time when she had confessed to Darion she had betrayed him and kissed Lawrence. She had a feeling there would soon be another confession too.

"Are you okay?" Tara asked, her forehead creased with concern.

Gabi shook her head, as if ridding the nasty thoughts. "I'm fine." She picked up the glass of wine Jasmine had placed before her.

"Are the girls here yet?" Darion asked Carl.

"No, but they should be here soon. Shall we head upstairs? I'll give you a tour."

"Why not?" Darion handed his cigarette to Jasmine to put out, having found no ashtrays, and gave her a wink.

Upstairs was livelier than ever. A mixture of people, all different ages, were occupying the sofas, bar area, and dance floor. Gabi admired the room. Carl had done an amazing job with the whole place. She lifted her head to take in the familiar black door, which led to the playrooms. It wasn't yet open, but it soon would be. She could feel the sexual tension in the air, and she observed people flirting and touching one another. They couldn't wait to get down and dirty, and she still couldn't understand it one little bit. She hadn't changed her mind about being able to share Darion. The thought terrified her.

Feeling protective over him, she stroked his sexy, firm buttocks, and froze when she felt the outline of something in his pocket. It was the key to the playrooms.

"Why do you have the key?"

His brows pinched together in confusion. Then they shot up as if suddenly remembering. "I wanted to return it." He took the key out of his pocket, and handed it to Carl. "I've been in these playrooms more times than I've had hot dinners. Let someone else enjoy them."

"I thought you would have wanted to go in them one last time," Gabi said.

"We don't need the playrooms, darlin'."

Carl told Gabi to make herself comfortable on the sofas and that a bartender would be over with bottles of champagne and glasses. She lifted her head searching for Tara, but she was chatting with a group of women. Giving Darion a chaste kiss on the lips, she wove through the dancing and talking crowd, and sat on a leather sofa. When the champagne was before her, she poured a glass, and downed a quarter of it. She wondered when Lexi and Marnie would be arriving.

A few minutes later, Darion excused himself from Carl, and was sitting beside her. Gabi asked again if he was okay, to which he replied he was. Then he stroked her thigh, his touch leaving tingles in its wake. When he kissed her passionately, he sent her senses whirling, and her heart racing. She was overwhelmed with lust.

She was surprised when his body then tensed, and he shifted away slightly. Glancing over her shoulder was Gina. Lexi, Marnie, Wendy, Tiana, Lennie, Travis and a few others followed. She and Darion greeted them. Excited and eager, they rushed to the bar, except for Gina. When she sat on the opposite sofa, Gabi sensed the animosity between Gina and Darion. They hadn't seen one another in so long. She thought they would have been ecstatic to be reunited. Making polite chit chat, and receiving short answers, Gabi couldn't help but feel she had offended Gina in some way.

An uncomfortable silence loomed over them, leaving Gabi with no choice but to break the ice. Gina then shocked her with a snort, and said Darion had something to say. With neither of them revealing anything, Gabi continued to stare at them at regular intervals, questioning them. She almost choked when Darion tried to silence Gina, and that they'd already discussed whatever secret they were hiding. Darion had Gina had been in contact, without her knowledge. Why would Darion hide that? The hairs on the back of her neck prickled, and her stomach somersaulted rapidly. Had Darion and Gina been having an affair?

When Darion apologised, Gabi pushed herself to her feet, afraid of what she would be told. She had a feeling the confession would be worse than his previous one. The last thing she heard from Darion before her brain shut off was, "Me and Gina…"

Chapter
Twenty-Two

Gabi blinked rapidly, and shook her head as she was brought back to reality. Taking in Gina's tearstained face, and Darion's remorseful expression, she was terrified to ask him to repeat his and Gina's confession, *their* confession. But she had to know.

"You and Gina what?" she asked, her voice trembling with emotion.

"We have a son."

Gabi staggered back, her mouth dropping open. *What?* She moved her lips to speak, but speech eluded her, her brain aching. Feeling light-headed and faint, she slid onto the sofa, and stared at the floor for what seemed like the longest time. "Since when?" she managed to mumble.

Braving a glance at Darion, she noticed his hands were clamped together; his expression pained, like he had the weight of the world on his shoulders. "I only found out yesterday that he was mine."

153

"He was conceived before you and Darion got together," Gina said quickly.

"I don't understand. How old is he? Why didn't you tell Darion sooner?"

"He's two months old. And I wasn't sure who the dad was." Her head dropped in shame. "Darion, along with a few other men, were potential fathers. I wanted to be certain." Gina wiped away a tear. "Darion had to take a paternity test."

"You should have said something as soon as you fell pregnant." Gabi shook her head in disbelief, her heart breaking. "How did nobody know?"

"I didn't even know. I was just over five months pregnant when I left for London." She snivelled. "It wasn't until I kept getting sick that my mom forced me to take a test." Gina's bottom lip trembled, and she inhaled as if to hold in tears.

Gabi shoved her hands through her hair and then released it. "How did you not know you were pregnant?"

"My periods have been irregular since I was like twenty-one, sometimes they don't come at all." She hung her head in her hands. "I thought it was normal weight gain. The bump was so small...the...um...the baby has growth problems." The tears came flooding out again. Gabi had never seen Gina so vulnerable.

At that moment Lexi, Marnie, Wendy, Tiana, Lennie, and Travis stopped before the sofas, concern etched on their faces.

"Is everything okay?" Lexi asked.

Darion straightened his posture. "Can you um...give us a moment, Lex?"

"Sure." She threw Gina a sympathetic look. "We'll be at the bar."

"He was diagnosed with intrauterine growth restriction," Darion continued for Gina, drumming his fingers on his knee. "The baby was small in the womb. We've been back and forth at the hospital for results of abnormalities, heart defects, and whatnot."

Gabi swallowed. "I'm sorry to hear that." She fiddled with her nails, not knowing what to do, think, or say next. "How is he?"

"We need to keep monitoring his growth and development."

Gabi nodded. "Are you pair going to give things another go?" She couldn't look at them. She felt tightness in her chest and a heavy ache in her throat.

"No, we're not," Darion said firmly.

Gabi noticed Gina's head drop in disappointment. It was obvious she still loved Darion. Gabi would be lying if she said she didn't feel threatened by Gina. She and Darion had once had an adventurous sex life. They'd always been there for one another. Would Darion look at her in a different light now she had his child? Maybe he'd finally love her in the way she wanted.

Gabi flinched when Darion slid across the sofa and reached for her hand. She denied his affections. "I need some space." She tightened her grip on her handbag, and slowly stood. She needed to be alone so she could let out her emotions. Darion and Gina had a child together. It was sinking in, and the future looked more uncertain than ever.

"Don't go," Darion pleaded.

"I *need* to be alone," she repeated. "This is a lot to take in."

"I know that," he said, rising to his feet and meeting her gaze. "Shall I take you home?"

"I'll call a taxi."

Gabi turned on her heel and pushed through the crowd as fast as she could. She needed to get away from The Black Door, Darion, and Gina. Her head was pounding, and she'd never been so heartbroken. The happy ending she craved with Darion could be no more. The fairytale ending she wanted was ruined.

Lawrence had known all along. She felt foolish. She didn't know where he'd gotten the information from. She wasn't sure whether she would have preferred to hear it from Lawrence, or straight from Darion and Gina. One thing she was certain of was that she was definitely running, but back to Lawrence wasn't her intention ever. She didn't make the same mistake twice.

"Trouble in paradise?" a sultry voice asked, pulling her back to the present.

Looking up, she came face to face with Eva's smug face. Darion's past lovers were everywhere. She could never escape them. It was as if she was always fighting a battle, trying her hardest for their relationship to succeed. Surely it shouldn't be that difficult.

"Move, Eva," she spat.

"Leaving Darion in the playrooms with all of these beautiful women?" She cocked an eyebrow. "Aren't you brave?"

"At this moment in time, I couldn't give a shit."

She pushed past her. Could it get any worse? The man she was in love with, and who she wanted a future with, had a baby with someone other than her. Many times she had fantasised about having the whole marriage and kids thing with Darion. It was everything she looked forward to. She hated the fact he'd been a playboy, and had slept around. How could he have been so careless? His wild days had certainly came back to bite him in the ass. Her whole relationship with Darion was one big rollercoaster ride, except there was no end. The drama never stopped.

Hurrying down the steps, she sucked in air as soon as she was outside. Hot tears trickled down her cheeks, and she hated how selfish she was being, for caring more about her own feelings than his. The news must have shocked him to the core.

"Gabi!"

Shit. She hastily wiped her eyes, and continued striding down the street. The quicker she hailed down a taxi, the better. She heard Darion's loud footsteps behind her, and groaned inwardly. Why couldn't he just leave her in peace?

"Gabi, stop." He grabbed her by the arm firmly, and spun her around to face him. "Can we talk?"

"Not now," she snapped, yanking her arm free. Closing her lids, she tried to gather patience. "Please, Darion. Not now."

"I can't let you leave like this." He focused on the sky, as if blinking back tears. But Darion didn't cry. She knew that. He believed it was a sign of weakness. "I have a son. It doesn't change anything between us."

"It changes everything," she mumbled, tears spilling again. "When I met you, I didn't sign up to play stepmom."

"I'm not asking you to."

"So I'm meant to sit on the sideline and watch you and Gina play happy families?" She stared at him incredulously. "I can't do that!"

"It won't be like that." He ran his hands up and down his tired looking face.

"What will it be like then?"

He shrugged, obviously at a loss for words.

"Why didn't you use protection?" She turned her back on him, not wanting him to see how heartbroken she was.

"I always use protection." He stepped around her, tipping her face up so their stares met. "It must have split. I didn't ask for any of this."

"When did you find out that you *could* be the father?"

He chewed his bottom lip, and then inhaled deeply. "The night we made up, and I told you I was selling the club, I got a call from Gina."

Gabi glared at him. "So you've known for months, and you didn't tell me." She shoved him. "I asked you in the hotel if you had anything to tell me, and you lied."

"I didn't have the results then. I didn't wanna say anything until I knew for certain." He ran a hand through his hair. "I was scared of losing you."

Gabi laughed mirthlessly. "I can't believe this." She shook her head. "We get rid of one ex, and now there's another one in the picture, who will *always* be in the picture because she has *your* baby."

"She's not my ex."

"Well, someone you fucked then," she yelled, feeling her face heat with rage. She sobbed uncontrollably, her chest jerking, her shoulders bouncing. "There's always something that comes between us, Darion."

"It doesn't need to come between us."

"But it will." She wiped her eyes. "Gina loves you. She always has. It's only a matter of time before she worms her way back in."

"That's not gonna happen," he said sternly.

"Whatever," she mumbled.

"What do you want me to do, Gabi?" he screamed. "You want me to leave Gina and that baby with no money, nowhere to live?"

She remained silent.

"What kind of woman are you if you want me to be the man who turns his back on his kid, neglects his responsibilities? Why would you want a man like that?"

"I have to go."

"Go ahead then." She saw the veins protruding in his neck. "Leave!"

She had never seen Darion so angry before. His chest was heaving, his breathing loud, his eyes hooded, his expression one of exhaustion and sadness. She hated that a part of her still found him unbelievably sexy and so tempting.

"Life isn't all perfect like the romance books and movies you fill your head with. Sometimes life doesn't go as planned. Shit happens," he spat. "It's how we handle it that matters the most. So go on." He waved his arm in the air. "Go and run back to your perfect little life."

"You know it wasn't perfect," she said through gritted teeth.

"It couldn't have been that bad. You went running back to him when things got rough. Go do it again."

Gabi flew toward him and slapped him forcefully across the cheek. The impact heated her palm and sent his face to the side. When he slowly dragged his gaze back, Gabi's breath held tight inside in anticipation. She remained frozen to the spot, not knowing what he'd do.

He shoved her against the wall, his solid body preventing her from moving. Her treacherous body ached with longing, wanting him desperately, whereas her brain wanted him as far away from her as possible. Darion's fingers gripped hold of her hair. Tilting her face up, his mouth crashed against hers as he kissed her frantically. His tongue swept in and silenced her pleasured moans. He lifted her into his arms, grinding and circling his hips. Gabi's head rolled back on a soft sigh, helpless to the attraction between them. Her core ached as she became wildly aroused. *Stop, stop, stop!* the sensible side of her screamed.

When Darion buried his head in the crook of her neck, kissing, nibbling and sucking, she spotted Gina over his shoulder. Mouthing "Sorry" for disturbing them, she vanished back into the club.

"Stop," Gabi pleaded, coming to her senses. When Darion failed to put her down, she yelled, "Let me go, Darion."

Shock etched on his face as he freed her.

"Go and see to Gina. I need some time to think."

"Gabi…"

Ignoring him, she took out her mobile and called a taxi. She continued walking away from the club as fast as her legs would take her. Glancing back, she saw Darion was frozen to the spot where she had left him. So Gina had no money, and nowhere to live. Darion was obviously going to come to her rescue and let her shack up in his apartment. Gabi believed it was only a matter of time before she was replaced.

It was the most painful feeling ever.

Chapter Twenty-Three

Darion

When Darion returned to the club, everyone was sitting around Gina, laughing and chatting, obviously none the wiser. Grabbing a drink, he tossed it back quickly, and poured another. He was about to scold Gina for telling Gabi, like he suspected she would, but as he took in her red, puffy eyes and downturned mouth, looking like she'd crumble, he kept his mouth shut. Gina hadn't told Gabi to hurt him. She'd never do that. She'd told him several times to tell Gabi there was a possibility he had a child. She'd even called and texted him at inconvenient times to ensure he was caught out. He wasn't stupid. He'd known of her game. She'd believed Gabi needed to know, that it wasn't fair for her to be kept in the dark. Maybe she had been right. If he had told Gabi earlier on, would things have been different? He doubted it. Gabi was heartbroken. The news had shattered their world. He wasn't sure if their relationship could survive it.

"Hey, Daz, where's Gabi?" Lexi asked.

Darion swallowed and leant toward Gina. "Shall we tell them?"

She shrugged a shoulder. "It's only a matter of time before they find out anyway."

"There's something I think you should know." Darion took a deep breath. At that moment, Eva joined them, perching on the arm of the sofa. Darion clenched his teeth. Damn Eva. She always had a way of popping up at the wrong moment. He saw her brow rise, her lips pursed, as she nosily awaited his announcement. "Gina gave birth to my son a couple of months back."

"What?" Lexi, Marnie and Tiana said in unison, shock in their tones.

Out the corner of his eye, he checked Eva's expression. Her jaw was practically on the floor. Her eyes were bigger than he'd ever seen them. The devastation was apparent on her face. He'd thought his heart breaking days were over. Obviously not.

"So, this was obviously before you met Gabi, right?" Marnie asked.

He nodded.

"Are you still with Gabi?" Panic flashed in Lexi's eyes. He knew she was fond of Gabi. She believed he was a better man when he was with her.

"I think so."

"Well then, congratulations." Carl grinned and held his champagne flute in the air.

"Yeah, congrats, Daz." Wendy beamed, clinking her glass with Carl's.

"Darion's a daddy." Lennie approached him and patted him on the back.

"Never thought I'd see the day," Travis joked.

"How about we congratulate Gina too?" Eva said sourly. "After all, she did do most of the work."

Lexi, Marnie and Tiana rushed over to Gina, pulling her into a tight hug.

"How did we not notice you were pregnant?" Lexi gasped.

"I didn't know myself," Gina told her. She then explained the situation with the baby.

"I hope everything will be okay." Lexi squeezed her hand. "If there's ever anything I can do, you know where to find me."

"Thanks."

After everyone was up to speed, they resumed their seating positions. Although it was a shitty situation to be in—having a child with a woman who wasn't his girlfriend—Darion's heart swelled. The times he had attended the hospital appointments with Gina and seen his son had been overwhelming. It hadn't properly sunk in yet. He hadn't picked up the baby; he was so tiny, he was afraid of breaking him. His skin was grey, and all he wanted was for him to be healthy. It worried him sick.

"So, what's his name?" Lexi clapped her hands in excitement.

"You thought of a name yet, G?" It suddenly dawned on him she'd never referred to the baby with a name.

Gina took another sip of her drink before responding, "I still haven't named him. I wanted us to choose together."

"Awww," Lexi gushed. "Pick a name," she urged.

"Did you have anything in mind?"

"Yeah," Gina mumbled. "Axl, Ryder, Preston, Morgan, Brody…"

"You have quite a list," Darion cut her off and chuckled. "I like Preston."

Gina smiled properly for the first time that night. "He looks like a Preston."

He nodded in agreement. "He does."

"Well?" Lexi was unable to contain her excitement. "Do I hear a baby name?"

Darion responded, loud enough for everyone to hear, "Preston."

Claps and cheers echoed around the room. Darion lifted his glass to his lips, and finished the rest of his drink. Then he turned to Gina. He could never turn his back on the girls when they needed him most, and especially when he was partly to blame for the position they were in.

"You're not staying in that hostel anymore," he told her sternly.

"I have nowhere else to go, Daz."

"You can both move in my place until you find somewhere."

"I wouldn't want to come between you and Gabi—"

"Sssh." He silenced her, pressing his finger against her mouth. "It's just temporary. And that's if there is still a 'me and Gabi.' She's hurting."

"I understand," Gina said glumly. "But I'm hurting too. I've lost Johnny because of this."

"Let's hope they both see sense and realise how much we care for them," Darion said softly, staring into the distance.

If he lost Gabi, the only woman he had ever truly loved, he didn't know how he'd get over it.

***

Gabi

Gabi pulled the covers up and stared out of the window in a trance-like state. The room was bathed in the gentle, white illumination of the streetlamps. She couldn't hear a single sound. Her eyes were sore from all of the crying, her throat dry, and her chest was aching. She could smell Darion's cologne on her pillow, and she missed him already. She wondered what he was doing at The Black Door.

Rolling onto her back with a yawn, she closed her lids and attempted to sleep. Instead of her brain shutting off, it tortured her with memories of Darion: eating out at restaurants, getting merry at clubs, strolling around town sightseeing or shopping, the romantic weekend in London, even just laying together watching television. She missed it all. She had gotten so used to being around him, that being apart left her feeling empty inside, like a part of her was missing. He'd been more than just her boyfriend, he'd been the world's most amazing lover, and caring, protective friend she'd ever known.

His wickedly glinting eyes invaded her mind, his sexy, devilish smirk, his dirty sounding laugh, and *that* body. *Fucking hell!* She groaned inwardly, gripping her hair in frustration. *Think of the bad stuff, Gabi.* Ignoring her raging hormones, she forced herself to think of his faults. He'd owned an adult club for years, enjoyed the lifestyle of a swinger, had hundreds of sexual partners, whom they could never escape, and worst of all, he had a son with Gina.

She tried to hold in the tears. Even all of the bad stuff didn't put her off him. He'd changed for her, and had given it all up. Then the baby news popped up, throwing a massive spanner in the works. This was something that would *never* go away. He couldn't change it. If she stayed with him, Gina would be in their lives forever. It wasn't like Gina had just been a one night stand, either. This was a woman Darion had known for years, someone he trusted with his life, who he always went to when he had a problem. She knew him inside out, and vice versa. How could she compete with that? What if Darion and Gina reunited? She'd be left devastated. Was it worth taking a risk and trusting him?

Sighing heavily, she opened her eyes and stared at the ceiling for what seemed like an eternity. Eventually, she fell asleep, although most of the night was spent tossing and turning.

Chapter Twenty-Four

Five painfully slow days passed, and Gabi didn't know whether to feel hurt Darion hadn't contacted her, or relieved he'd listened to her, and was giving her space. She'd thought the space would do her good, and she could decide what the best thing to do was, however she was none the wiser. Whatever route she took, it was a massive risk. She could stay with Darion, and there was a chance she could lose him to Gina, or she could leave Darion, and always wonder 'what if.' She wasn't sure which was the least painful.

She wished she had Mallory to speak with. Many times, she'd been tempted to call her, but decided against it, not wanting to put a dampener on her friend's holiday. She'd called Suzie a few times, to no answer. She was probably too busy with baby stuff, just as she believed Darion would be.

Sighing heavily, she picked up her mobile. She stared at the screensaver of Darion. He was wearing all black, as he mostly always did, and was sitting on his Yamaha R1. His expression was one of mischief and pure seduction. He could seduce women without even trying by his cool, confident manner, his sultry sounding voice, and the fact he had trouble, but excitement written all over him, a bad-boy who many girls would love to tame.

She kept wondering what he was doing, whether he and Gina were already playing happy families. She must have moved into his apartment already. Did she stroll around half-naked like she had done at the club? Did Darion spend his nights keeping her company? Was their baby bringing them closer together? *Stop it, Gabi,* she scolded herself, rubbing her aching temples.

Clambering to her feet, she took a book from her bookshelf, and dropped back onto the sofa. She started to read the first page, but then gave up. Darion's words echoed loud in her head, *"Life isn't all perfect like the romance books and movies you fill your head with. Sometimes life doesn't go as planned. Shit happens."* Darion was right. Had she been foolish to have believed their relationship could have been perfect? Was any relationship perfect?

Not wanting to be left alone with her thoughts, she picked up the stereo remote, and pressed the power button. "Something In The Way" by Nirvana was playing on the radio. Shuffling down on the sofa, Gabi lay there listening to the lyrics. She ignored her stomach which was rumbling in hunger. Physically and mentally drained, she didn't have the energy or the appetite to rustle something up.

Three songs later, she dragged herself to bed.

***

Darion

Darion inspected the boy lying in the plastic crib. He appeared too small, too fragile, like he shouldn't have been born yet. His skin had a grey tinge to it, and it almost looked see-through, his veins visible. Tubes were secured with tape to his nostrils. Slightly kicking his feet, he whimpered softly, as if he was too weak to cry.

Darion averted his stare. A painful lump lodged in his throat. He wished he could reach out and touch him, but he was afraid of hurting him. He was also terrified of getting attached to a baby who could turn out not to be his after all.

Hearing a loud cry, he spotted another baby in a nearby crib. He was much bigger than this baby. His skin was a healthy pink colour, his arms and legs were chubby, and he kicked and moved his arms, full of energy.

It pained him Gina had given birth to a child who faced several health problems. He could tell by her quiet, withdrawn mood that she blamed herself. He hated telling her everything would be okay, when he was unsure as to whether it would be.

***

Darion blinked his eyes open. He rolled over on

a loud groan. Clutching his forehead, it did little to stop his pounding headache. It took him a few seconds to work out where he was. He must have fallen asleep on the sofa in his new office. Gripping the back of the sofa for support, he pulled himself into a seating position. *Fuck!* He clenched his teeth at his aching limbs. He must have slept in a funny position. Licking his lips, he searched for a drink, feeling completely dehydrated.

Flashbacks of the last few nights began to seep into his brain. He had slept at the club. Gina had moved into his apartment and Preston had done nothing but scream the place down. Gina didn't know what to do to stop his crying and she'd done everything she could think of: feed him, wind him, change him, play with him, rock him to sleep, yet nothing worked. Being an only child, and never having been around babies, she was at a loss at what to do. He'd caught her sobbing to herself when Preston slept for a single hour. He'd wanted to comfort her, to cuddle her, but stopped himself from doing so. He was terrified Gina would get the wrong impression and make a move on him. She'd done it many times before. He wasn't taking any chances.

He didn't know what to do to help her. Apart from minding his niece Odelia here and there, he was also clueless when it came to children. He still couldn't believe he was a dad. He'd only recently just learnt to look after himself, and now he had a son to raise, to teach right from wrong, and to set a good example. Frustrated, he'd fled to the club and locked himself in the office. The peace and quiet had been the best and worst thing for him. Being able to actually get some sleep was a bonus, but being left alone with his thoughts had been punishment. How could he be a good role model? He hadn't learnt anything from his neglectful parents. Affection and showing emotions was also newish to him. When he looked down at Preston, he didn't even know where to start. A part of him believed he'd be better off without him.

He hadn't heard a thing from Gabi either, which had sent him over the edge. If she left him, he knew he'd forever hate himself for ruining what they had. It was his own fault for sleeping around. Did he really think he could be that careless fucking anything and everything and not have to deal with any of the repercussions? It was probably only a matter of time before someone got pregnant. In a way, he was relieved the condom had split with Gina, and not with some one-night stand from the playrooms.

Feeling around the sofa, he searched for his mobile. When he located it and glanced at the screen, he shook his head, completely bewildered. Was Gabi not missing him at all? He contemplated ringing her, but decided to give her the space she had asked for.

A knock at the door caused him to drag himself to his feet. Smoothing his hair back with his hands, he gripped the door handle and yanked it open. Addilyn, the barmaid, flashed him a tight smile.

"Everything okay?" she asked, handing him a glass of juice.

He nodded, took the juice, and searched his

pockets for his cigarettes. "How's it going out there?"

"Real busy. Me and Raina have been serving non-stop all night."

Downing half of his drink, he set it on the side. He was glad to hear business was booming. At least his professional life was one less thing to worry about. A steady cash flow was definitely what he needed.

Stuffing the cigarette into his mouth and lighting it, he took a long drag. He closed his eyes in contentment, enjoying the nicotine rush. He perched on his desk and observed Addilyn as she stooped down, and began collecting empty Coke bottles. Throwing them in the bin, she then stood before him. She was a pretty twenty-four-year-old with black hair, complete with blue streaks in. She had a hoop in her nose and a piercing in her tongue. Her feisty side reminded him a little of Eva and Gina. The punters loved her. He'd spotted a few groups of men check her out through the windows as they'd walked past earlier. Darion knew he'd done well in hiring her. The club didn't have exotic dancers, so the next best thing was hot barmaids.

"Fancy another drink?"

He shook his head.

"If you need anything, let me know."

"Thanks." He blew out more smoke.

"Oh." She paused at the door. "There's a woman at the bar asking for you."

Darion froze on the spot. He hoped it was Gabi. "Who is she?"

"Lexi, I think she said."

Darion hoped the disappointment wasn't apparent on his face. He'd hate to look like some little bitch moping about the place. Grabbing his jacket and keys, he followed Addilyn out of the office. He locked the door, and within minutes he was in the bar area. Rock music was playing at a decent volume, and the room was packed. People were sitting in the booths, on the stools at the bar, and standing in groups on the floor, chatting away, and some even dancing near the window. He nodded his head in approval. It wasn't like there was much choice in Westhaven when it came to nights out, but he hadn't expected it to be that busy.

He noticed Lexi propped on a stool, a cocktail in hand, nodding her head along to the music. He poured himself a whisky, and slid on the stool beside her.

"Daz." She grinned and flung her arms around his neck. She was tipsy. He could smell the alcohol on her.

"Hey, Lex. What are you doing here?"

"I finished work a couple of hours early so I could check in on you."

He was touched by how much she cared about him. The girls knew when he was distressed, and in the past when he'd slept in his office to try and block out nightmares and flashbacks, they'd always check in on him.

"Marnie and Tiana are gonna pop in when they've finished their shift." She downed some of her pink drink. "Mmmm. This is good." She laughed. "Retox seems to be doing well." She craned her neck to examine the room.

"How's things at the club?"

"Not too bad. Carl loves it there. When his wife isn't around, he likes to have a private dance or two." She winked.

Darion grinned. "Sounds like me when I first opened it."

"Oh, you couldn't get enough of the dances." Her gaze fell on the barmaids. "Cute staff. Gabi's got her work cut out for her," she teased.

"Gabi never needs to worry about other women," he told her. "Not Gina, not Eva. No one."

"Aw." Lexi nudged him with her elbow. "True love that."

He chewed his bottom lip before saying, "I haven't seen her since the opening party."

"What? Why?"

"Me having a kid has freaked her out. She must think I'll get back with Gina, or something."

"I can understand the insecurity she must be feeling, Daz. How would you feel if she had a child with Lawrence?"

Darion frowned. He hadn't noticed he was tapping his foot on his stool repeatedly. Gabi had kissed Lawrence. If she had a child with him, he knew he'd find it difficult. It would definitely spark feelings of insecurity and jealousy in him. He wouldn't turn his back on her though. He'd give it a shot, and see how it went. He just hoped Gabi did the same. "It wouldn't be the best news I'd ever heard, but it'd take a lot to keep me away from her."

"Gina can be quite intimidating."

"She's not like that anymore. Ever since she's had Preston she's like a different woman. She blames herself for his condition."

"Well, it can be related to drink and drug abuse. Gina didn't exactly look after herself."

"It's not her fault," he said firmly, and meant it.

They were both silent for a moment whilst they gulped back some of their drinks. Darion then reached for Lexi's hand and squeezed it. "I'm glad you popped in, Lex."

"Me too. We miss you being at the club."

"You're always welcome here."

"Just you try and get rid of us." She beamed.

"Eva giving you any shit?"

"No." Lexi's mouth dropped. "I fucking forgot to tell you," she shrieked.

"What is it?" Panic began to set in and he hoped it wasn't bad news.

"Eva hooked up with Carl."

"Are you serious?"

"Wendy walked in on them. They were in the office."

"He's got a wife."

"Like that would stop Eva."

Darion screwed his face up in disgust. "The best thing I did was finish with her."

"I agree."

Relief swept over Darion and he actually found himself amused at the situation. Eva didn't have a care for anyone in the world except for herself. She wasn't bothered people got hurt by her actions. He could have forgiven Eva, and she could have cheated on him again, or even worse, he never would have found out. She knew Carl was married. She really mustn't have had any shame at all. Any tiny ounce of respect he had left for her completely vanished. It also proved she hadn't loved him as much as she claimed she had. If she did, then she wouldn't have given up fighting for him so easily. He knew he loved Gabi, and he'd do anything in his power to get her back should she leave him.

"So, have you told your family about Preston?" Lexi's voice brought him back to the present.

He nodded. "They didn't really say much. Dion's excited, though. She can't wait to meet him."

"I wonder if Gabi's told her family about it."

Darion's posture went rigid at the thought. He liked Gabi's family. Unlike his cold, judgemental parents, hers had seemed kind, and had welcomed him into their home with open arms. He'd felt accepted for once. Gabi's father had congratulated him on owning The Black Door at the time, even knowing it had been a gentlemen's club. His parents had never congratulated him on anything in his life. He could just imagine Gabi telling them about Gina and Preston. Would they think less of him? Would they advise Gabi she was better off without him? He hoped not.

"I better head home." Lexi pulled her jacket on.

"Me too. Reece can lock up."

"Your security man?" Lexi giggled. "He's quite cute, Daz. Is he single?"

"Nope. He's Addilyn's boyfriend."

"Damn." Lexi pursed her lips.

"Why don't you give Trav a go?"

"Travis doesn't fancy me."

Darion pushed up the sleeves of his shirt. "He

does."

Darion leant over the bar and informed Addilyn and Raina he was leaving. They waved at him with flirtatious smiles, thrusting their chests out, and told him they'd see him tomorrow. He and Lexi then stepped out into the cool air.

"I'll walk you home," he told Lexi.

"Daz, it's not far. I'll be fine."

"I insist," he said. "I can get a taxi from your place."

"Okay."

They walked side by side in a comfortable silence. The streets were quiet, and it wouldn't be too long until people were getting up for work, pedestrians rushing about, and traffic clogging the roads.

When they finally reached Lexi's apartment, he accepted a hug goodbye. He waited until she was safely indoors, and then found a wall to sit on. Before he went to ring a taxi on his mobile, he noticed he had several text messages.

Gina: Daz, Preston is still crying! I don't know what to do.

Gina: Daz, I need to take him to the hospital. Maybe he's sick.

Gina: He seems okay now. He's sleeping. Hope you're not doing anything stupid.

Gina had seen him at his worst when he'd split up with Eva. He would have done anything to block out the pain. The easiest option had been to escape reality, to be so out of it he almost forgot the hurt she had caused him. He hadn't realised at the time he'd been hurting himself in the process.

Dialling a local taxi company, he waited patiently for it to arrive. He had never wanted his own bed so much. For some reason, he was completely shattered. He wondered if he'd get any sleep with Preston waking up every couple of hours.

When he was eventually on his way home, he thought of Gabi and what she was doing. It was strange going home to a place packed out with baby stuff, and Gina being there. How his life had really changed.

Chapter Twenty-Five

Gabi

Gabi chewed the end of her pen as she read the manuscript before her. She rolled her eyes at the romantic declaration from one of the characters. Usually she would have melted on the spot, feeling giddy at such a sweet story. Now, she believed the majority of romance movies, shows, and books were probably, in fact, bullshit. Could Darion be correct? Did women have high expectations and an unrealistic perception of what romance should be like due to the sweet heroes they read about or watched? Were they really expecting a knight in shining armour to come and rescue them and make everything in their world right?

Tossing her pen aside, she slipped back into the Jimmy Choo heels she had kicked off, and grabbed her cup. She needed a caffeine fix. She hadn't slept much last night. Her worrying thoughts had given her a migraine, and prevented her from nodding off. A hot bubble bath and some pills hadn't even helped.

After she made a fresh cup of coffee, she quickly checked her emails. A few clients were querying the changes she had made to their manuscripts. Others had sent new manuscripts. Taking out her diary, she added some entries and then shoved it into the top drawer.

Swinging around in her chair, she took in the dull, grey sky, which reflected her dismal mood. She had dance class later. She wasn't sure she had the energy. Her limbs were achy, and her eyelids heavy. She really didn't want to miss it, though. She needed to keep her mind as busy as possible.

When her mobile began ringing, she grabbed her handbag, and rummaged through it until she located it. She couldn't stop a huge grin from crossing her face at Mallory's name. She was just the person she needed to talk to. If anyone was good at listening, dishing out advice, and knowing Darion, from what she'd revealed about him anyway, it was Mallory.

"Hi, Mal," she sang cheerily. "How are you?"

"Hi, sweetie. I'm fantastic! How are you?"

"Hmm. Not too bad."

"What's up?"

"Can we talk about you first? How's the holiday going? It's so quiet without you here." She groaned.

"I'm literally on the beach as we speak. Steve has just gone to get some drinks. It's amazing here, Gab. The weather, the hotel…it's just perfect."

"I'm so glad to hear that."

"And don't worry, I've taken plenty of photos."

"I can't wait to see them. How's Steve?"

"He loves it here. It was just the break we needed. But I miss you, and wanted to check in. How's everything going?"

"Everything's going wrong, Mal."

"Aw, why, honey?"

"I didn't tell you any of this because I was uncertain about what was going on," she began, tapping her nails on the desk. "But to cut a long story short, I saw some text messages in Darion's phone, and missed calls from a number not stored. He'd then deleted them and his call log. He'd obviously been meeting this person, so I followed him." She sighed heavily. "I know it sounds crazy, but I needed peace of mind. I had to know who was contacting him."

"It's understandable. Lawrence cheated on you. You need to have your wits about you this time around."

"Well, anyway, he was visiting the hospital. And then he was being shifty, not wanting to go to the opening party at The Black Door. I thought he was hiding something, avoiding someone."

"Uh huh," Mallory mumbled, urging her to continue.

"And it turns out he was meeting up with Gina."

"Why would he hide that?" Mallory gasped. "Oh fuck. Don't tell me him and Gina were hooking up."

"No." Gabi's lower lip trembled as tears filled her eyes. "It's worse than that."

"How can it be worse than that?"

"He was obviously avoiding the club because he knew Gina would be there, and she'd tell me everything." Taking a deep breath for courage, she continued, "As you know, Gina and Darion used to sleep together before I met him."

"Yeah."

"She um…got pregnant."

"What?" Mallory yelled in surprise.

Gabi bit her lip to suppress her cries. Holding the mobile away from her ear for a moment, she sobbed silently. When she pulled herself together, she added, "She gave birth just over two months ago. He has a son with Gina, Mal." Unable to hold it in again, tears trickled down her cheeks.

"Oh, Gab. I can't believe it. Why didn't Gina tell him sooner?" she spat. "Didn't they use protection?"

"She didn't know she was pregnant for a while. She put it down to normal weight gain, as she was so small. The baby had problems growing in the womb. They have to monitor his health."

"Oh, shit."

"And they did use protection. The condom split."

Mallory was silent for a moment, obviously as shocked as Gabi was.

"It feels like my whole world has fallen apart. First there was me being concerned about his history with the dancers, then there was the return of Eva, and now Gina's back in the picture, not only as his friend, but as the mother of his baby."

"Do you trust him?"

"I think so," she murmured. "But I'm not sure if I trust Gina."

"Gabi, if you love Darion and you trust him, then you can get over anything. Yes, this will completely change your lives, and it will be testing at times, but surely he needs you now more than ever."

"But what if he falls for Gina? The baby could bring them closer together. I'm always going to be afraid of that."

"It's a risk you'll have to take."

"It feels like I'm fighting a losing battle."

"You don't know that. How does Darion feel about it all?"

"He stepped up to his responsibilities. He said he wouldn't turn his back on his child."

"I respect him for that. It shows the type of man he is, someone you can always rely on."

"I guess so." Gabi took out her compact mirror and checked her reflection. She hated how exhausted she looked. "I haven't spoken to him since I found out. I don't know what to think, do, or say."

"Do you want to be with him?"

"I can't imagine not being with him."

"Well, then you have to stand by him when times get tough. This is life. Sometimes things happen that are out of our control. It wasn't Gina's fault, and it wasn't Darion's fault. They weren't careless, they used protection. You can't punish him for it and give him the silent treatment."

"I'm not…I just needed time to think."

"You need to call him and talk about it, Gab."

"You're right."

"Oh, hi, baby…it's Gabi." She paused. "Steve said hello."

"Tell him hi," she said before adding, "I'll leave you to it, Mal, and we'll talk as soon as you're back."

"Okay. And remember that saying, take risks. If you win, you will be happy. If you lose, you will be wise, and it's true. What's meant to be will be."

"Hmmm," she mumbled softly, but agreed it did make sense.

"If you need me, you know where I am. Call me."

"Bye. Enjoy the rest of your holiday."

"Bye, honey."

Gabi placed the mobile on her desk, and slouched in her chair on a long, heartfelt sigh. She really did need to speak to Darion. Well, if he hadn't already formed a relationship with Gina. She knew Gina could be tempting. She hoped Darion had the willpower to resist.

Tapping her computer keyboard, she was halfway through an email when her office phone rang. She snatched it up, balancing it in the crook of her neck whilst she typed.

"Gabriella Woods, Miller & Co. Can I help?"

"How are you, Gabi?"

"What do you want, Lawrence?" she asked drily.

"I take it Darion came clean."

She froze. "Have you been following us again?"

"No, I haven't."

"Well, it sure sounds like it," she snapped. "Do I really have to call the police and file harassment charges?"

"That's not necessary," he replied with an incredulous laugh. "Have you thought anymore about us?"

"There is no 'us,' there will never be an 'us,'

Lawrence. How many times?"

"You're seriously going to stay with that man when he has a child with another woman?" He snorted. "You really are desperate, Gabi. It's only a matter of time before they get back together, and you're kicked to the gutter."

"Even then I wouldn't come back to you. Now leave me alone!"

She slammed the phone down and clamped her lips together, determined not to cry. Squeezing her lids shut, she then reopened them, and summoned a smile. *Don't let Lawrence get to you,* she told herself. She needed to take everything one day at a time.

Chapter Twenty-Six

Darion

"It's rocking in here tonight." Addilyn grinned. Leaning on the bar, her cleavage in his line of sight.

"It is." He lifted his glass of lemonade to his lips. "How are you and Raina getting on?"

"We love working here."

"I'm glad to hear it."

"So, um…" She toyed with her fringe. "I hear you used to own The Black Door."

He nodded.

"I knew what that place was about." She giggled. "Do you still participate in the playrooms?"

"No, I don't." Darion held her stare. Was she coming on to him? "Why do you ask?"

"I'm always up for a bit of fun." She licked her lips enticingly.

Fuck, she really is as fiery as Gina, he thought. "I thought you were with Reece?"

"I am, but we have an open relationship."

Darion finished the last of his drink and stood up, towering over Addilyn. "Well, then I suggest *you* participate in the playrooms," he advised her. "I have a girlfriend, and a son with an…ex-girlfriend," he added, not knowing how else to explain Gina.

"Damn." She pouted. "A lot of women are gonna be disappointed to hear that." She jerked her head toward the crowd.

Darion craned his neck to view the dance floor. A few women had their stares fixed on him. They were giggling, and appeared to be talking about him. He wasn't particularly fazed. He'd gotten used to the attention he was lavished with at The Black Door. If he could resist nude, hot dancers, then resisting these women was easy.

"So, have I met your girlfriend?" she asked.

"No." He wasn't even sure if he was still in a relationship with Gabi. He was now at a point where he was desperate to call her. He didn't want to pressure her though, and end up losing her, if he hadn't already.

"She's a lucky lady."

"Addy, I'm the lucky man, believe me." He turned to walk away, but added, "Reece can lock up. I'll see you tomorrow."

"Daz, are you going?" Raina rushed toward him.

"Yeah."

"Okay." She waved. "See you tomorrow."

Shoving his hands in his pockets, he gave them a little wink. Raina's cheeks went a deeper shade of pink. As he made his way toward the exit, he shook his head. What was wrong with these women?

Couldn't they see he had trouble written all over him? Not only was he complex in every way, he had an extremely colourful past, emotional issues due to his childhood, a kinky sexual appetite which some found hard to deal with, and now he had a baby with an ex-stripper-lover. The term 'baggage' was an understatement.

***

Darion had just parked his motorbike and removed his helmet when his mobile started vibrating in his pocket. He turned his attention to his apartment building. He could see from the balcony that the living room light was still on. He guessed Gina was still awake. As he rummaged for his mobile, he assumed it was Gina calling him to ask questions about the baby, of which he never knew the answer, or that she needed nappies, wipes, or milk powder or whatever.

Staring at the screen, he stilled. It was Gabi. He stared up at the heavens above, and silently prayed she wasn't calling to break up with him. Strolling toward the building, he answered the call.

"Gabi," he said, and then coughed to clear his throat. "Everything okay?"

"Not really," she mumbled. He respected her for being honest. "I miss you so much."

His lips tilted at the corners. "I miss you too."

"We really need to talk."

"I agree."

"When do you want to meet?"

"Now."

Her giggle was like music to his ears. He'd missed hearing her laugh and seeing her smile. Most of all he missed holding her against him, burying his head in her hair, and breathing in her sweet perfume. He missed her soft mouth, her smooth body...*fuck!* He groaned inwardly. He was so aroused, he thought he'd explode from the frustration alone.

"It's late."

"Why aren't you asleep?" he asked her.

"I can't sleep."

"Me either." He changed direction and headed to his Audi. Pressing the button on his keychain, the car bleeped, the doors automatically opening. "I'll be there soon."

***

Gabi

Gabi jumped out of bed and raced to the bathroom. Smoothing down her pink silk nightie, which just about skimmed her buttocks, and dipped low to reveal her cleavage, she decided to keep it on. She ruffled her blonde locks in the mirror, and grabbed her bronzer pallet. Stroking some gold colour into her cheeks, satisfied she looked reasonable, she re-entered the bedroom. She spritzed on some perfume, and dropped onto the bed. Her hands were shaking ever so slightly, her heart beating wildly. She scolded herself for being so nervous. How could she still feel coy around a man she had been with for a long while? She believed the giddy effect he had on her would never cease. Even now, when things weren't exactly going smooth, she loved him all the same. She knew it would be hard given the circumstances. She couldn't leave him, though. She missed him like crazy.

When she had left Lawrence, it had been difficult, and upsetting, but she had gotten over it quite quickly, except for feelings of guilt here and there. Lawrence had treated her badly, which is why it had probably been easier. She had learnt to focus on the bad things about him, the way he controlled, criticised, neglected, and cheated on her.

Darion hadn't treated her badly. Not ever. Even when it came to the playrooms, and involving herself in the dark lifestyle he enjoyed, he had never once pressured her to take part. He always asked if she was comfortable, and assured her she didn't have to do anything she didn't want to do. He supported her in whatever she did, and would move mountains for her. He was attentive and protective. Would she ever find someone like that again? She wasn't confident she would.

Forty minutes later when she had finished concentrating on the book before her to calm her nerves, the bell rang. *Shit, shit, shit.* She fiddled with her nails as she approached the front door. She was unsure of what to say to him.

Unlocking the door and gently pulling it open, nervousness crept in. His back was facing her. She could see his broad physique, his perfect ass her fingers ached to reach out and grab. When he turned around, desire assailed her. The ambient glow from the moon sparkled in his green eyes. His hair and stubble was a little longer than usual. He still managed to look smart, whilst rough and rugged at the same time. When he flashed his wicked, sexy grin, she melted on the spot.

"Hey, darlin'," the sultry sound of his voice played havoc with her emotions.

She marvelled at his perfection, tongue-tied. She was so aroused her mind couldn't focus enough to articulate a sentence. When his brow rose, she managed to mumble "Hello," whilst trying to stabilise her breathing.

Stepping forward, he regarded her cautiously, and tucked a stray hair behind her ear. His gaze slowly swept over her body, making her cheeks warm. He seized her face in the palms of his hands, his lips hovering precariously close to hers. His expression reflected a deep hunger.

"I *need* to kiss you." His tone was both a demand and a plea.

When Gabi didn't reject him, he tightened his hold on her face, and kissed her powerfully. He knocked the air out of her lungs, and caused her body to tremble in delight. She gripped hold of his ass, pulling him into her. They kissed frantically, groaning and tasting one another's tongues greedily. When he backed her into the hallway and kicked the door shut behind him, the pit of her stomach began to burn. She had never wanted him so much.

Pinning her to the wall, she could feel the hard ridge of his arousal. Grinding her hips into his, she continued to kiss him like she hadn't seen him in years. It may as well have been, as the time without him had been torturous. By the way his hands fondled every part of her body, she knew it hadn't been easy for him either.

"I want you now," he growled in her ear, before pulling on it with his teeth.

She didn't speak. She slowly unbuttoned his shirt like he was a delicious prize she was unwrapping. As his smooth chest came into view, she couldn't help but kneel slightly, and lick up from his navel to his chest. Then she kissed his neck continuously, threading her fingers through his hair. Darion's head rolled back on a groan, and she heard the loosening of his zip. Lifting her into his arms, he carried her to the bedroom.

He dropped her onto the bed and kicked off his shoes. Ordering her to remove her clothing, he stripped off his shirt, followed by his jeans and boxers. Peeling her nightie down, she spread her legs invitingly as his glorious nakedness loomed over her. The sexual tension between them hung heavy in the air.

"How about a bit of music?" he suggested. He selected a playlist on his mobile. Setting it on the bedside table, the first song that played was "Lucky You" by Deftones.

Darion then crawled up the bed. His head dipped and he sealed his mouth over hers. Her lips moved desperately over his, her hands delving into his hair. When his smooth erection skimmed across her sex, the tingling in her stomach became a plaguing, needy ache. Darion began kissing and nipping at her neck, causing her to arch her back. Her nipples tightened under the pads of his circling thumbs.

Whimpering lightly, she thrust her chest upwards. Her body screamed for more contact.

Darion blew on her nipple gently, the cold air making it tingle. She clenched her eyes shut as she waited for his next move. He lasciviously took the nipple between his teeth and tugged on it. She grimaced at the pleasure-pain sensation. Her eyes shot open when he stopped. He licked his lips, his eyes alight with lust. Her breasts were tender and swollen, and unable to take the teasing, she yanked his head down. With a low chuckle, she received a vicious flick of his tongue. *Ah!* She wriggled. His suction was now fast and greedy, and his hand was dipping between her legs. She spread them wider.

His fingers rubbed at her sex, and her core clenched in retaliation to the teasing.

"Mmm," he murmured huskily. "You're so turned on."

His fingers slipped into her easily. Gabi gripped the sheets, and as he pummelled in and out of her, she became dizzy, feverish. His long, skilled fingers curled, massaging her inner walls. How she'd missed feeling him. Her chest expanded sharply. The slapping sounds of him hitting into her filled her ears. His mouth was back on her pink nipple, and he lapped at it with his tongue.

"Oh, yes…"

He watched her as his tongue and fingers pleasured her. She knew how he loved to see how she reacted to his touch. His cock jerked against her leg again, and knowing he must be insanely frustrated too, she reached down for it. It was rock hard and warm in her palm. She slid her hand up and down, wrenching a low, feral growl from his throat. She circled her thumb over the tip, spreading the moisture around. He clenched his teeth. She loved seeing him aroused, it made her want him even more. Darion removed her hand, to her astonishment. Then he gathered saliva in his mouth, and licked up her palm, soaking it. His face was shadowed with a dark hunger, and he positioned her hand back on his cock. Now, when she moved, she slid over him with ease, his erection slippery.

"Ah, Gabi…" He plunged into her deeper, matching the rhythm of her movements on him. "Get up."

She was left hanging, her body burning at the absence of his fingers and mouth. "What?"

He shuffled up the bed, and made himself comfortable. "Dance for me."

"Now?" her voice was high pitched with shock.

His fingers curled around his penis, and his tongue swiped across his lower lip. "Now."

"Darion," she tried to protest, not sure if she could concentrate when her lower region was on fire, at the urgency for release.

He didn't speak. He nodded his head in the direction of his mobile. Reluctantly clambering off the bed, Gabi obeyed. It had been a while since she'd given him a private dance. She remembered what Mallory had told her before, *"Darion is clearly a man who easily gets bored sexually. Just keep him on his toes."* She didn't know why she hesitated. She liked dancing. She also liked the way her confidence soared under his appreciative stare at her nakedness. She picked up his mobile and scrolled through his music albums. She settled on "Sexy Boy" by Air.

A smirk surfaced on Darion's face, a dangerous gleam appearing in his pupils as if he liked her song choice. Her stomach clenched nervously as she began to slowly sway her hips. Then she scolded herself for being silly. She'd known Darion quite a while now. They had experienced so much together sexually, and she'd bared herself to him completely.

She swivelled her hips, whilst running her fingers gently down her neck. When she reached her nipples, and fondled them, Darion bit his lip. The jerking movements on his cock slowed, as if he were trying to hold off the climax.

"So...fucking...sexy..." he panted.

Gabi turned her back on him, circling her hips, giving him a full view of her behind. At a steady pace, she leant forward, and touched the floor. She wiggled her ass from side to side, which provoked a muffled grunt from him. Skimming her hands up her legs, she straightened again. Darion hands were now either side of him, his chest rising and falling. His lip curled back into a snarl, and his gaze swept over her.

"Do you want me?" she asked, sliding her palm down her smooth, firm stomach.

"Don't stop."

Following his instructions, she lowered her hand. As she massaged her clit, the burn amplified. A soft sigh seeped through her parted mouth. Delighted vibrations spread through her. It felt good, but she wished it were his fingers. Her ego swelled under his intense stare. Darion squirmed, his legs stiffening. He inhaled audibly.

She sashayed toward him and straddled him, her legs either side of his. She moved her body in 'S' shapes, and resumed fondling her clit. When she slipped a finger in on a gasp, Darion made a sound of agonised ecstasy.

"That's it, baby…" His head rolled back slightly so he could take in the erotic scene. His eyelids narrowed as if he was hazy and drunk with lust. He was clearly seduced.

Gabi's thighs trembled with each plunge of her fingers. Every nerve was pulsing. As she withdrew and rubbed at her clit, Darion quickly slid down the bed. She yelped when he guided her over his face. His tongue swept over her entrance. Her body quivered and she gripped the top of the bed for support. Heat spread up her chest as he sucked and licked with his warm, wide tongue.

Hearing his ferocious groans, she straightened, and glanced over her shoulder. He was sliding his hands up and down his shaft again. The image of herself sitting on his face in the mirror piqued her arousal. He jabbed at her with the tip of his tongue, lapping away. Her body twisted and turned in pleasure. He was so good with that mouth. She cupped her sensitive breasts for a second, before stimulating her clit again.

"You…taste…so…good," Darion mumbled.

"Come here…" she pleaded, shuddering with rising excitement as his fingers filled her.

Needing his own release, his hands caught hold of her hips. He pushed her onto her back, and positioned himself over her.

"Do you want me?" he asked, his cock jerking before her face.

She took it into her mouth and swirled her tongue around it. "Yes."

She didn't get time to prepare herself, as he withdrew and thrust between her legs swiftly. *Ah!* She wriggled at the impressive length and width that stretched and filled her. Darion flexed his hips, driving into her deeper. Her legs instinctively encircled his waist. Gabi perved at his lean, muscular torso which glistened with sweat. His body was built to pleasure. He was an expert between the sheets, and she knew the women in the playrooms must have missed him like crazy.

With merciless pounds, his hands came up and gripped the sides of her throat. His expression was both menacing and pained. "I fucking love you, Gabriella Woods," his tone was vicious, his pupils blazing. "Don't you ever forget it."

Her heart rate sped up at his aggressiveness during sex which sent her delirious with lust. She knew he'd never hurt her. "I love you too."

Enjoying every deep, forceful plunge, Gabi felt the ache of an orgasm lurking inside. Darion pushed in as deep as he could. The pressure built in her groin, and she feared she'd lose control. She shattered underneath him on a loud moan, her body trembling, her sex tightening and contracting around him. Darion's brutal slams were fast and frantic. He came on a long, drawn out moan, his face screwed up. He continued to rock his hips until the last tremors died down.

"Ah, fuck…" His body went rigid and he

collapsed on top of her. "That was amazing."

"It was," she agreed, feeling satisfied and exhausted.

Darion lifted himself up, and lazily reclined back on the bed. Always one to sleep naked, he scurried under the covers. Gabi joined him, draping an arm and a leg over him.

"Darlin'." He nibbled her lips gently before pulling away. "Are you sure you wanna be with me?" She noticed the flash of distress on his face.

"Are you crazy?" She sat up. "Yes, Darion. I do. More than anything."

She couldn't comprehend how this man who was handsome and confident on the outside, could be so insecure, and uncertain on the inside. His vulnerabilities made her love him even more, even though at times it worried her. She liked how only she and a few select others got to see the *real* him.

She snuggled up to him again, her head resting on his chest. She yawned, and knew it wouldn't take her long to fall to sleep. When she peeked up at Darion, she saw he was gazing into the distance and it was clear there was an internal battle going on in his head. Lines of worry creased his forehead. As much as Gabi wanted to question him, she was unable to keep her heavy lids from closing.

Chapter Twenty-Seven

Darion

The next morning Darion couldn't refrain from grinning like an idiot. He may not have had a chat with Gabi about everything yet, but she'd said she still wanted to be with him. At least that was one less thing to worry about.

Unlocking the door to his apartment, he was met with the loud crying of Preston. Dropping his keys on the side, he headed toward the living room area. Gina was rocking him back and forth, trying to comfort him. Darion raked a hand through his hair, and tentatively took a few steps forward. He desperately wanted to help Gina, but he was afraid of holding the baby. He was so tiny and fragile he worried he'd accidentally hurt him.

Settling on the sofa, he peered over at Preston, who was pressed against Gina's bosom. She had chosen not to breastfeed and used a bottle.

He swallowed as he took in Preston's skinny legs and arms. He was definitely underweight. Odelia had been much bigger at that age. His colouring was also still a tad greyish. Gripping onto Gina's finger, Preston wailed at the top of his lungs before his cries became soft moans, due to him getting tired.

"Are you okay?"

"I'm knackered," Gina murmured. When she lifted her head, he noticed she really did appear exhausted. Her face was paler than usual, her eyes red and puffy, and her blonde hair a tangled mess down her back. She definitely wasn't the Gina he used to know.

He was about to offer to take Preston, but kept his mouth shut when she lowered him into a Moses basket. The baby was now snoring gently.

"Do you need anything?" he asked, taking hold of her hand and squeezing it.

"No. I've got everything I need."

"Have you eaten?"

"I had a sandwich earlier." She yawned.

"How was he last night?"

"He cried every hour."

Darion chewed his lip. "I'm sorry, G. I should have been here."

She scraped her waves up into a high ponytail. "Where were you?"

"At Gabi's." He studied her expression, but it was unreadable. He guessed she didn't even have the energy to show her emotions. "Have we got any hospital appointments coming up?"

"Next week."

Silence loomed over them for a moment. Darion

then broke it. "I'm sorry I'm not much help. This whole baby thing is all new to me, G. I don't even know where to begin."

"It's okay. I guess we're both learning as we go along." She shuffled closer to him. "You need to hold him soon. He won't know who you are."

"I will."

Gina leant down and rummaged through a blue bag with an elephant on the front. She retrieved some white mitts and put them on Preston's hands, careful not to wake him.

"It's not that cold, is it?" he asked.

"He needs to wear these. He keeps scratching his face." Gina looked at him and grinned for the first time in a while. "Did you think these were winter gloves?"

He shrugged a shoulder.

"Come on." She held out her hand. "I need to teach you how to prepare his milk, how to bathe him, wind him, and get him to sleep."

He hooked his hand in hers and allowed her to drag him to his feet. Once in the kitchen she explained to him how to make his bottles. Then she flipped through a baby book, and read the important parts. Darion fidgeted the whole time, drumming his fingers on the counter, chewing his lip, tapping his foot on the floor. It still hadn't properly sunk in that he was a father. It was crazy.

"You need to read this." Gina shoved the book at him once she'd closed it. "One of these days you'll need to look after him on your own."

Blowing out a puff of air in exasperation, he shook his head. His confidence diminished rapidly.

"I don't think I can do it, G."

"You can." Switching the kettle on, she grabbed two mugs and began making coffee.

Darion slid onto the stool at the breakfast bar. "Have you heard anything from Johnny?"

"No. But I miss him real bad."

When tears started to roll down her face, Darion strode toward her, and he wrapped her in his arms. Stroking her back, he soothed her, and told her everything would be okay. She tightened her hold on him. Closing his lids, he buried his face in her hair. The usual fruity smell of her shampoo didn't fill his nostrils. Her hair didn't smell of anything.

"Go and have a hot bath. I'll watch Preston."

"Are you sure?"

He nodded.

"Let me have my coffee first."

They both sat side by side sipping their drinks. Darion paid an interest in Gina's mom's wellbeing, who she said was doing well. Gina was hoping to travel down to London with the baby at some point to see her. Gina asked how Gabi was, although he wasn't sure she actually cared. He hoped she didn't get any ideas about him and her having a relationship. Baby or no baby, he and Gina weren't suited. Both fond of the playrooms, drinking and living carelessly, they were a bad influence on one another.

When they'd finished their drinks, Gina scampered to the bathroom. At that moment Preston's screams filled the air again. Darion rushed over to him. *Shit!* He tried to pick him up, however his head rolled back and he screamed even louder.

Placing him back down, he scanned the floor for something to distract him. Picking up a toy, he pressed the 'on' button to which music blared from the speakers. Holding it above the basket, he prayed it would help settle the baby. It didn't.

"Gina." He stared at her helplessly. "What the fuck do I do?"

"Nothing. I'll take care of him." She lifted the baby and started to rock him.

Darion tossed the toy to the side. He felt like the worst dad in the world. He tried to think back to how his parents had made him feel better when he'd been upset. He couldn't think of anything. They usually left him to it, or his dad told him to 'Man up and stop being a wimp.' His mom wasn't comfortable with expressing her feelings, so was rarely ever affectionate. Then he thought of Dion and how she handled Odelia. Usually she'd bribe her with sweets. He shook his head as if to rid the idea. Preston was way too young for solids even.

"Let me hold him," he said once the baby had stopped crying.

Gina held the baby out to him. Darion's arms were outstretched.

"I'm handing you a baby, not a bomb." She laughed. "You're not ready yet, Daz. I don't wanna push you. Let's wait until you're comfortable, okay?"

"It's fine."

She placed the baby in his arms. Darion studied his tiny features. Rocking him gently, he whispered, "Hello." Preston's face screwed up, and Darion prayed for some resemblance of a smile. Instead, he cried hysterically. Darion resumed rocking him, and stroking his head tenderly. It made the baby scream even more.

"He doesn't like me, G." He held Preston out for her to take.

"Don't be stupid. He needs to get to know you, that's all." As soon as Preston was in Gina's arms, the crying stopped. Darion reached out and stroked his head once more. It set him off again. Gina looked at him sympathetically. "It'll take time. Be patient."

When Gina started feeding Preston, he escaped into the bedroom. What if the baby never liked him? What if he never got used to him? A sharp pain pierced through his heart. He had been rejected by his own son. He scolded himself for being so sensitive.

Stripping his clothes off, a hot, relaxing shower had never seemed so appealing. When he was completely naked and sauntering toward the en-suite bathroom, Gina burst into the room, still holding the baby.

"Daz, can you—" Her eyes widened and her face flushed pink. "Shit, Daz. I'm so sorry."

Darion covered himself with his hand. "Don't worry. It's nothing you ain't seen before," he said calmly, trying not to embarrass her further. "What did you want?"

She spun around so her back was facing him. "I was going to ask if you go out today, if you could pick up some baby wipes? I thought I had another pack, but I haven't."

"Sure. Just write a list of everything you need."

"Okay."

"And G," he called her back before she vanished. "I'll start giving you more money every week. Retox is doing well."

"You don't have to do that."

"I insist. My son will never go without. Do you understand?"

"Thanks," Gina said with a nod before leaving the room.

If it was one thing Darion was certain of, it was that Preston was not having the childhood he'd had. Darion had been bullied by other children for wearing the same crappy clothes. He hadn't had the latest toys, or trainers. He was a loner for the majority of his teen years. Women barely even glanced at him. He partly blamed his earlier life, lack of affection, and often going without things as a reason why he'd adored The Black Door. In the playrooms, he had all of the affection and attention he needed from many women, and as the club pulled in a lot of money, he could buy whatever he wanted, whenever he wanted.

Continuing to the bathroom, he examined himself in the mirror for a moment. His eyelids were heavy, and leaning closer, he was almost certain there were a couple of extra lines creasing his forehead. On a loud sigh, he massaged the aching muscles in his neck. He never got much sleep with Preston always crying throughout the night. His usually immaculate apartment was also cluttered with Gina's stuff. He had zero privacy, even in his own bedroom. He hated himself for being a little annoyed about it.

As he stepped into the shower, he winced as he trod on something sharp. *Fucking hell!* He crouched down and picked up a pumice stone. He'd asked Gina several times if she could use the other bathroom, but she'd complained it only had a bath, and she only had time for quick showers. Throwing the stone forcefully to the wall, he slid down the tiles, and squeezed his eyes shut. The water rained down on him. It was far too hot, burning his skin. He didn't care. He didn't have the energy to adjust the temperature.

He missed his old, carefree, fun life. He missed working at The Black Door. He missed being able to have a beer and a cigar, and play cards with Lennie and Travis. He missed having no responsibilities, and being able to do as he pleased. He wondered if he'd ever adapt to his new life.

Chapter Twenty-Eight

Gabi

Gabi binned the coffee capsule and lifted the cup to her lips. She gasped in delight as the warm liquid went down. It was just what she needed. She was about to exit the kitchen when Ben walked in.

"Hi." He grinned.

His eyes ran the full length of her body. She was wearing a figure-hugging, red, knee-length dress, and black Louboutin heels. Her hair was scraped up in a long ponytail, and hung glamorously down her back. Her lips had also been stained in Max Factor's Ruby Red. She'd made a bit more of an effort that morning. She was meeting Darion after work at his new bar. She was excited and curious to see what it was like.

"Hello," she responded cheerily.

"It's nice and bright today, isn't it?" he asked, filling a glass with water, and leaning against the counter.

Gabi smiled at the polite weather chit-chat, and peered out of the window. The blue sky was clear of clouds. The sun blared through the window. It was times like this when she wished she was sitting at a pub terrace, shopping along the high street, or reading a book in the garden.

"How are you finding Miller & Co?"

Ben nodded vehemently. "I like it. Everyone I've met so far has been really nice."

"That's good to hear. What do you enjoy reading?"

"Thrillers, mystery, crime, non-fiction. You?"

Chick-lit, romance, erotica. Gabi averted her gaze, deciding not to reveal her guilty pleasure reads, and said, "Contemporary fiction mostly."

Ben was attractive in a clean shaven, pretty-boy way, with dark, short hair, and brown eyes. When he asked her how her weekend had been, and she'd disclosed her antics, he revealed he'd been to the library, visited art museums, and seen family. He was the complete opposite of Darion. She had been so used to Darion's complex lifestyle, she'd almost forgotten how nice and easy it was to speak to other men, who appeared not to have a past of dark desires, and baggage. It was actually refreshing.

"Well, um...I better get some work done." He placed his glass down. "It was nice to properly meet you, Gabi."

"Yes. You too."

"I'll see you around."

When he left, Mallory dashed in. "Ooh. Did you just meet Ben?" she asked.

Mallory had been back from the Maldives for a few days. Gabi envied her golden suntan, and the hundreds of photographs she'd shown her. It had looked like complete paradise. Mallory had gushed at how she and Steve were even closer. Gabi had always believed Mallory had found her perfect match. They complemented, rather than complicated one another's lives. It made her question her relationship with Darion again. Was love meant to be so hard?

"So, do you think he's cute?" Mallory asked.

"He's okay."

"How's your morning going?" She rinsed her cup under the tap.

"Busy. Yours?"

"Same."

"You heard much from Suzie?"

"I spoke to her yesterday. She loves being pregnant. She's got a few months left now." She threw Gabi a sympathetic look. "You know, I still can't believe Darion has a son."

"Me either."

"It wouldn't be so bad if it wasn't with Gina."

"Yeah, and they're living together." She shrugged a shoulder. "But then again, I don't think it matters much who it's with."

"Have you seen the baby yet?"

"No. I should be meeting him tonight."

"I hope it goes okay, Gab. Remember, this is all new to Darion too."

"I know," she mumbled. "I'll also be seeing his new bar Retox, later."

"What sort of bar is it?" She eyed her

suspiciously.

Gabi threw her head back with a soft laugh. "A normal bar, Mal."

"Good. The last thing you need is more stuff to worry about."

"Don't I know it."

Gabi gave her a little wave and headed to her office. The photograph on her desk caught her attention. It was of her and Darion standing on the bridge in London. They looked happy, like they didn't have a single care in the world, although, the picture had been taken before she'd been hit with his news. She picked it up, and ran her finger across his face. He was so sexy. She was completely seduced by everything about him. She wished he was before her so she could kiss his full lips, and run her fingers through his hair. She placed the photo flat down on the table. She'd find it hard to concentrate otherwise.

It was an hour later of editing a manuscript when her mobile rang.

"Hi."

"Hey, darlin'." The provocative tone of his voice sent shivers up her spine. "How's your day going?"

"Not too bad. How about yours?"

"Noisy. I'm about to cook up some dinner."

The loud crying of the baby in the background filled the line. Gabi held the mobile away from her ear for a moment. "Is everything okay?"

"Yeah. We've got a hospital appointment later so they can do some checks on Preston."

"I hope it goes okay."

"Thanks...Gina," he yelled. "Do you want some

food?"

Gabi heard Gina's voice and her stomach somersaulted. She hated the jealousy that took over her. She got to spend every single day with Darion. She was able to wake up with him there, have breakfast and dinner with him, and see him at night, when he wasn't with Gabi. She wondered if they watched TV or films together, if they shared a bottle of wine on the night, chatting. Rubbing her aching temple, she tried to rein in her worrying thoughts. She'd see for herself later what the relationship between them was now like. She hoped it was civil for the baby, and not because Gina had other motives.

"Gabi, I've gotta go. I'll see you at Retox later."

"Sure."

She was about to end the call on a miserable sigh when he added, "I love you. You know that, right?"

"I love you too."

She was pleased he was expressing his feelings more. Eva had made him feel needy and pathetic when he'd declared his love. Gabi needed him to say it, and not just show her he cared through sex. It had taken a while to get Darion to trust her and open up. She hoped it stayed that way.

Later that evening, Gabi was in Westhaven outside Retox. Through the window she could see it was fairly busy. The music was loud enough to hear from the street, a mixture of rock and vocal metal. Clutching her bag, she smiled at the doorman, and entered the premises. She surveyed her surroundings in awe. It was modern, elegant, and so different from his last club. The fact everyone was fully clothed made her feel much more secure.

Sliding onto a stool at the bar, she curiously examined the barmaids. She couldn't help but notice how pretty they were. She knew it was expected really, if Darion wanted to lure in customers. Her mouth fell when she noticed a barman also, and a good looking one at that. She was pleasantly surprised. She'd thought Darion hated competition. Perhaps he'd saw sense and realised the women needed eye-candy too.

"What can I get you?" The brunette with blue streaks in her hair approached her.

"Is Darion here?"

"He's in his office. Want me to get him?"

"Please."

"Who shall I say is asking?"

"His girlfriend."

Gabi noticed her stare sweep over her entire body. Her lips curled at the sides, as if in approval. When she disappeared through the door, Gabi ordered a glass of white wine. When "Tainted Love" by Marilyn Manson pounded from the speakers, she had a sudden urge to dance. Finishing her wine in several gulps, she ordered another. The dancing crowd around her seemed to be enjoying themselves. The cute barman handed her another drink with a wink.

"What's the strongest drink you have?" she shouted over the music. She wondered if Darion was still stocking the devil's drink.

"Absinthe."

She couldn't help but laugh. Darion didn't mess about. "I'll have a shot please."

His brow rose. "You sure you can handle it?"

"I'm sure." Darion had taught her well. The very first time she had met him he'd persuaded her into having two shots of Absinthe. At eighty percent, it was harsh to the throat but got you merry quickly.

When the barman handed her a shot of the green liquid, she tossed it back. As always it tore through her throat like hot flames. She grimaced.

"Honey, Darion's on a call. He'll be out in a sec." The brunette had returned.

"Okay."

Gabi gulped back her second glass of wine, and stood up. She didn't know whether it was the alcohol, or desperately needing to let her hair down, but her confidence soared. She wove through the crowd until she was in the middle of dancing bodies. Then she swayed her hips and arms from side to side. As the music and laughter rang loud in her ears, all of her worries seemed to dissipate.

Spinning around, she took in the DJ, who she hadn't noticed before. The drunken crowd were really letting loose considering it was only mid-week. Continuing to grind her hips, she twirled around again on a giggle. The absinthe was really taking effect.

Heat flooded through her body, and she was certain she could feel Darion's presence. The hairs on her neck stood on end. A girl moved out of the way. Then she saw him. Her dancing slowed down. At the corner of the bar Darion stood looking as delicious and tempting as ever. Dressed smartly in navy jeans, a matching shirt, with the sleeves rolled up, and his hair neatly gelled back, she understood why several sets of eyes were on him. When he casually strolled toward her, her heartbeat quickened.

She gasped when a hand gripped her buttocks. Her head shot around to the culprit. A stumbling blond man smirked at her. Before Gabi could scold him, Darion had him gripped by the collar.

"Touch her again and you'll never set foot in this club again. Understand?" His tone was low and vicious, his glare murderous.

"Okay." The man stepped back with a scowl, smoothing his shirt down.

Darion's eyes were then back on her. His features softened, and he snaked his arm around her waist, and pulled her into him.

"Having fun?" A wicked glint flashed in his pupils.

"I'd have more fun if you stopped threatening people."

"I didn't hit him." He smiled, appearing somewhat pleased.

"Fair enough." She shrugged.

"Don't stop dancing," he ordered, greedily taking her in.

"Lucky bitch," Gabi heard a girl behind her giggle to her friend.

"I wouldn't mind a bit of him," the other said.

Gabi shook her head in amusement, whilst Darion laughed his usual dirty-sounding laugh. *Yeah, they couldn't handle you,* Gabi wanted to say. They looked way too innocent to enter the dark world of Darion Milano.

"I love the new bar," she told him.

"Me too. It's less stressful than the club."

His arm anchored her against his solid body. Her nostrils were invaded with the scent of his cologne. Heat radiated from him, and lust assailed her. As she felt him hardening in his trousers, her internal muscles began to spasm as he ignited all of her senses. Not breaking their hard stares, she ran her hands down his impressive biceps, all the way to his ass, where she yanked him even closer. Their hips collided as their bodies fell in sync with the music.

"I thought you didn't dance," Gabi murmured against his ear before tugging on it with her teeth.

"This isn't dancing," his voice was low and husky. He winked suggestively.

Gabi dropped her head with a laugh. His erection skimming between her legs caused her to groan in pleasure. He was rock hard. Her insatiable need for him increased. Her sex clenched and throbbed, aching for contact.

"I've a new office desk that needs christening." He continued to grind into her teasingly, causing the pressure to build in her groin.

"Let's go," she panted, flicking her tongue over his bottom lip.

Darion sucked her tongue into his mouth. Then he caressed firmly, licking and sucking. It was a full on kiss that left them both breathless. His fingers buried into her hair, where he gripped it roughly. Gabi retaliated by biting on his bottom lip. He grimaced and possessed her mouth again, savagely, trapping her moans.

"I want you," his breathing was harsh in her ear. "Now."

Taking her by the hand, he led her toward the bar area. He was met with his bar staff. Obviously not wanting to be rude, he introduced them to Gabi.

"Whenever she's here, all drinks are on the house. She's welcome to come on through to the office anytime. Okay?"

They all nodded in unison.

"It was nice meeting you all." Gabi waved before she was shoved through the door. She had to practically sprint to keep up with Darion's hurried strides. When she was in his office, and he was locking the door, she got a quick glimpse of her fancy surroundings.

"Get on the desk."

She rolled her eyes at his impatience, but did as she was told. Her heart swelled when she noticed his laptop screensaver was a photo of her sleeping that he'd taken in their early days of being together. He carefully placed the laptop on the side, and then pushed her further onto the desk. Papers and stationary scattered to the floor. Darion didn't waste any time in bunching up her dress and peeling off her underwear.

"Open your legs."

"Darion…" A blush flamed her cheeks.

"Gabi." He towered over her. He cocked his head to the side and gave her a salacious grin that unnerved her. "Surely you're not still shy around me."

"Sometimes," she confessed with a low giggle. *You make me fucking nervous.* Anticipation coursed through her veins and she never knew what his next move would be. She hesitated for a second, but then

217

parted her legs.

Darion's stare swept over her slowly and admiringly. His tongue traced along his bottom lip. She slid across the wood as he settled her on the edge. Then he crouched down, and his wet, flickering tongue was between her legs.

"Oh…" she moaned, her head rolling back.

Grabbing fistfuls of his hair, she silently begged him not to stop. His tongue licked up and down her clit, causing heat to suffuse the area. Her inner muscles throbbed as a needy ache loomed in her stomach. His swirling tongue and the feel of his hot breath made her cry out. When Darion glanced up at her, she could see the animalistic hunger on his face. With no warning, his fingers plunged into her deeply.

"Ah…" She bit her lip.

The slow thrusting then became pleasurable as her body accepted it. Her breaths were short and sharp, and she was shuddering. She couldn't resist from watching him, and noticing how the muscles in his biceps swelled with each movement.

Returning to pleasure her with his skilled tongue, she rocked her hips against his face. When he met her sensitive spot, she gripped the edge of the desk. It was so good she feared she'd orgasm any second. Delightful vibrations rushed through her whole body. Her pelvis was burning up, needing release.

"Don't stop," she pleaded.

Then he stopped, wiping his mouth with the back of his hand.

"What are you doing?" She sat up.

He pushed himself to his feet, and didn't say a

word. Stripping himself of his shirt, he then unzipped his jeans, and allowed them, and his boxers to fall down his legs. Gabi swallowed as he stepped out of them. She was level with his erection, which was close to her lips. She reached out and closed her palm around the shaft. When she took him in her mouth, she heard him grunt in pleasure. She circled her tongue around the glistening head, before taking all of him deep in her throat.

"Fuck, Gabi..." he groaned, bucking upwards. "That...feels...so...good," he murmured breathlessly.

She tugged back and forth with her hand whilst sucking firmly. She loved seeing him aroused. When she licked the groove under the tip, his groaning got louder, as if it was torturous and he urgently needed to come. As she placed her palms on his smooth buttocks, she guided him back and forth. She could feel his thighs trembling. He was soaking with her saliva as she took as much of him as she could.

"Fuck." He wriggled.

Gently massaging his balls, he thrust into her deeper. In and out fast. When his grunts were more frequent, and she felt his whole body shuddering, she stopped.

"Don't stop."

She stood up and pushed him. His legs hit the sofa, and he dropped onto it with a thud. As he lay there completely naked, she studied his perfect physique and impressive cock. Crawling up the sofa, she straddled him. Darion's lips were parted, his chest rising and falling with his heavy breathing. Lifting herself up, she lowered herself onto him. His lubricated shaft made it easier for her body to connect with his.

"Oh, Gabi…"

She moved up and down, riding him slowly and teasingly. His nails dug into her hips and she knew he wanted it faster, harder. So she gave him everything she had. She rocked her hips, taking all of him. Each time she dropped onto his length, they cried out together. Darion gripped her buttocks and helped push her body up and down.

Clenching his teeth, he then tore her dress over her head. Gabi frantically unclasped her bra, her nipples swelling, needing some sort of pleasure. Sitting up, Darion's mouth wrapped around her breast. His tongue sucked and flicked against her nipple. Then he bit it roughly.

"Hmmm…" She winced.

"You like that?" he asked, closing his teeth around it again and pulling.

"Ah. Stop," she warned, shooting him with a look, and continuing to push herself against him.

"Or what?" he asked, with a challenging lift of his brows.

To show him she wasn't afraid of him, she sunk her teeth into his neck, hard. He screamed out. When she looked at his face, which was red with rage, she giggled. Gritting his teeth, Darion withdrew. She didn't get chance to move as he spun her around. He positioned himself behind her, and pushed her face into the sofa. On all fours, her buttocks was pulled up, and he rammed into her forcefully. Darion preferred it when he had full control. She didn't mind one bit. She loved being dominated.

She reached down to stroke her clit simultaneously, causing tingles to race through her body. Darion swivelled his hips, and then pulled back to teasingly graze her entrance with the tip of his cock. She *hated* it when he kept her waiting. Then he pounded into her again, filling her completely, making her body shoot forwards. His thrusts were merciless and relentless.

He fucked her aggressively, possessively. Every forward motion was sending her toward the release that was burning her sex, and making her clench her fists. She writhed at the intensity of pleasure. She wasn't sure if she could take it. She fought to keep her heartbeat steady, but it was no use.

"Oh yes…" Darion groaned. "Come with me."

The pressure built and Gabi knew she could no longer resist it. She pushed backwards, inviting him to increase the pace. The muscles in her sex tightened around him, throbbing. He slammed into her a few final times and she was gone. Her whole body trembled, and she came on a loud, drawn out moan. Darion jerked inside her, riding out his own climax. Cursing and grunting, she waited until he fully emptied himself. When he separated their bodies, she fell flat on the sofa, exhausted. He dropped onto her, and she didn't care he was heavy, just as long as she felt the warmth of his naked body against her skin. They lay silent, catching their breath for a moment, and for their muscles to regain energy. Then Darion rolled onto his side. Gabi turned over to face him.

He wiped drops of sweat from his forehead and stared at her, love and admiration visible in his eyes. He stroked her hair gently before planting a tender kiss on her lips. When he told her he loved her, she said it back. She would never tire of hearing him say it. Silence hung in the air, and they remained staring at one another, sheepish grins on both of their faces. She loved that the chemistry and passion still existed between them, as strong as ever.

"Marry me, Gabi," he said barely above a whisper.

She almost choked and wasn't sure whether she'd heard right. "What?" She sat up.

"When things get tough, all you do is run. I'm not letting you run anymore." Darion sat up also, and took hold of her hands.

Gabi wanted to be settled with Darion. Some sort of normalcy. Then in the future, children even.

"I know what I want, and that's you. So, what's the point in waiting?" His expression was serious, but she also noticed a hint of fear whilst he waited for her answer.

"Darion, all I've ever wanted is for what we have to become serious." She squeezed his hands. "Of course I'll marry you."

"Really?" his voice trembled with insecurity, as if he couldn't quite believe it. "Are you sure?"

"Why wouldn't I marry you?"

He bowed his head with a soft chuckle, and shrugged. "I dunno. I just thought with everything that's happened between us, you'd want someone more deserving of you."

"You *do* deserve me," she said sternly. "Just because you come with a whole lot of issues, it doesn't mean you aren't a good person, Darion. I have never felt more loved, desired, or safer than when I'm with you." She stroked his cheek gently. "I wish you could see what I see."

His mouth curled into a grin. "Gabriella Milano," he tested the name. "I like it."

"Me too." Her lips lingered on his for a few seconds, and when they parted, her tongue swept in. She cupped his face in her hands, and kissed him with such softness, it created butterflies in her tummy.

"We'll look for a ring in the week." He leant down to locate his jeans. He rummaged in the pockets and retrieved a cigarette.

"I get to choose?"

"Whatever you want, darlin'." He wrapped his lips around the cigarette, and lit it. Blowing out smoke, he gave her a wink that sent shivers of excitement up her spine.

She crossed the room, and started to get dressed. She had never in a million years expected Darion to propose to her any time soon. She was utterly bewildered. It didn't even matter that it wasn't romantic, and in front of the Eiffel Tower in Paris how Lawrence had done it. Lawrence had been the wrong man for her. Darion was definitely the right man. A lifetime with him would be testing, but never dull. She was certain of it.

"Are you ready to meet Preston?" he asked, towering over her.

Gabi nodded. She tucked a stray hair behind her ear. Had he proposed because he feared she'd run off once she saw how tough things could be? Or did he really want to spend the rest of his life with her?

Scrambling to her feet, she said, "Let's go and meet your son."

Chapter Twenty-Nine

Darion unlocked the door to his apartment. It was midnight, and he assured her Gina and the baby would still be awake. Her hands were shaking, and her heart was pounding faster than ever. She was terrified of facing Gina, of seeing her all comfortable in Darion's home, and whether she'd feel like a third wheel when she saw the three of them together. Was she standing in the way of them being a perfect little family? She opened her mouth to speak, yet no words came out. She swallowed, in urgent need of a drink.

"Hey, G. I'm back," Darion called out.

Gabi took a few tentative steps into the room. She expected to see Gina sitting on the couch, looking her usual pretty made-up self, baby in arms, and the apartment decorated with her belongings. Instead she saw a vulnerable, exhausted looking woman, rocking a whimpering baby to sleep. The floor was trashed with baby things, and she had to tread carefully to avoid stepping on anything.

"Sorry about the mess," Darion said.

"It's my fault." Gina stood up, and balancing the baby on her hip, she leant down and started to pick up things.

"It's okay," Gabi said, perching on the edge of the sofa.

"G, leave it," Darion instructed. "I'll clean up in the morning." Darion made his way toward Gina, and peered down at the baby. "How has he been?"

"He's still crying every hour or two."

"Gabi, this is Preston," Darion said.

Gabi leant forward and took in the baby before her. She was certain her heart skipped a beat. He was beautiful. He looked like a mini Darion. She knew instantly he would break hearts when he was older. His features were perfect. When her gaze dropped to his body, her eyes widened when she noticed how small he actually was. His legs and arms were tiny.

"He's gorgeous," she whispered.

They all watched him for a few minutes, until he blinked his eyes open. His screams pierced through her ears. She couldn't believe how something that small could make so much noise. Gina groaned and began to rock him. He stopped almost immediately.

"How did it go at the hospital?" she asked, remembering she'd forgotten to.

"We actually had some good news for once." Darion ran his hands through his hair. "The nurse said he's put on weight, and seems taller and healthier."

"I'm glad."

"She did say though that he may have a harder time fighting infections, should he get sick. Low blood sugar may be a concern, and some other stuff." Darion traced his fingers across Preston's cheek. "She said most babies with growth problems reach a normal height when they're around three. All we can do is be positive."

Preston started to cry again. Darion held out his arms, and Gina handed him over. He rocked him gently. Gabi melted on the spot. Seeing Darion Milano holding a baby was probably the best thing she'd ever seen. His forehead crinkled with concern, and she could see how much he adored his son. He may be unpredictable at times, and difficult to work out, but he was reliable. Gabi knew she, Gina, and Preston would always be able to count on him.

When Preston's cries got even louder, a confused and frustrated Darion gave him back to Gina. "What am I doing wrong?"

"Nothing, Daz." Gina sighed heavily. "I've told you already, he needs to get used to you."

"He won't get used to you if you keep on handing him back," Gabi said softly.

"You wanna try again?" Gina asked.

Darion chewed his bottom lip and then nodded. When Preston was in his arms, and continuing to scream the apartment down, he tried to return him to Gina.

"No." She took a step back.

Darion rocked him, and rubbed circles on his belly at the same time. "Maybe he's got wind." He sat down, and arranged the baby into a seating position. Holding his chin with his hand, he leant him slightly forward, and began rubbing and tapping his back gently with the other hand.

"Have you been reading the baby books?" Gina's brow rose.

"I flipped through one when I was taking a bath."

Gina swept her hair up quickly and turned to Gabi. "You want a drink?"

"No. I'm fine, thanks." She held her hand to her mouth to hide her yawn.

"Gabi, go to bed. You've got work in the morning."

"Okay."

"We'll get up early and collect your car."

"Sure."

"I won't be too long."

Stepping into his bedroom, she stared at his big, comfortable looking bed. She couldn't wait to get under the covers. She stripped and brushed her teeth quickly. When she buried herself under the warm covers, she closed her eyes on a delighted sigh. She could still hear Preston wailing through the wall.

Two hours later, Gabi woke to the sound of laughing. Rolling onto her side with a groan, she caught sight of the wall clock. It displayed it was 2.30 a.m. Stretching, she expected to find Darion beside her. She was disheartened when she spotted his side of the bed was empty. Surely Preston had fallen asleep. Sitting up, she waited for his screams to fill the air. They didn't. Why hadn't Darion come to bed?

Slipping out of bed, she crossed the room, and

stood behind the door to hear if he had fallen asleep. He hadn't. His and Gina's voices were clear. She wondered what they were talking about. Had he told her about them being engaged? She was about to return to bed when she heard Gina mention The Black Door. Gabi stepped closer to catch the whole conversation.

"I can't believe how much our lives have changed in such a short space of time." She laughed. "More wine?"

"No," Darion responded. "I was only meant to have one glass."

"Well, we needed more than one after tonight. I seriously didn't think we'd get Preston to sleep."

"Me either."

"Fuck. Can you believe we're parents?" Gina's tone was high-pitched with disbelief.

"No, I can't."

"Not so long ago, we'd both be at the club, drinking there. I'd be on the stage; you'd be at the bar gambling, or in the playrooms." She giggled.

"Yeah. Times have definitely changed."

"I miss that place. We had so much fun. Do you miss it sometimes?"

"Yeah, I do."

"Will you not use the playrooms with Gabi?"

Gabi froze, waiting for his response. Was he craving the playrooms again? Did he want other women? Would Gina, a constant reminder of The Black Door, sway him from a life he now had, to a life he once led? When silence followed, her shoulders drooped in disappointment. Had he nodded, or shaken his head?

"Do you remember that time with Karla?"

"Oh yeah." He chuckled. "That was crazy."

"What was your favourite room?"

"Probably the dungeon suite. What about you?"

"I quite liked the fantasy suite."

"Yeah, you would do, with all of those toys." He laughed.

"No," she shrieked. "Well, maybe. But it was the outfits I loved. I enjoyed role playing."

"Dominatrix was your favourite, if I remember correctly. All that PVC."

"It was the nurse, and schoolgirl I liked playing best."

"Yeah…I remember now. It was Eva who loved the dominatrix role."

It was quiet for a moment, and then Gabi heard Gina ask for a cigarette. Darion stated he'd join her on the balcony. When the sound of a door opened and closed, she was unable to hear what was being said. Bile rose in her throat, as insecurity set in. Why did Gina have to bring up the club? Gabi wanted Darion's past and dark desires put behind him. The last thing she wanted was him reminiscing about the times he'd had. If he was ever tempted to return to that lifestyle, she knew the relationship would have to end for good.

***

Gabi pulled the covers over her head, blocking out the light. She wished blocking out Preston's cries was as easy. She'd been tossing and turning in bed for most of the night. When Darion finally made it to bed and wrapped his arms around her, she didn't feel like the adored fiancée she had only hours earlier. How could he miss The Black Door? She knew it had played a huge part in his life. She had believed he had finally seen sense and was over it. He said he could never share her with anyone else. But that wasn't to say he didn't fantasise about sharing another woman with others. She hoped he wasn't having second thoughts already about their engagement.

Rolling onto her side, she wasn't surprised to see Darion was no longer in bed. The baby had woken him too, and she knew he needed to tend to him. She hated that she felt left out. It wasn't Preston that bothered her. It was his close relationship with Gina. She could never compete with her.

"Fucking hell, G!"

The sound of Darion's scream caused her to jolt out of bed, and race to the living room. Darion was clutching his bleeding foot.

"I tidied up last night, and toys are all over the floor again."

"Sorry." Gina rushed in and bent down to pick up the mess off the floor. Gabi's mouth dropped as she took in the flimsy nightie Gina was wearing. Her breasts were spilling out, and as it was see-through, her nipples were visible. Gabi clamped her lips together to prevent angry words from escaping. Did Gina always parade around the apartment dressed inappropriately? Also, did they always keep one another company, whilst sharing a bottle of wine?

"Shit." Darion grimaced, falling onto the sofa.

"Where's the first aid kit?" Gabi asked.

"I'll get it." Gina darted into the kitchen area and rummaged through cupboards.

A moment later she was tending to Darion's foot. Gabi's body temperature rose. She sucked in air through clenched teeth. Not only was she pissed off with Gina for dressing like a tart, but for bringing up the playrooms last night, and now she was taking over where it concerned Darion.

Returning to the bedroom, Gabi gathered her work clothes, showered quickly, and then dressed. When she was back in the living room, she sensed Darion was still agitated. He was staring at the television absentmindedly. His fingers were drumming on his leg, and the veins in his forehead were protruding. To top off an awful start to the morning, Preston started to cry.

"Fuck." Darion hung his head in his hands.

"Daz," Gina yelled. "I've ran out of nappies. Can you get me some, please?"

Closing his eyes to gather patience, Darion slowly rose to his feet. "I asked you the other day if you had everything you needed."

"I thought I had an extra pack." Gina was in the room again, with Preston in her arms.

"Gina, please," Darion pleaded, rubbing his forehead. "You've gotta be more organised. I'll go get dressed."

Gabi moved aside to let Darion pass. Taking up residence on the sofa, she scowled when she got another eyeful of Gina's breasts. She wasn't on the stripper pole now. Did she not have any respect?

Unable to hold her tongue any longer, Gabi

asked, "Any chance you could dress appropriately when you're around Darion please?"

"Oh for fuck's sake, Gabi," she snapped. "I didn't have anything clean. I'm sorry. I don't usually wear stuff like this around him."

"Okay," Gabi said in a bid to end the conversation.

"You think I still want Darion?" She shook her head. "I bet you think I got pregnant on purpose, don't you?" Tears spilled down her cheeks.

"What?" Gabi knew disbelief must have shown on her face. "No, Gina, I—"

"It wasn't my fault. We used a condom! I'm always careful when it comes to sex," she shouted to be heard over Preston's wails. "I'm not after Darion. You don't need to worry about me."

"I don't. I—"

"What's going on?" Darion asked, now fully dressed.

"Gabi thinks I'm dressing like a slut because I still want you."

Darion sighed heavily, fixing Gabi with a look.

"No, I did not," she exclaimed.

"You may as well have. Daz, please tell her I don't usually dress like this."

Darion rubbed his temples as if to alleviate the pain of a migraine. "Girls, please don't fucking argue. It's 7 a.m. and I can't handle it."

"Well, I don't want Darion." Gina huffed. "I've been there, done that."

"Yeah, I bet you have," she muttered, remembering last night's conversation she'd eavesdropped on.

"Oh. Is that how it is? How dare you look down your nose at me. I was there for you when you needed me."

"I don't want to argue. I asked you politely if you could cover up, that's all."

"I'm sorry I have nothing clean," she yelled. "Preston won't stop crying. Can't you see my hair?" She tugged on it. "It hasn't been washed in days! I only have time to wash my body. Darion can't get him to sleep, and all he does is cry."

"Sorry for being a shit dad, G," Darion snapped. "I'm trying my best. It's hard."

"I know it's hard," she roared. "I'm fucking exhausted. I've had about ten hours sleep in the last three days. I can't remember the last time I actually had a bath, not a rushed shower. I can't remember the last non-microwaveable meal I had, either. My clothes smell of vomit. And then Gabi's bitching about my nightie. I rushed in here because you hurt your foot." She shook her head, her face red with rage. "Sorry for trying to help."

"Gina," Gabi said softly, wanting to apologise.

"Just leave it," she spat. She vanished into her bedroom, slamming the door behind her.

Darion clenched his teeth. He scanned the floor as if searching for something to throw out of frustration.

"Maybe me and Preston should leave?" Gina returned.

"You're not putting him in that hostel. It's full of druggies."

"No, it's not."

"It is," he roared, his eyes flashing dangerously.

"Great." Gina waved her arms in the air. "Now you've woke the baby. Thanks a lot." She shot daggers at him.

Darion looked up at the heavens above. He seemed at a loss of what to do. Gabi had never seen him so stressed before. It was as if he was trying his hardest to help out, but felt like a failure. "I can't handle this," he muttered quietly.

Grabbing his car keys, he left the apartment, instructing Gabi to follow him. Glancing back, she witnessed Gina crumple to the floor, sobbing. She instantly pitied her, desperately wanting to help.

"You get the nappies. I'll wait with Gina."

"You'll be late for work."

"I'll phone in sick."

"Gabi—"

"Just go."

Gabi folded her arms across her chest and approached Gina. The bitterness she had for her turned to compassion. She hadn't realised how hard it must have been for Gina and Darion. Having a baby, unplanned, was a shock to the system. Both of them being clueless she was pregnant; they'd had no time to prepare themselves.

Dropping to her knees, she embraced her tightly. Gina was right. She had been there for her when times had gotten tough with Darion. Stroking her hair repeatedly, she soothed her, and told her everything would be okay.

"It won't," she snivelled. "Everything's a mess."

"No, it's not. You're both new at this stuff. It'll get easier, I promise."

"We're terrible parents."

"That's not true. You both love that baby. You'd do anything for him. I know you would." Gabi stood up and held out her hand. "Go and have a nice, hot bath. Then style your hair and do your make-up. I want to see the old Gina."

"I can't."

"You can. I'll watch Preston," she said firmly.

"Are you sure?"

Gabi rolled her eyes, and took hold of Preston. Sitting down on the sofa, she placed him on her lap.

"What's the matter with you, huh?" she cooed, stroking his soft head of hair. "What's all this noise about?"

The baby continued to cry. Gabi took in the fluffy outfit he was wearing. Her brow furrowed in confusion. "Gina, how long has he been wearing this?" The room temperature was hot even to Gabi. In a flimsy shirt, she couldn't imagine how hot Preston felt wrapped in wool. He resembled a stuffed teddy bear.

"Um, a couple of days."

"Do you always dress him in these sorts of clothes?"

She nodded. "The nurse said he could have trouble maintaining his body temperature." Gina burst into hysterics again. "It's my fault he's like this. The nurse said smoking, drinking, and abusing drugs can play a part in a baby's health."

"Don't blame yourself." Gabi began stripping the clothes off a still screaming Preston. "There are drug addicts and alcoholics that have healthy babies. There are also extremely healthy people who have unhealthy babies. Sometimes these things

236

just happen."

As soon as the outfit was off Preston, he stopped crying. Gabi stroked his babygrow of which he'd also had under the fluffy number. It was soaked in sweat. "Gina, he's been boiling hot for days. No wonder he was crying. Has he been sleeping in this?"

She nodded meekly. "I didn't want him to get cold." She wiped her cheeks.

"You can't put him in these types of clothes. It's not even winter."

Preston began gurgling, and moving his arms and legs. Gabi's heart swelled with love. He was the cutest baby she'd ever seen. He looked perfect, and healthy in her eyes. She peeled off the babygrow. "Bring me his bathtub please, and some light clothes. Another babygrow, or a vest and shorts."

"Okay."

A few minutes later, Gina placed everything Gabi had asked for on the floor.

"Now, go and have a relaxing bath. I'll take care of him."

Gina paused in the doorway. "Thank you for helping me, Gabi."

"I'd do anything for Darion," she responded. "And I'd like to help make things a little easier for you if I can."

"I really didn't plan this. I lost Johnny and everything."

"I believe you."

"Thank you for not taking Darion away from Preston."

"I'd never do that."

When Gabi was left alone with Preston, she placed him in his Moses basket, and quickly filled his tub. She then spent the next hour bathing him, dressing him, feeding him, and rocking him to sleep. She had read and edited quite a few books on motherhood and enjoyed the odd self-help book here and there. She was pleasantly surprised how natural handling Preston came to her. She was broody as hell. Her heart tightened in her chest. How she wished it was her baby Darion had and not Gina's.

Chapter Thirty

Darion

Darion drained his beer quickly, and ordered another. His legs almost gave way, and he had to grip hold of the bar to steady himself. *Shit!* He chuckled. Jasmine collected his empty glass and handed him another beer. She told him he'd had more than enough, and it was the last one she was serving him. He slapped the bar in frustration. Just because he didn't own The Black Door anymore didn't mean she had a right to refuse him another drink. He sighed heavily, and as he retrieved a silver tin from his pocket, his stare landed on the stage. Wendy and Lexi were seductively dancing, half-naked. Marnie was flirting with a customer. It was like old times. He liked it.

Popping the cigar in his mouth, he fiddled with the lighter to get it to work. He cursed under his breath. Rolling her eyes, Jasmine took a black strip of matches, decorated with the club's gold logo, and lit one. He thanked her and took a long drag. As the nicotine filled his lungs, he exhaled on a smile. He'd had to get away from his now messy apartment, from Preston's screaming, and from Gabi and Gina's arguing. It was all too much for him to handle. He never seemed to be able to do anything right. He was just like his own dad: a shit one.

He winked when Lexi gave him a little wave. He could have had a drink at Retox, but he'd needed to see familiar friendly faces. The Black Door was like home, and he was more than comfortable there. Well, he was until he heard a sultry voice.

"Back so soon?"

Lifting his head, he took in the sight of Eva before him. Her long, black hair hung silkily down her back, like it always did. Her mouth curled at the corners, as if amused at the drunken sight of him. "Trouble in paradise?"

"Paradise," he blurted out. "I wish."

"What's wrong?" Eva slid onto the stool next to him, and ordered Jasmine to fetch her a drink.

"Nothing that concerns you," he mumbled, blowing out smoke.

"You know Carl doesn't permit smoking in his club."

Darion glared at her. "Don't piss me off, Eva."

"So." She took a sip of her drink when she received it. "How's parenthood treating you?"

"What do you think…Marnie!" he called out. "Can you get rid of this cigar, darlin'?"

"Sure." She took it from his outstretched hand.

"That tough, huh?"

He didn't respond. He wished Eva would leave

him in peace to drown his sorrows. Taking another swig of his drink, he then slammed the glass on the bar, causing beer to spill. He shakily clambered to his feet, and grabbed the keys to his motorbike. He wanted the adrenaline rush the speed gave him. He was about to exit the club when Eva blocked his view. Placing her palms on his chest, she shook her head.

"You're not driving in that state."

"Watch me." He pushed past her.

He was yanked back around when she gripped hold of his t-shirt. "Darion, you're drunk. You can't drive," she yelled. "Lennie!"

Darion scoffed when Lennie marched over, and hooked his arm through his. "Come on, Daz. I can take you to the office, or to Retox. Whichever you fancy."

"I'm not going anywhere."

"He needs to stay here," Eva agreed, snatching his keys. "Don't let his new employees see him in this state. It doesn't set a good example."

"I'm going upstairs." Darion yanked his arms back, freeing himself. "I want my VIP booth, champagne, the full fucking works."

"It's not a good idea, Daz," Lennie warned him.

"Len, he's drunk. He won't listen. I'll take him upstairs."

Lennie sighed heavily. "Has anyone got Gabi or Gina's number?"

"Don't call them," Darion spat. "I need to be here, where I belong..." he slurred.

He rubbed his palms up and down his face, exhaustion having kicked in. The beers were starting to take effect. Ascending the stairs on his shaky legs, he had to grip the rail to prevent from falling. He couldn't remember the last time he'd been this drunk.

"Leave him to me," he heard Eva sternly tell Lennie. Then she was helping him up the stairs.

"I wanna see what Carl's done with the playrooms." He hadn't seen them since Carl had taken over. Curiosity got the better of him, and he couldn't wait to see if there was anything new in store.

"I'll show you." Eva smirked, a twinkle appearing in her eye. "It will be just my pleasure."

***

Gabi

It was a day later, and Gabi hadn't heard a word from Darion. He hadn't called or sent her a text. She had tried to ring him several times, but his mobile had been switched off. She had even rung the office to Retox, and had been told he hadn't been seen. She silently prayed nothing bad had happened to him. Or that he hadn't done anything stupid. He had taken his motorbike, and she always worried when he drove that thing. When her mobile vibrated on her desk, she snatched it up without even checking the caller ID.

"Hello."

"Gabi."

"Gina. Have you heard anything?"

"No. I'm really worried. I know what he's

capable of when he goes missing for days on end."

"What do you mean?" She straightened her back, and inhaled air, fearing the worst.

"He used to go on benders. He would do nothing but drink, gamble...and use the playrooms."

Oh no. Gabi tugged at her collar, feeling hot and claustrophobic. Perhaps Gina's walk down memory lane had sent him running back to the playrooms. She cranked opened the window, and allowed a light breeze to enter the room. "Have you rung the club?"

"Yeah. Carl hasn't seen him."

Gabi tapped her heel-clad foot on the floor, and searched her brain for ideas on where he could be. "Do you think I should call the police? What if he's had an accident or something?"

"I don't know. Maybe try the club again."

"I will." Collapsing onto her chair, she said, "How's Preston doing?"

"Really well. You're a lifesaver, Gabi. He's sleeping so much better. I honestly didn't think his clothes were the problem. I feel terrible."

"You were only doing what you thought was best. And other things probably played a part too."

"Let me know if you hear anything."

"You too. Bye, Gina."

Gabi searched her mobile contact list for the number of the club. Her stomach somersaulted at what she would hear. If he was there, would she be relieved or terrified? When the tone filled her ears, she almost ended the call. Surely Darion wouldn't have gotten so drunk as to not know what he was doing. Building up the courage with a mental pep talk, telling herself he wouldn't betray her, she waited patiently for an answer.

"Hello," a soft voice purred down the line.

Gabi tasted something sour in her mouth. "Hi, Eva. It's Gabi."

"Oh. I was wondering when you'd call."

Her spine went rigid. "Why is that?"

"Your boyfriend has been here for almost two days."

"Is he okay?"

"He's been paralytic drunk. But he's okay. He was having a bit of fun, that's all."

"What do you mean, fun?" she asked slowly.

"Before you get your knickers in a twist, it wasn't with me." She giggled. "As much as I wanted to fuck the life out of him, it was the hundred other girls in the playrooms you needed to worry about."

Gabi's lower lids filled with tears. "Is he still there now?"

"No. He left about an hour ago. You should thank me, by the way."

Gabi remained silent, trying her hardest not to scream abuse down the phone.

"He wanted to drive in the state he was in."

"Do you know where he was going?" She didn't have time to make small talk with Eva Rhodes, the bitch ex-wife she despised. She could bet Eva had been in her element when she had the company of a drunken Darion. Had she made a move on him? More so, had Darion given into temptation? She trusted him when he was sober, but when intoxicated, she had no idea of how he'd behave.

She couldn't believe he had been in the playrooms without her. She instantly began thinking of the worst. He had been surrounded by many women, probably beautiful, daring, sexually adventurous women. She swallowed back vomit.

"He didn't say where he was going. Sorry." With that the line disconnected.

Gabi stared at her mobile, her eyes wide. Then the shock turned to rage. Eva was purposely trying to rile her up. She decided to contact Lexi and see if she could get some sense out of her.

"Hey, pretty lady," she answered cheerily. "Long time, no speak."

"Hi, Lex. Everything okay?"

"Yeah. Everything's great. Did you give your devilish boyfriend a couple of nights off? He was causing all kinds of havoc at the club." She laughed.

"I haven't heard from him in two days. I'm calling because me and Gina have been sick with worry."

"Oh."

"I rang Carl and he hadn't seen him."

"He wouldn't have. Carl's been cooped up in his office for the past week."

"Do you know where Darion is now?"

"I don't."

Gabi licked her dry lips to moisten them. She mustered up the courage to ask what was niggling away at her, "Did he do anything stupid?"

"I wouldn't know. I was downstairs working."

"Okay, thanks, Lex. I need to find him." Gabi stood up. "I'll see you soon."

"Sure. Let me know when he's found safe and

sound."

"I will do. Bye."

Gabi strode out of her office, past Mallory's desk, and the elevators. She entered the bathroom and splashed cold water on her heated face. If Darion had sent her a text message stating he was safe, but needed time out, she wouldn't have minded. It was being kept in the dark which hurt and worried her. Was it she, Gina, or Preston he was trying to get away from, or all three of them? What happened to facing his responsibilities?

What if he had let loose in the playrooms, and betrayed her? Had he tried to get one over on her by punishing her for the time she had kissed Lawrence? She hoped he wasn't that petty.

Back in the office she glanced at the wall clock. She'd really been looking forward to dance class that evening. Now her high spirits had plummeted. If Darion wasn't around to be there for Gina and Preston, then she'd have to step in. Seeing Gina unrecognisable, and in that state had broken her heart. Johnny, the man she loved, had left her, Darion had now left her, and she was struggling with motherhood. Gabi knew sometimes in life you had to do the right thing, not necessarily the easiest thing.

Chapter Thirty-One

"Hi, Gina." Gabi smiled when Gina opened the door. She was pleased to see Gina was looking more her usual self. Her blonde waves tumbled down her back. Her make-up consisted of smoky eyes and pink lips, which accentuated her features, and her impressive cleavage was peeping out through her vest top. Her body was still petite, but curvaceous, and one would never guess she had been pregnant. "How are you?"

"I'm good." She bent down and picked up a few toys, tossing them into a basket. "I managed to do a bit of cleaning today." She placed her hand on her hip. "Preston has been sleeping for a few hours straight."

"Oh, good." Gabi scanned the room. It was much tidier. She peered into the Moses basket to see Preston asleep. He was dressed in a blue babygrow, and had matching mitts on his hands. The blanket was only covering his legs. His colouring looked better. He appeared to have even put on weight. Gabi had an urge to reach out and stroke him, but she stopped herself, not wanting to wake him. "Fancy a coffee?" she asked Gina, heading for the kitchen.

"I would *love* a coffee," she groaned in delight.

Gabi switched on the kettle, and took two cups, along with coffee out of the cupboard. She found it weird being in Darion's apartment without him being there. "I can't believe Darion isn't home yet."

"Yeah." Gina sighed. "But as I said, this isn't out of character for Darion."

"Eva told me he was in the playrooms, with hundreds of beautiful women."

Gina rolled her eyes. "Eva would say anything if she believed it would put a strain on your relationship."

"Why else would he go to the club?" Gabi spooned coffee granules into the cups.

"Maybe to visit everyone." She shrugged a shoulder. "Unless…"

"What is it?" Gabi swivelled around to face her.

"I'm sorry, Gabi." She crossed her arms over her chest, causing her breasts to rise. "I brought up the times at The Black Door with Darion. I was just thinking of the old days." She threw her a sympathetic look. "I shouldn't have done that. I was comforting myself, trying to remember before I had Preston I at least had a good time."

Gabi tried to keep a straight face, and not reveal she'd heard the conversation. She rubbed her forehead. "Did it sound like he wanted to return to that lifestyle?" Would his dark desires ever be a thing of the past?

Gina closed the door gently, and placed a cigarette between her lips. Lighting it, she took a puff and said, "He's bound to miss that lifestyle, Gabi. He loved being a ladies' man, and living carefree and wild." She blew out smoke. "Do you miss your fun teenage years?"

"I spent most of my teens studying. My early twenties were some of my best years, though." She smiled at memories she had with her friends.

"Well, it's the same for Darion. He's insecure deep down. He could be hanging onto his youth. The club makes him feel alive, adored, wanted. He thinks he's invincible there, that he can do whatever he wants."

"So Eva could have been right, that he was in the playrooms?"

"Do you trust him?"

"I like to think that I can. It's the women I don't trust. If Darion's drunk, would he be swayed easily to use the playrooms?"

"Before he met you, he didn't even need to be drunk. But when he was drunk, he was an animal." She laughed, as if remembering something. Obviously noticing Gabi's wide, worried eyes, she straightened her face and said, "But he's with you now. He's a changed man."

"I hope so, Gina. Or else it's over between us."

When the kettle boiled, Gabi poured water into the cups, added milk, and took them into the living room. Gina stubbed her cigarette out and joined her on the sofa.

"It's good to see you looking well again."

"I feel a lot better. But it's still hard with Preston. It will always be hard." She blew her hot drink. "I can't do it alone."

"Darion wouldn't expect you to. He'll come around." She glanced at the television for a moment to see cartoons were playing. "Have you heard anything from Johnny?"

She shook her head. "He ignores my calls."

"Did he think the baby could have been his?"

"Yeah. He thought because my bump was small, that I wasn't too far along. He thought it could have been his. Then I had the scan and it revealed how far in the pregnancy I actually was."

"It must have devastated him."

"He's probably feeling how you are." Gina surprised her by taking hold of her hand and squeezing it. "I know this news has shattered your world. I'm sorry. I hate myself for it."

"These things happen, I guess."

"Sometimes I sit here and wonder what it would be like if he was Johnny's. And then I look at him and see Darion, and he's just so handsome, Gabi. I don't think I'd want Preston any other way."

"He's beautiful," Gabi agreed.

"How are things with you and Darion?"

Gabi clamped her hands together, and suddenly remembered her own news. "He proposed to me."

"What?" Her mouth fell, before turning into a wide grin. "Congratulations!"

"I hope he didn't propose because he was afraid of me running for the hills."

"Gabi, you're the one for him." Her expression was serious. "I had feelings for Darion for a long,

long time. And it pained me to tell him I thought you were right for him."

Gabi remained silent.

"When we found out he was the dad, I almost booked a train to London. I didn't want to come between you, or spoil what you and Darion had." She toyed with the bracelet on her wrist. "But I couldn't do it to Preston. I grew up without a dad and it fucked me up. I looked for love and comfort in other men and slept around. I was that insecure I even had relationships with women."

Gabi nodded in understanding. She was glad Gina was opening up to her. She supposed it could have been worse. He could have had a child with Eva. She shuddered at the thought. Now that was something she definitely wouldn't have been able to handle. At least Gina wasn't malicious, with ulterior motives. She now understood it all. Gina wasn't back to try to trick Darion into having a relationship with her. All she wanted was a father for Preston. She actually respected her for it.

***

Two hours later, Gabi grabbed her car keys and stood up, ready to leave. She had spent some time helping Gina feed, change, and entertain Preston. He cried here and there due to an upset stomach, but other than that, he was like a different baby. His irises twinkled in merriment, and he energetically waved his arms and kicked his legs. She felt a deep connection with him. She loved him already, as if he were her own.

She bent down and placed a tender kiss on his soft cheek. His clean baby smell invaded her nostrils. Stroking his silky hair, she beamed, and mumbled goodbye. The sound of the front door opening caused her to freeze on the spot. Her heart skipped a beat. Darion.

She didn't think it was possible for him to look any sexier, or it could have been the fact she had missed him that made her greedily take in his appearance. In grey sweatpants, a matching t-shirt, and a jacket dangling from his hand, his perfect physique made her mouth water. He casually strolled into the room, all cool and confident, like nothing had happened. Smoothing his dishevelled hair back with his hand, he slid onto a stool and didn't speak.

A part of her wanted to race up to him and kiss him repeatedly, tell him she'd been worried about him, and had missed him. The sensible part, however, wanted to question him before storming out of the apartment. It had to be the latter. Him running off like that was selfish. Plus, if he really had been in the playrooms, then she knew she couldn't forgive him.

As he sat there, his green eyes boring into hers, she felt that undeniable, strong chemistry between them, that magnetic pull. Goosebumps raced across her skin, and she ached for his touch.

"I'll leave you to it," Gina mumbled, scooping up Preston and vanishing into the bedroom.

Gabi folded her arms across her chest, and waited patiently for an explanation.

"Gabi…" The provocative tone of his voice

stirred feelings of arousal, but then he said, "I'm sorry."

She closed her eyes for a second; afraid to open them in case what came next made her hate looking at him. "For what?" she croaked out. Her hands were shaking, and a tightening pain appeared in her chest.

"For disappearing and not contacting you." He stood up. With a few steps across the room, he was towering over her, and she had to lift her head to accommodate his height. She could smell a mixture of cologne, smoke, and alcohol.

"Anything else you're sorry for?"

"Yes." He lowered his head to hers, and his lips were so close she could feel the heat of his breath. "I'm sorry for everything I've ever done wrong in our relationship."

Gabi didn't speak. It took all of her willpower not to grab hold of his hair and smash her lips against his. She hated how much of an effect he had on her. She was weak when it came to him, needy for him, for his kiss, his touch, his voice, his smell. Darion Milano. How he infuriated, but excited her.

"I needed to get away from it all," he continued. "It got too much for me." His throat dipped as he swallowed. She could see the exhaustion on his face, and the worry in his eyes. "You, Gina, and Preston deserve better." Turning away from her, he dropped onto the sofa and rubbed his palms up and down his face.

"Why would you say that?" She sat beside him, but not too close in case Darion's statement was right.

"I'm fucked up," he said barely above a whisper. "I'm just gonna drag you all down with me."

"You're not making sense," she said sternly.

"Why do you want a man with a fucked up past?" he asked through gritted teeth, shooting to his feet. "Why would Preston want a dad who has no clue how to raise him? I'm not a role model," he spat. "I was stupid to think I could have had a normal life."

"You can."

"No, I can't." His fists were clenched as if he were fighting to stay in control. "That child hates me. Every time I go near him, he screams. I don't know how to be affectionate with him, how to teach him right from wrong, how to set a good example. If he found out who I was, he would be ashamed."

"That's not true." Gabi clambered to her feet.

"What if I'm like my own parents?" He shot her a questioning look.

"You won't be. Dion isn't like them."

"I don't think I can be the type of father he needs." He sucked in air. "And I don't think I can be the type of partner that you need."

Was he breaking up with her? Gabi felt all of the air leave her lungs. Her sight was going blurry from the tears teetering on her lower lids.

"I don't want the same things you want." He looked her squarely in the eye. "My own childhood put me off kids. Eva put me off marriage," his tone was low, but vicious. "I don't want a repeat of that."

The love she had for him crystallised into hate. "So why did you propose to me?" she yelled.

His eyes were glazed, his lips in a thin line, but

his expression was devoid of emotion. How could he not feel bad for the words leaving his mouth? She didn't think she had ever seen him act so cruel. "I thought I wanted those things. But it would never work."

Gabi flew toward him and punched him in the chest repeatedly. Tears were now streaming down her cheeks as she sobbed hysterically. She had done *everything* for Darion. She had turned her back on a normal life to experiment in his seedy, sexual world. She had done things for him she never would have done for anyone. She had trusted him with her heart. She had stood by him when he'd confessed to things that devastated her. She had even been willing to help him raise *his* child. How stupid had she been?

"You visit The Black Door, and all of a sudden you've changed your mind about everything," she screamed. "You asshole!"

"Gabi..." Darion grabbed her by the face and pressed his lips against hers, kissing away the tears. His full, soft lips didn't soothe her this time.

"Get off!" She pushed him forcefully. "Don't you dare break up with me, then try to kiss me." She grabbed her handbag and marched to the door. She ignored him calling her back. Pausing for a second, she said, "Don't contact me again. Ever."

Instead of taking the elevator, Gabi raced down the stairs as fast as her legs would take her. She hated him. How could he get her hopes up and propose to her, only to dump her, all because he'd had a failed marriage before? Eva had ruined everything once again. Judging by his cold, heartless behaviour, she wouldn't be surprised if he had fucked Eva in the playrooms, or loads of other women. Had he gotten a reminder of how perfect everything had been before he met her?

Her shoulders bounced with each loud sob. Her heart was breaking. She noticed Darion didn't chase after her this time, like he usually did. But then again, did she even want him to? She was worth a million women who visited The Black Door. If Darion couldn't see that, then he really didn't deserve her. Gabi had wanted it all: love, passion, marriage, a family. She thought he had too. He'd fed her some bullshit about his past as an excuse. He was right. He was insecure and fucked up.

She never wanted to see him again.

Chapter Thirty-Two

Darion

Darion leisurely walked toward the window. Moving the curtain aside, he could see Gabi marching out of the building. An empty ache lingered in his chest. His heart had broken into a million little pieces. He swallowed down the emotions building in his throat. She was better off without him, though. So was Gina and Preston. Eva had been right. He could play *normal* all he wanted, but deep down, he would always be insecure, needy, fucked up, and an embarrassment to them with a dirty past.

"Look at you," Eva had sneered. *"If you really loved them, you'd let them go. They deserve better,"* her words haunted his mind. *"We were perfect together because we were the same. We were selfish, doing whatever we wanted, whenever we*

257

wanted with no regards for anyone else. You can play happy families all you like, but it won't last. You're Darion Milano, a wild playboy. You can only be tamed for so long. Sooner or later, you'll get bored of the monogamous relationship. End it now before you hurt them further down the line."

Eva had showed him the playrooms that night. He'd wanted to see what Carl had done with the place, in respect of the décor, and to say hello to his old employees, the girls that role played at the club. The erotic scenes displayed before him in the playrooms had caused him to stare in awe. He'd thought he was over that period in his life. He knew he could never share Gabi with other people, but did he want to share someone else with other people?

As if reading his mind, Eva had said, *"Gabi isn't enough for you. Give it a year or two, and you'll be back here."*

As Gabi's car sped off, he clenched his teeth, willing himself not to get upset. She needed someone like Lawrence. A man who wore a suit to work, played golf on the weekends, and would never fantasise over dirty orgies, and kinky fetishes. He was too much for her to handle. He had warned Gabi away from the very start. He had known things would end in tears.

"Darion?" His head lifted when Gina entered the room, Preston in her arms. "Are you okay?"

He shrugged a shoulder. "I think I need to get away for a bit, G." He stared at the wall before him in a trance. "You're welcome to stay here."

"Do you think that's wise?"

When she was before him, he took in his tiny, perfect son. His lips curled slightly at the corners. When his big eyes met his, and he gurgled, Darion felt a love stronger than he ever had before. It terrified him. He wanted to love him so bad, wanted to raise him, make him proud of him, and be the dad his dad never was. But what if he messed it up? He would never forgive himself.

As Preston kicked his arms and legs excitedly, he had an urge to pick him up, and squeeze him into a tight hug. He wanted to hold him and never let go. What if he could be a good dad? Taking a deep breath, he reached over and stroked Preston's cheek. He prayed to God his son would give him some sort of a smile, a chuckle, a widening of the eyes, anything to give him a bit of hope. One sign was all he needed. He waited for Preston to accept him. Then, as expected, his features screwed up, and he screamed loudly. His cries made Darion's shoulders droop in disappointment and rejection.

He turned to face Gina, and held her face in his hands. "Gina…take care of my son."

"How long will you be gone for?" her voice shook with emotion.

He didn't respond. He didn't know. Pressing his lips on her forehead, he gave her a gentle kiss goodbye.

***

Gabi

"Hey, Gab," Mallory said cheerfully, kicking the

office door shut behind her. She waved a paper bag in the air. "I've got doughnuts."

Gabi manufactured a smile. She was exhausted, and didn't have the energy to speak. Perhaps the sugar rush would help. As Mallory plopped onto the chair at the other side of her desk, she picked up the bag. The sugary custard smell hit her nostrils. Taking a doughnut out, she bit into it. They were her favourite. Usually she would have groaned in delight, yet nothing seemed to lift her spirits lately, not the sunny weather, dance class, pamper sessions with Mallory, or gossip time with Suzie. Although she and Darion had split up a few times, it never got any easier. She felt like she was trapped in a big black hole and there was no escape.

She hadn't seen or heard from him in a week. Although she had told him never to contact her again, a part of her had hoped he would.

Gina had called her, though. She'd informed her Darion was going away for a bit. He'd left Retox with a friend to run. Gabi had visited Gina every couple of days to help out with Preston. She hated being in Darion's apartment, though. Everywhere she looked, she was reminded of him. She'd tried to think of every reason possible as to why Darion would have left Preston. Gina was none the wiser. She'd stated Darion had told her of his intentions, and then packed some stuff. He'd hugged her goodbye, and that was it. Something had changed in him. Something had happened at The Black Door. She knew it. Maybe he had done something so bad he believed he didn't deserve forgiveness.

Gabi wasn't sure what to feel anymore. What

was the point in holding onto a relationship that would never progress? He didn't want a family, and he didn't want marriage. She needed to deal with the sleepless nights, and the pain of missing him, and then move on as best as she could. It had been fun whilst it lasted. He had opened her eyes to a completely different world. The relationship had had so many good points, and the memories they had created were unforgettable. She still loved him, and a small part of her bet she always would.

"Have you heard anything from Darion?"

Gabi's posture stiffened, the doughnut hovering near her lips. "No," she said softly. "I'd rather not talk about him again, if that's okay, Mal?"

"Okay, sweetie." She pursed her lips, a sad expression forming on her face. "Anything I can do to help?"

"Yeah. Keep bringing me doughnuts." She laughed.

"You might need a truckload," she joked.

"I'll be fine in a few weeks," she said, although she knew it would probably be months until she got over Darion, if she ever did. "How's Steve?"

"He's good."

"Suzie looked well the other day, didn't she?"

"Yeah. And Marcus. Fancy seeing them again this weekend?"

Gabi nodded. Anything to take her mind off things. "We could have a night out too. Sasha's bar?"

"I'm in."

Gabi's stomach rumbled, and all of a sudden the smell of custard made her heave. Placing the doughnut on the side, she stood up quickly and excused herself. Rushing to the bathroom, she emptied her stomach in the toilet. The acidy burning feel in her throat made her vomit again. She sat on the floor for a moment, grabbing handfuls of tissue. Her diet had been poor lately. She hadn't eaten a proper meal in days. The doughnut wasn't what her body needed. She had to replace the crisps, chocolate, and Fanta she'd been having with fruit, vegetables, and water in order to feel better. Wiping her mouth, she eased herself off the floor. She almost didn't confront her reflection in the mirror, but curiosity got the better of her. As predicted, her face was paler than usual and her hair hung flat down her back. Peering down at her coral knee-length dress, matching nails and black platforms, she was glad the rest of her appeared put together and stylish.

She crouched down, and cupped water in her hand to swill her mouth out. After she washed her hands, she returned to her office. She instantly spotted the concern on Mallory's face. "I'm fine."

"What did you have for dinner yesterday?"

"Food."

"Very funny. Seriously?"

"Um…" She racked her brain. "I had crisps and a cake."

Mallory shook her head in disapproval. "You need to eat properly."

"I know." She groaned. "I will." Tapping the spacebar of her computer she noticed her inbox was flooded with emails. She was displeased she was in for a busy day. "So, Suzie's Friday night, and

Sasha's Saturday night?"

"Sure." Mallory stood up. "Are you going to dance class later?"

Gabi nodded.

"Good." She yanked the door open. "You know where I am if you need me, sweetie."

"Thanks, Mal."

When Gabi was alone in her quiet office, she slouched in her chair. Kicking her shoes off, she closed her eyes. How she wished she could take a nap right then. Her eyelids were heavy, and her mind was aching with information overload. Rubbing circles into her temples, she then mustered up the energy to get some work done. Unable to locate a pen on her desk, she pulled open the drawer. She was met with the photograph of her and Darion in London that she had shoved in there. She grabbed a pen and slammed it shut. She wasn't in the mood to be tormented by happy memories.

When the working day finished, she headed straight to dance class. She quickly changed into leggings, a crop top and trainers, and stalked to the lesson. The tutor was fiddling about with the stereo. Greeting Kalli with a wave, she placed her bag on the windowsill.

"How are you, Gabi?"

"I'm fine," she said, plastering on a brave face. She didn't want to discuss Darion and dampen her mood, which at that moment was excitement for dancing, and releasing some pent-up energy. "How are you?"

"I'm really good. The kids and hubby are still driving me nuts, but I wouldn't change them for the world."

"Why do you choose a noisy dance class to get away from it all, and not some relaxing spa treatment, or quiet gym?"

"I used to dance when I was younger, so it makes me feel like *me* again." She beamed.

Gabi nodded understandably.

"Everyone ready?" the tutor yelled. "Let's do our usual warm up." She pressed play on the stereo and hip hop music followed.

Gabi stretched her muscles, mirroring the tutor's movements. She could see herself in the gigantic mirror before her. She looked noticeably thinner. She made a mental note to cook a decent meal once she got home.

"Okay. Are you ready for some footwork?" the tutor asked. "Kick your right leg forward like this." She kicked her leg out. "Then bring it back in." She returned to her normal position. "Now do the same with the left leg...kick forward...bring in."

Gabi followed her instructions.

"Let's do that again, but faster and twice this time. Then we'll move our arms in the same way."

An hour and a half later after intricate dance moves, Gabi finally got home. It didn't take long to make some pasta, which she ate before the television. She tried her hardest to concentrate on the show, but she felt empty, sad. Dancing had given her a happiness boost, but it hadn't lasted. Being in her empty apartment, with no Darion to call or cuddle up to, was hell. Even when she was in the bath, the vanilla candle scent filling her nostrils, and the hot water soothing her muscles, she was still restless. If only she had answers as to why he had ended it, then maybe it would be easier to get over him. If she had something that made her hate him, she could convince herself them being apart was for the best. But her feelings for him were far from hatred. Questions swirled round in her head. Should she call him and ask for an explanation? It just didn't make sense.

Closing her lids and holding her breath, she submerged her entire body into the water. At least her tears would be washed away.

Chapter Thirty-Three

Darion

Darion kicked the covers away and pulled himself off Lennie's sofa. The past week had been lonely. He'd shut himself away from everything and everyone. He'd needed time to think. He'd thought being away from The Black Door, Retox, and his drinking and gambling buddies would prevent him from going down the self-destruction path. He couldn't afford to throw everything away he had worked hard for. The savings he had were for Retox and to support Preston. He wasn't about to let personal issues get in the way of business, and so keeping away had seemed like the best idea.

Many times he had wanted to call Gabi, to apologise and beg for forgiveness. He desperately wanted everything to go back to normal. Then Eva's words echoed in his mind and he forced himself to do the right thing, to let Gabi go. She would be happier without him in the long run. He couldn't be everything she wanted him to be. Could he?

"Hey, Daz, you're awake." Lennie looked up, a cigarette dangling from his mouth. He was sat at the kitchen table, tapping away on his mobile. "Sleep good?"

He shrugged a shoulder. "I suppose."

"How long do you intend on staying here?"

"Why?" He sauntered to the sink and poured himself a glass of water. "Do you want me gone?"

"Nah. You're welcome here for as long as you like. I just think you'll regret not being there for that kid."

"He doesn't need me, Len." He screwed up his face before gulping back his drink.

"Everybody needs a dad." He doused his cigarette in the ashtray. "My dad wasn't perfect. He fucked up. He made a lot of mistakes, but he was there. That's all that matters."

"I don't wanna ruin his life by being the wrong sort of dad." He set the glass down and leant against the counter. "What if Eva's right? What if, one day, it all gets too much, and I do return to my old habits? I can't change overnight. I was foolish to think I could."

"Eva doesn't know shit. She'd say anything to mess up things for you, and make you as miserable as her. If she hasn't got you, she doesn't want anyone else to have you." Lennie pushed himself to his feet and searched the cupboards. Taking hold of a large bag of crisps, he popped the bag open, and sat back down. "You know what your problem is?"

he said, crunching noisily. "You live in the past, and worry about the future. You never live in the present, and appreciate it for what it is in that moment. Your head is always someplace else."

Darion nodded in agreement. "You're right. I thought being in a normal relationship was hard, but being a dad is even harder. I'm constantly fucking worrying that I'll mess up."

The sound of the doorbell made him straighten his posture. Lennie trudged to answer it. When Lexi walked in, he perked up a little. She grinned, before pulling him into a tight hug.

"How's it going, Daddy?" She giggled.

"Enough of that."

"I've been trying to get hold of you for days."

"Sorry, Lex. I needed time out."

"Time out?" She shoved him playfully. "Do you think Gina gets time out when she wants it?"

He chuckled. "You're right. That's why I've gotta head back."

"So, what's been going on?" She pulled herself up onto the counter, and snatched a crisp from Lennie's bag. "How's Gabi?"

"We split up."

"What?" Her mouth dropped. "Why? She was perfect for you, Daz."

"Yeah, but I wasn't perfect for her."

"What do mean?"

He raked his hand through his hair. "She deserves better."

"Better? How? You love her, protect her, have changed your life for her, and you make her happy. It doesn't get much better than that."

Darion chewed his bottom lip, not knowing what to respond with. It must get better than that.

"I don't understand the change of heart," she mumbled, shaking her head. "I thought you decided you and Gabi were good for one another?"

"I did." He crossed his arms over his chest.

"Until Eva poked her nose in," Lennie huffed. "I'll be in there if you need me." He nodded to Darion, and vanished into the living room.

Lexi turned to him, her face displaying anger. "What did Eva say to you?"

"It doesn't matter," he mumbled, digging into his pocket for his cigarettes. When he couldn't find a lighter, he sighed heavily, and gave up.

"Daz, tell me," she commanded icily.

"She said some shit about me being able to change my ways temporarily, but I'd be back to how I was within a certain amount of time." He dropped onto a chair and hung his head in his hands. "She's probably right. The playrooms still fascinate me."

"Of course they still fascinate you." She pulled up a chair beside him. "You enjoyed that lifestyle for a long time. Do you think anyone with an addiction doesn't miss and think about what it was they were addicted to from time to time? It's normal. I bet if you returned to that life, you'd miss Gabi, and you'd be thinking about her, about the normal life you could have had. The grass is greener where you water it."

"I just don't wanna hurt her, Gina, or Preston."

"You won't. You've changed a lot since you've met Gabi. And I know you have the potential to be a good father." Lexi rubbed up and down his arm supportively. "I don't know why you let Eva mind-fuck you. She tried to make you feel weak and pathetic for being in love. She's poison. Don't let her perception of you define you. You're a good person, and *everyone* has a past."

Darion drummed his fingers on the table, saying nothing.

"Please don't let her ruin your happiness. Put your all into it with Gabi and with Preston. At least then you can say you tried."

"Gabi won't take me back now. She hates me."

"Unfortunately, love doesn't go away that easily. Trust me, I've fucking tried."

"I'd proposed to her not so long ago."

"What?" she shrieked, bewilderment showing on her face. "And you're trying to tell me you haven't changed?" She slapped his arm. "You proposed because you love her, you want to change, you want to be a better man. Tell me I'm wrong." She challenged him with a lift of her brows.

"You're not wrong."

"How did you propose?" She clapped her hands together in excitement.

"Right after sex."

She gasped. "Whoever said romance was dead was right. And the ring?"

"I told her I'd take her shopping for one."

"Darion Milano, you've topped the ranks for the most-insensitive-asshole-way-of-proposing."

He licked his dry lips to moisten them. "You know me and romance don't exactly go hand in hand."

"You've got some *serious* making up to do." She laughed. "And there's no time like the present. Come on." She jumped up.

"Where are we going?"

"Home. I want to see Gina and that beautiful little boy of yours, and you're ordering an engagement ring online."

He groaned. "I'm not doing that. Gabi won't take me back."

"Well, at least try," she snapped. "We need to find out her ring size."

"Like it's that easy."

"Do you have her friend Mallory's number?"

"No, but she works at the same place as Gabi, so I could call there."

"Do you think she'd know her size?"

He pushed himself to his feet. "Actually, she might. She returned her old engagement ring to Lawrence."

"Ah." Her eyes lit up. "I bet she tried it on first to see how it looked. Us women are suckers for a pretty rock." She beamed. "Failing which, I bet she'd find out."

Darion didn't know whether to laugh or cry at the craziness of his unpredictable life. He was being pushed and pulled like a ragdoll. Eva was in one ear telling him to end his relationship, that Gabi deserved better, and Lexi was in the other ear telling him to propose to Gabi again, and that he was good enough for her. He remained rooted to the spot for a moment, thinking long and hard about what it was that *he* wanted. It really was decision time. Be a doting, faithful boyfriend to Gabi, and give her what she wanted, should she forgive him: marriage and a family. Or continue to live his life spontaneously, and enjoy his sexual freedom forever, without a care in the world.

He knew which option was the easiest, and which he couldn't fail at. The question was, would that make him happy in years to come?

***

Gabi

"Cheers!" Gabi tapped her glass against Suzie's and Mallory's.

They were in Sasha's bar, sitting in a booth, with several drinks before them. Suzie was on fruit cocktails, and she and Mallory were on the good, strong stuff. All week she had waited for Saturday to come. Dancing, drinking, and letting loose was just what she needed. Even though Mallory was gushing about her perfect relationship and relaying the details of her holiday to Suzie, and Suzie was pregnant and now showing, Gabi wasn't envious. She was happy for her friends. She was as excited for Suzie's baby to arrive as she was.

For the first time ever though, Gabi didn't have much to talk about. She had no boyfriend, or nothing interesting to gossip about. They knew all about the break-up. Rather than feeling single and fabulous, she felt single and horrendous. They said time was a great healer, but she didn't believe it. Not at that moment anyway.

"It was nice you both popped by yesterday,"

Suzie said, twirling her straw in her drink. "Marcus was pleased he could brag about the baby." She laughed. "Honestly, it's all he ever talks about."

"It was nice seeing him too," Mallory responded. "I'll bring Steve next time."

"You should." Suzie slid in her chair and stroked her stomach. "I'm so impatient, I just want to meet her now," she gushed, studying her bump.

"Not too long left."

Gabi fidgeted in her chair. As she took in the dancing crowd, she had an urge to join them. Taking hold of her drink, she drained it back, and then started on another drink. *Shit!* She grimaced. It was whisky. She hadn't even looked at the drink. Mallory had ordered a variety of everything. Her heart tightened. It was Darion's favourite drink. Many times she had kissed him and tasted it on his lips. Her high spirits plummeted. She missed kissing him so much. *Stop thinking about him, he's an asshole,* she scolded herself.

"Mind if I dance?" she asked the girls.

"No, go ahead." Suzie grinned. "You go too, Mal. I'll be fine here, honey. Honestly."

"I'm not leaving you here on your own."

"I insist," she said sharply.

Reluctantly Mallory stood up. They wove through the dancing, excited crowd, and settled in the middle of the dance floor. Swaying and dancing from side to side, she began to relax. Spinning around, her hair flying about behind her, the alcohol began to take effect. She giggled as she stumbled slightly in her heels. A large palm pressed against her stomach to steady her. Instinctively she bolted backwards.

"Sorry." A man held his hands up in defence.

"She's okay," Mallory told him, and twisted her round to face her. "Everything good?"

She nodded. "I'm going to the ladies'."

As Gabi pushed through the crowd, couples caught her attention. They were either dancing together, kissing, or laughing. She wished she knew what Darion was doing. Was he missing her, or was he coping just fine? When she was in the privacy of a cubicle, she took out her mobile. There were no notifications on the screen. The rejection was unsettling. Tilting her head back, she stared up at the ceiling. She contemplated messaging him to see how he was. Deciding against it, she stuffed the mobile into her bag. He'd ended the relationship. He was obviously standing by his decision. She hung her head in her hands with a heartfelt sigh.

She wondered if other men would help take her mind off Darion. She'd spotted a couple of cute men amongst the crowd. Getting to her feet, she touched up her make-up before the mirror, and strutted back into the main room.

When she noticed a figure leant casually against the bar surface, she stilled. He had his back to her. His tall, broad frame was concealed in black clothing, and his dark hair was neatly styled. A few giggling women surrounded him.

Gabi's heart skipped a beat when he slowly turned around. Lifting his head, their eyes locked. It wasn't Darion. She didn't know whether she was more relieved, or disappointed.

Chapter Thirty-Four

Darion

After the nurse had weighed Preston, taken his measurements, and checked his heartbeat, she carefully handed him back to Gina. Sitting on the opposite side of the table, she began scribbling notes down before she looked up and smiled. Pulling the stethoscope out of her ears, she said, "This baby is a fighter, just like his mommy and daddy."

Darion almost scoffed. He wasn't a fighter. He was a coward. All he'd done since Preston was born was run away. He intended to make up for it though, and ensure he was there for him.

"He seems healthy, he's put on weight, and his heartbeat is perfectly normal."

Gina smiled weakly, tears forming. The nurse cocked her head to the side, and stared at her questioningly. Darion took hold of Gina's hand and squeezed it.

"She expected the worst," Darion told her. "She blames herself for his condition." He tapped his foot on the floor anxiously. "The, um, smoking, drinking...drugs."

"You shouldn't blame yourself," the nurse said softly. "Whilst that is one cause, there are many causes as to why babies are born with intrauterine growth restriction. It could be due to abnormalities in the placenta, chromosomal abnormalities, carrying twins or higher multiples, severe malnutrition. It can even occur if the mother is perfectly healthy." Her features softened in sympathy. "You were very lucky. Sometimes there are complications during pregnancy and delivery."

"I almost nearly had to have a caesarean," Gina told her.

"Well, as I said, he's a fighter." She glanced down at Preston. "Whilst Preston is smaller than babies his age, I really do believe by the time he's three, he'll catch up in height with others his age." The nurse looked from Darion to Gina to see if they had any further questions.

Darion cleared his throat. "Um." He inhaled. "Preston hasn't really taken to me. Every time I pick him up, he screams the place down. Any suggestions?"

"Mr. Milano, there are many ways in which you can build a bond with your baby." She opened her drawer and took out a booklet. Sliding it toward Darion, she continued, "Learn to understand Preston's unique cues, watch his facial expressions, listen to the sounds he makes, see what he enjoys, whether it's being rocked, listening to music, or sounds you make, and even a change of environment such as being outside."

Darion nodded.

"Play a part in feeding him and putting him to sleep. Don't leave it all to Gina. Talk and play with him. And let go of trying to be the 'perfect parent,' just do your best."

Darion's tense muscles relaxed a little. He definitely did need to let go of trying to be the 'perfect parent.'

"Darion worries about being the perfect parent a lot," Gina told her.

Darion swallowed, wishing she hadn't revealed that about him.

"His parents weren't the best, so he worries he won't know how to be a good parent."

She nodded in understanding. "Those who didn't experience a secure bond with their own parents can have trouble emotionally connecting with babies. It can range from having an abusive childhood, being neglected, or it simply being chaotic." She tapped Darion on the arm lightly. "It will take time. But you'll get there."

He hoped so.

"Then you'll experience the 'falling in love' experience, as they call it." She beamed. "The rewards are huge for you, in respect of the joy and happiness you will feel for Preston."

Five minutes later, they were leaving the hospital. Darion felt like a weight had been lifted off his shoulders. Being terrified of being a parent was perfectly normal, and so was stressing about

277

being the perfect parent. If Preston could fight to be in his life, and to be healthy, then he could fight right back for him. He made a silent pact he would *never* leave his son again. No matter how tough it got, he would never run away. He was a dad and he was going to try to be the best dad he could be.

***

Back at the apartment, after Darion had showered and changed into some sweatpants, he lounged on the sofa. He flicked through the channels using the remote and settled on a romance film. He knew Gina would more than likely enjoy it. His stomach cramped with guilt and sorrow as he remembered Gabi loved romance movies too.

"Still hungry?" Gina asked, sitting next to him, Preston asleep in her arms.

He shook his head. "The takeaway was good."

"It was. I hadn't had Chinese food in a while."

"I'll start cooking again soon," he promised. "I can cook up some mean dishes."

"As ever the talented Darion Milano." She nudged him playfully. "Have you not heard anything from Gabi?"

He shook his head. "I think I've lost her this time, G."

"I thought you were a fighter?" Her brow rose.

"Hmmm," he mumbled.

"If you don't try, you'll never know."

When silence fell upon them, he studied the messy room. He weighed up in his mind whether it'd be best for Gina if she had her own apartment.

He could settle the rent fees for her. She could probably do with the extra space and privacy.

"Do you think you'd be more comfortable if you had your own place?" he asked, rubbing at the stubble on his jaw.

"I can't afford it."

"I'll sort it, don't worry."

She pursed her lips as if mulling it over. "It might make things a little easier. I could start looking for places online."

"You do that. Just make sure it's close by so I can visit all the time."

She clasped her hands to her chest in excitement. "Preston can have a nursery," she squealed.

Preston cries then filled the air. Darion glanced down at his scrunched up face and open mouth. Gina stared at him, urging him to hold him. Inhaling and exhaling slowly, he picked Preston up. He laid him on his lap so he was facing him. Preston cried even louder.

"What's the matter, little man?" he said softly, and widened his eyes in shock to make the baby laugh. Preston stopped crying for a second. Darion's spirits lifted. "G, he's stopped crying." He nudged her, unable to contain his excitement. Preston began whimpering again. "Oi." He rubbed his hand across his belly repeatedly. "I thought you were a fighter?" He tickled his ribs. Preston stopped crying again, his eyes bulging. Darion tickled him once more. When Preston kicked his legs and a gurgle escaped his mouth, Darion looked at Gina for confirmation he'd heard right. She nodded. "You like that?" he asked, tickling him again. When

Preston let out a little squeal, his mouth curling at the sides, Darion melted on the spot. "He's laughing, G."

"See?" She ruffled his hair. "He does like you." She placed her hand on his shoulder. "How could he not?"

Darion doubted he'd ever been that happy before. His son was smiling and laughing at him. The best thing about it was that no matter what happened, he would forever love Preston, and he'd love him right back. His heart swelled in his chest. He'd never been interested in having children before, and didn't believe he'd miss out on much. Now, with Preston lying on his lap, staring up at him like he was the most important person in the world, he knew he'd been stupid. Maybe this is what had been missing from his life all along: a purpose, someone to really love, and someone to love him right back unconditionally. Gina's news at having his baby wasn't meant to shatter his world, sure it would change it, but now he believed it was meant to repair his world.

When Preston squealed and his tiny fingers clamped around his finger, he was gone. He was on cloud nine. Preston's big eyes stared up at him. It was the 'falling in love' experience the nurse had told him about. He didn't think he could love anything more. Now he realised no experience had ever come close to being a father.

***

Gabi rolled over in bed and blinked her eyes

open. She moaned as the light poured through the room. The ache of her heavy limbs prevented her from moving. Her attention darted frantically around the room, searching for water to soothe her dry throat. It was Monday morning and she was still fragile from Saturday night's antics. Her feet were swollen from dancing for hours, her head pounding from the excessive drinking, and her throat sore from shouting above the music.

She had woken at 8 a.m. and called Human Resources to advise them she wouldn't be present at work. She'd then fallen asleep for another 4 hours.

Rubbing her forehead, she wondered if she could get away with spending the whole day in bed. Yanking the covers over her face, she buried herself in the warmth and closed her eyes. She lay there for many minutes before she dragged herself up. She couldn't sleep.

She'd allowed several men to flirt with her on Saturday. She'd shown genuine interest in what they had to say, and had even danced with some of them. There had been no spark though, not like there was with Darion. She wondered if she'd ever feel that chemistry and passion again.

Her mood continued to slip from loneliness to anger at how Darion had ended it. She loved him, and yet she hated him at the same time. Padding toward the kitchen for breakfast, she figured she may as well have a lazy day to recover. The sofa, a blanket, a book, and junk food should help.

Chapter Thirty-Five

Darion

Darion climbed off his Yamaha R1 and pulled off his helmet. As he neared to Retox, he noticed Reece in his usual position at the door, and Addilyn having a fag break. He nodded to both of them in acknowledgement. When Addilyn offered him a cigarette, he didn't refuse. Positioning it between his lips, he lowered his head so she was able to light it.

"How have things been here?" he asked, blowing smoke from the side of his mouth.

"Everything's been fine, Daz," Addilyn responded. "I've been managing bars for the past eight years. You never have to worry about this place when you're away."

"Good." He grinned. "I'll be spending less time here. I've gotta take care of other things first."

"Like your son?" Addilyn clasped her hand to

her chest, staring at him adoringly.

"That's one of the things." *And winning Gabi back,* he thought. If she forgave him, he would ensure he really worked on the relationship. He knew he couldn't keep letting his past affect their future. It wasn't fair on her.

"How is Preston?"

He couldn't stop the huge grin that strained his cheeks. "He's perfect."

"You'll have to bring him in one of the days. We'd love to meet him."

He nodded in agreement. Flicking his cigarette butt to the gutter, he said, "I'll see you inside."

As soon as he stepped into Retox, he was met with the sound of rock music and a lively crowd. He lowered himself onto a stool at the far end of the bar and greeted Raina. She offered him whisky, which he declined in favour of water. When she handed it to him, as he slowly sipped it, he retrieved his mobile from his pocket. The screensaver of Gabi's beautiful face smiling up at him made his heart tighten. He pressed the call button and held it to his ear. He hoped she wouldn't reject his call and switch her mobile off again. Having no contact in a while had been painful. When he didn't get an answer, he ended the call. He tapped in a text message asking her if she'd meet him tomorrow night.

"Raina, I'll be in my office if you need me," he told her, gulping back the last of his drink. Setting the glass on the bar, he strolled toward his office.

Once he was comfortable in his leather chair, he switched his laptop on. As it loaded, he thought of the busy day he'd had with Gina. They'd been apartment hunting for her and Preston. They'd found a perfect place opposite the building in which he lived in. He knew he'd feel secure with her being close by.

His mobile bleeping caused his body to go rigid. Gabi's name was displayed on the screen. He smoothed his hair back with his hands, and inhaled deeply. The excited part of him made him reach for the mobile, but the anxious part of him avoided looking at the screen. He didn't know what he'd do should she refuse to meet him. Chewing his bottom lip, he opened the message.

Gabi: Where shall I meet you?

Relief swept over him. It was a good start, at least.

***

Gabi

Scooping her hair up into a high ponytail, Gabi studied her reflection for the final time. She'd dressed in a short, black skirt and a tight, white vest, complete with heels. Her make-up had been applied to perfection, gold, shimmering eye shadow, and nude, shiny lips. She wanted Darion to see what he was missing out on. Satisfied she looked decent, she grabbed her handbag and left the apartment.

Darion had asked her to meet him at his favourite restaurant. As she climbed into her car, it was only when she put the key in the ignition did she notice her hands were shaking slightly. She hated how Darion played havoc with her emotions. She was still livid with him at the way he'd ended things. She wasn't sure what he wanted to meet her for. Was it to apologise for the way he'd handled things and for them to remain just friends? Or did he want to give things another go? If he hadn't betrayed her in the playrooms, and he wanted to work on things, then she knew she'd be unable to refuse. She couldn't turn her back on him. She needed him. She felt whole and safe when she was with him. She looked forward to the future. She appreciated the world and everything in it. With him, she believed she could do *anything*.

One thing was certain though; she wasn't changing her life for him anymore. She definitely wanted children in her future, and she had high hopes of having the big, white wedding. She needed the security of a fully committed relationship. If he still didn't want the same things, then how could it work?

Turning on the stereo, she played "Habits" by Tove Lo. She nodded her head along to it. The lyrics hit close to home. Her days without Darion had been lonely. It had been torture trying to keep him off her mind. When raindrops hit the windscreen, she flipped on the wipers. A flashback of sex with Darion on the car bonnet in the pouring rain teased her. She rolled her eyes. She wasn't sure whether to feel amused at some of their sessions, or hurt that there may be no more.

When she was parked outside the restaurant, she

studied it for the longest time. She wasn't aware she was fiddling with her cross necklace. Having seen Darion's Audi parked close by, she'd had a sudden urge to turn around and drive off. What if it wasn't good news? She wasn't sure she could handle it. Closing her lids for a brief moment, she gathered the courage to face him. Rolling her shoulders back, she reapplied her lip gloss, and exited the car.

The rain had stopped, which perked her up a little. She strolled toward the restaurant, head high, and feigned confidence. If Darion couldn't see what was in front of him, then more fool him. Gripping the handle of the door, she tried to control her emotions. *Relax,* she told herself. Pulling it open, she stepped inside.

There were only a handful of tables occupied. Waitresses tended to tables, and the atmosphere was chilled. The leafy surroundings were hidden due to the condensation on the huge windows. She lifted her head and then she spotted him.

Darion was sat at the back on a table. His glass was held in mid-air, as if he'd noticed her and stopped what he'd been doing. As she approached him, he placed it on the table, and leant back. His predatory stare swept over her slowly, but she had no idea what he was thinking. He was dressed smartly as usual, and his hair was neatly brushed back. She found him irresistibly sexy. It took all of her strength not to rush forward and hug him. She wanted to kiss him so much. Instead she played it cool. She offered him a tight smile, and sat down.

Neither of them said anything for a few seconds. They took one another in, examining every little detail. She spotted his hand on the table, twitching slightly, as if he was fighting not to take hold of hers.

"Can I get you a drink?"

Gabi tore her stare away, relieved a waitress had broken the ice. "Um…a sparkling water, please."

"Sure. And for you, sir?"

Darion tilted his head back to look at her. "I'll have the same," he responded, his seductive tone no longer present. He didn't flash his killer smile, or wink, or make her blush with his confident demeanour. It was then did Gabi realise he was nervous.

When the waitress fled off, Darion licked his lips slowly to moisten them. Gabi's pelvic region flooded with hot arousal. Shifting uncomfortably in her chair, she crossed her legs and waited for him to speak.

"Thanks for meeting me."

She nodded, at a loss at what to say.

Casually draping his arm on the back of the chair, he remained staring at her. She was certain she detected humour in his twinkling pupils. She fiddled with her nails, all confidence rapidly diminishing.

"You look good," he told her, taking in her body once more. The salacious longing was apparent on his face.

"Thanks." *You too,* she wanted to add, but left it out. She wanted to be clear on what he wanted first.

"Two sparkling waters." The waitress beamed at them, and placed two bottled waters and glasses before them.

Gabi poured hers quickly, and took a long sip. Darion did the same, but he didn't seem in a rush. When he lifted it to his lips, she hated he was watching her intently. When he set his glass back down and took hold of her hand, she drew in a breath. His thumb tracing along her skin sent tingles in its wake.

"You know I'd never hurt you, don't you?" he said softly.

She shrugged a shoulder, deciding to be honest. She didn't know. She was terrified of him tearing her heart into a million little pieces. Whilst she wanted to give it to him to love, she was afraid he'd break it. Everything with Darion was always intense, and it was impossible to get away unscathed. Being with him had always been risky. Sometimes, unpredictability and spontaneity in a relationship wasn't always a good thing. It was like running excitedly along the edge of a cliff, appreciating the beautiful view, and getting a thrill from the danger, but deep down knowing there was a chance you could fall.

Withdrawing his hand, Darion's forehead creased with distress. Rubbing at the stubble on his chin, he continued, "If I've ever hurt you, it was never my intention."

Gabi waited patiently for him to continue. It wasn't often Darion opened up, or discussed his feelings, and she didn't want to say or do anything that may stop him.

"You thought I was up to something at the club." He shook his head. "When I told you I'd never betray you, I meant it." His expression was serious, his tone firm, and she believed him.

"What happened at The Black Door?" she couldn't help but ask. "You visited, and came back a completely different person."

He leant forward, resting his elbows on the table. "I lost my way for a short time." He chewed his bottom lip. "Eva made me feel I wasn't good enough for you or Preston." Raking his hands through his hair, he sighed heavily. "Sometimes I think she's right. But other times I don't think anyone could love either of you more."

Gabi felt a fluttering in her stomach. "You are good enough," she said firmly, as tears warmed her lower lids. "Why do you always doubt yourself?"

"It's easier to believe the bad stuff."

Gabi's nails dug into her palms when she clenched her fists. She could see how broken Darion was. Eva toyed with him, messing with his emotions. She should have known she'd be at the centre of their troubles. Why did Darion allow people to knock him down? How could he not see he was an overall decent person?

"How about I tell you some of the good stuff?" Rising to her feet, she settled down next to him, and took hold of his hand. "You've got a kind heart, Darion. You'd do anything for anyone. To those close to you, you're loyal, kind and real, and that's rare these days." She stroked his knuckles tenderly. "You may be complex, but I've never felt more loved, desired, or happy than when I'm with you."

Darion pursed his lips as if weighing up something in his mind.

"As for Preston, you may not have had a good

example with your own parents, but I know you've learnt from their mistakes. You'll be a wonderful father. I believe in you. And you have all of the support you'll ever need. You'll never have to do it alone."

He bowed his head with a soft chuckle. "He smiled at me the other day."

Gabi thought she'd explode with admiration. How could Darion doubt his parental skills when Preston made him happier than she'd ever seen him? Everything happened for a reason and she truly believed he was made to be a dad. It was probably just what he needed to feel things he never had before—unconditional love.

"Preston will be proud of you. You'll see."

"What about you?" he asked, worry etched on his face again. "All of this is too hard for you."

What did they do about wanting different things? "Darion." She paused for a moment. "I'll never change my mind about marriage and children. It's something I've always wanted."

He inhaled deeply. She waited, anxious at what he'd respond with. It would be the ultimate deal-breaker if he refused her that. Looking her squarely in the eye, he said, "If that's what you want, then that's what you'll have."

She was unable to stop the massive smile that surfaced on her face. "Do you want those things?"

"With you, I want it all." Sliding his hands either side of her throat, he tilted her head up. "I've missed you like crazy."

"I've missed you too," she confessed, swallowing the painful lump that lodged in her throat.

"I hate myself for treating you like I did. I thought letting you go was the best option."

"That's *never* the best option."

She squeezed her eyelids shut and pressed her lips gently against his. Darion reciprocated. He kissed her urgently, passionately, aggressively. His hands gripped her hair tightly as he pulled her as close as possible. Her heart swelled in her chest, and she was on the verge of tears. How could she love someone so much? How could it feel so good but scary at the same time?

As his tongue swept against hers, fast and needy, it was as if no one else in the room, in the world existed. Both of them had to stop running. Squeezing her arms around him, she felt an unfamiliar possessive streak. Darion was *hers*. She never wanted to let him go. She wouldn't allow anyone to come between them, especially Eva. She made a mental note in her mind this was it. This was the man she wanted to be with forever. There was no going back. She had fallen for him hook, line, and sinker. No one would ever come close to what she felt for him. Together they would smash down every obstacle that got in their way. No more running.

"Let's go home," she said, pulling back and wiping her mouth.

She couldn't wait to be lying in bed with his arms wrapped around her.

Chapter Thirty-Six

Gabi squirmed on a soft moan, her pulse racing. Slowly blinking her eyes open, it took a moment to recollect where she was. She was in her own bed. The light from the alarm clock came into focus. It displayed it was 5 a.m. When she properly woke, she could hear a song playing quietly in the background. She recognised it as "Blue Eye" by Menace Beach. She knew it was coming from Darion's mobile.

Before she could sit up, she was paralysed by tingles that trembled through her whole body. Then something warm and wet appeared between her legs. Glancing down, she noticed Darion was between her thighs. He was completely naked. On all fours, his perfect ass was in full view. As his tongue lapped at her clit again, she cried out in pleasure. Last night after the restaurant, they had barely made it through the front door when he'd pinned her to the floor. Darion had showed her how much he'd missed her. The sex had been hard, frantic, and mind-blowing as always. Now, he wanted her again. Even though she had to be up for work in two hours, she couldn't deny him.

"I couldn't sleep," he told her, his voice low and husky.

"Ah..." she panted, when his fingers plunged in deep. "Darion..."

As he parted her, meeting her sensitive spot, his tongue circling her clit, she wriggled again. His lips and hands then met her lower tummy. He shuffled up the bed, placing a trail of kisses along her hips and chest, until he reached her neck. It sent shivers of delight down her spine. When he captured her mouth with his, it was so tender, and passionate, like he was proving how much he loved her all in that one kiss. The sound of the sweet song and Darion lavishing her with attention sent an incredible warmth through her. She had never felt so in love.

He pulled back and the love and longing he felt for her in return was clear. He ran the pad of his thumb across her lower lip gently, and stared at her intently, as if he could see right into her soul. Leaning forward, he kissed her forehead tenderly.

"You're not going anywhere," he whispered, his voice trembling with emotion. "Ever again."

Sitting back on the heels of his feet, she took in his stunning nakedness. He wasn't yet aroused, and was obviously taking his time. Her silk nightie tickled her skin when he removed it patiently. When she was completely exposed, he trailed his fingertips down her neck right down to her thighs.

His eyes sparkled with lust, a small smile tilting his lips, as if she were perfect. He made her feel like the most beautiful woman alive. Her ego swelled at the way he worshipped her body.

Unable to wait for his next move, she gripped his arm and yanked him onto her. His bare chest pressed against hers was heavenly. She pushed her tongue into his mouth, massaging his greedily. They seemed to kiss for the longest time, until their lips were swollen, and their jaws aching. When Darion's now hard cock brushed against her leg, desire pumped through her body like a drug. She wanted him more than ever.

The tip nudged her entrance, and she bit her lip, as a needy ache loomed in her stomach. As much as she wanted to grip his buttocks and pull him into her, she needed to get a condom. She reached for the bedside drawer. Darion linking his fingers through hers, stopping her, made her glance up at him.

"We don't need one," his voice was soft. Did he mean what she thought he did? She studied him questioningly, needing clarification. "We're gonna want a family eventually." He held her other hand, so both of her arms were now pinned to the bed. "Why delay the inevitable?"

"Is this what you really want?"

He answered her by pushing into her slightly. Her inner muscles tightened around him, and she cried out. Moving in deeper, the feel of his bare, moist cock caused her to throw her head back.

"Oh, Gabi…" He clenched his teeth. He thrust his hips forward on a loud groan, plunging in all of the way.

"Ah…" She gripped the bed sheets.

"Does that feel good?" He teasingly rocked backwards and forwards.

She nodded. She was unable to tear her focus away from his tight, tanned abdomen, and bulging biceps as he restrained her. Her breasts were heavy and tender, in desperate need to be fondled. Darion, with the ability to read her like a book, withdrew. He sat back on the bed, and instructed her to sit on his lap. She did as commanded, wincing as she lowered herself onto his length. When he was in all of the way, he didn't move, but instead wrapped his mouth around her breast.

Her head rolled back, and his tongue circling her nipple wrenched a moan from her throat. Her insatiable body was burning up and aching, and she couldn't refrain from moving her hips. Her sex clenched and contracted around him. As he licked, sucked, and nibbled her breast, whilst cupping the other with his hand, the tension in her pelvic region built.

She buried her hands in his hair, lifting his head to find his mouth again. As their bodies connected, moving up and down in synchrony, their tongues wrestled. Their stares were fierce on one another, and their hands roaming. Every part of them was touching. The steady lovemaking was just perfect. They were taking their time, enjoying one another for as long as they possibly could.

"Hmmm…" she murmured, as he filled her even deeper. Her thighs trembled, her skin becoming hot and sweaty.

Taking hold of her chin, he forced her to look at him. She remained doing so, as he continued to swivel his hips and push into her. The leisurely pace was both torturous and pleasurable. She hooked her arms over his shoulders, and rocked back and forth.

"I'm close," she told him, her chest expanding on heavy breaths.

"Me too," he grunted, biting his bottom lip.

He rose to his feet, still holding her in his strong arms. She tightened her hold on him. With his fingers digging into her hips, he lifted her up and down. She whimpered each time she dropped onto him, unsure if she could take it. It was so good, it was almost too much. He increased the speed. A hot flush spread up her entire body. As she slid against his smooth, soaked chest, his cock filling her exquisitely, her stomach clenched. She was on the edge, getting closer and closer to an orgasm.

Darion's jaw was twitching, his head thrown back as he tried to stay in control also. He thrust upwards several more times. Their moans mingled, and they were soon panting. Her over-stimulated body shuddered. With a few last breaths, she shattered around him on a loud cry. Pleasure spread through every inch of her body, and she clung to him.

"Fuuuuuck," he growled.

His own climax met the last tingles of her own, and she felt his cock swelling. A hot throbbing sensation inside her signalled his release. He slammed into her, jerking and grunting. When the tremors died down, and he had nothing left, he sighed in total satisfaction.

Dropping onto the bed, he was still inside her as he softened. He buried his head in the nook of her neck, and she closed her lids, not wanting to move. Her limbs were weak, and exhaustion took over. Not only that but she didn't want to separate from him just yet. She hugged him tightly.

When their bodies eventually cooled off, they crawled up the bed. Darion switched the music off and they lay facing one another. She began to get sleepy when he stroked her hair. A part of her wanted another hour's sleep, yet the other part of her wanted to stay awake and talk to him about weird and interesting topics, which she loved doing.

Running her finger along his stubbled jaw, she whispered, "I love you."

"I love you too."

He wrapped his arms around her, pulling her against his chest. She drifted into a peaceful sleep, with a grin on her face of how far Darion had come since she'd met him. Not only could he now declare his feelings verbally, but he finally wanted all the things she did. Everything was perfect. She hoped nothing would come along and burst their bubble.

***

Gabi pressed send on the email to her client. She had returned their manuscript to them to revise the edits. She spent a few minutes reading and replying to emails. It was 11 a.m. and her morning had been productive. She'd thought she'd be tired for the long day ahead, after Darion waking her up for sex; however she was giddy, pleased they were back together. She opened her drawer and placed the photograph of them back on her desk. She was admiring it when Mallory walked in.

"Got you doughnuts." She shook the paper bag with a laugh.

"The doughnut deliveries are no longer necessary." Gabi leant back in her chair.

Mallory threw her head back with a laugh. "Well, I can certainly see someone got frisky last night. Look at you all glowing, and chirpy." Plopping onto the seat, she took out a doughnut and bit into it.

"Ah, what the hell." Gabi leant forward and snatched up one. "They're just too tempting."

"So." Mallory wiped the sugar from her lips. "I take it you and Darion sorted things out."

She nodded. "We met up, had a talk, and it went well. He's ready for commitment, Mal. No more running for either of us."

"Now you can stop worrying and feeling like you're in limbo. He doesn't want the fun of The Black Door. He doesn't want Eva, nor Gina, nor anyone else." She beamed. "I'm thrilled for you, sweetie."

"I just hope we can actually enjoy the relationship now, and not have to constantly fight battles."

"You'll be fine."

"How are things with you?"

"As good as ever."

"You heard much from Suze?"

She nodded. "Yeah. Me and Steve popped in to see her and Marcus yesterday evening. They're fine too."

A knock at the door disturbed them. Gabi yelled for them to enter. A man appeared carrying a large bouquet of red roses. The sweet smell invaded Gabi's nostrils.

"Gabriella Woods?"

"Yes."

"These are for you."

She thanked him when he placed the flowers on her desk. When he left the office, she took out the card.

Darion: I'll get better at this romance stuff, I promise. Love you. Can't wait to fuck you later. xx

She shook her head in amusement at the last part. Darion was as devilish as ever. Before she could tuck the card away, Mallory plucked it from her hand.

"Ooh, Darion's a sexy bastard." She giggled. "Let's swap. You can have Steve, and I'll have Darion for one night of passion," she joked.

"You'd want more than one night, Mal. Trust me."

She huffed. "Yeah, you're probably right."

They broke into laughter before continuing to eat their doughnuts. Gabi remembered Darion's words to her in the early days, *"I know that if I have you now, that you'll come back,"* and he'd been absolutely right. The first time they'd gotten intimate, she was unable to refuse seeing him again. Unlike all of the other women who had probably returned for more, and were unable to capture his interest, Darion Milano was now all hers to keep. She thought of their future with glee. She knew a lifetime with him would be nothing but amazing memories, as it already was. They had so much to experience and explore.

***

After work, Gabi drove straight to Retox. It was lively with rock music playing, but at a volume where people could talk to one another. After ordering a glass of wine, she found Darion at the back of the club playing pool with Lennie. Travis was sat on a stool, watching.

"Hi." She gave them all a little wave.

"Hi, Gabi." They grinned back at her.

"Long time, no speak," Lennie said. "Glad you pair sorted things out. There was only so much I could take of Daz moping around." He nudged him playfully.

"Moping around?" Gabi teased him.

Darion set his cue against the wall and sauntered toward her. Snaking his arms around her waist, he looked down at her. "It's the effect you have on me, darlin'." He placed his lips against hers.

"I was moping about too," she admitted. "Just a little bit, though."

When his tongue met hers, and wrestled hungrily, she giggled in his mouth, when Travis and Lennie yelled for them to get a room.

"I'll have her on this pool table right now if you don't shut it," Darion warned, his brows rising suggestively.

"No, you will not," Gabi argued.

He nibbled her ear. "Fuck. I wish I could shut the club now, and *really* have you on this pool table." He cupped her ass and squeezed it.

Gabi giggled, the image actually exciting her.

"I guess we've got time to do everything once."

She nodded in agreement.

"Wanna go to the office?" His voice was low and seductive, his eyes raw and glowing.

"Later." She turned on her heel. "I'm going to get to know your staff."

"You marking your territory?" He chuckled.

"Yes, I most definitely am."

After an hour of chatting away with Addilyn and Raina, Gabi found she actually liked them. They seemed friendly, and not at all threatening. They were a far cry from the once seductive Gina and Eva. Derek, the bar manager, also ensured the place ran smoothly, and the girls were pulling their weight. Judging from the packed bar, Gabi was thrilled business was going well for Darion.

As she observed him laughing with Lennie and Travis, she realised she hadn't seen him relaxed and cheerful in a while. She felt a rush of love for him. Finishing her drink, she ordered another. She was daydreaming about memories with Darion when her mobile bleeped. Fishing it out of the depths of her bag, she screwed up her face in confusion. Why was Darion messaging her? Opening the text, her pulse quickened as she read it.

Darion: I've got a surprise for you. x

301

Turning to face him she shifted in her seat. She watched as he slid his mobile into his pocket. When his gaze met hers, she noticed distress cross his face. What could the surprise possibly be? Usually his surprises were of a sexual nature, and sometimes they made her feel uneasy. Now The Black Door was gone, she hoped this surprise was something she'd enjoy.

When a glass of white wine was placed before her, she picked it up and crossed the room. As soon as she was before Darion, she questioned the surprise.

"If I told you, then it wouldn't be a surprise," he responded, his pupils lacking the usual playful twinkle.

Gabi failed to notice she was tapping the top of her glass repeatedly as nervousness crept in. When Darion returned to playing pool, she perched on a stool. She willed herself to stop overanalysing and worrying about what Darion had in store. Surely after everything they'd been through together, nothing could shock her now.

Chapter
Thirty-Seven

The working week flew by, along with Gabi's dance class. It was Saturday morning, and Darion's apartment was unrecognisable. Everywhere she looked she saw blue banners, balloons, and gifts. A large buffet had been spread out in the kitchen, complete with a huge cake. Gina was holding a baby shower for Preston.

Gabi helped herself to a crisp and peered out of the window. She spotted a few guests arriving, laden with presents. Returning to the living room, she smiled at Gina, who was bottle feeding Preston. Gina's blonde hair hung silkily down her back, and her make-up consisting of dark eyes and nude lips, made her appear like the old, confident Gina. Her vest was low cut, and her tight, black jeans complemented her figure. Gabi was pleased to see she was also finding it easier to handle Preston. He rarely ever cried these days, and when he did, it was only when he was hungry or tired.

303

The nights Gabi had stopped over at Darion's apartment, she had witnessed him feeding Preston more and putting him to sleep. It was unfamiliar seeing Darion in daddy-mode, but wonderful seeing the baby bring out emotions in him he usually tried to hide. The admiration and love on his face was visible every time he looked at his son. Gabi didn't think it was possible to fall for Darion any more, but she did.

"Everything set?" Darion entered the room, yanking a grey V-neck t-shirt over his head. It exposed the top of his chest.

"Yeah." Gina placed Preston carefully in his Moses basket. "I…um…invited Johnny. I hope you don't mind."

"You can invite whoever you want, G."

"I messaged him. I don't even know if he'll show up."

Gabi threw Gina a sympathetic look. She hoped Johnny did appear. Gina had found a new apartment, and if things went to plan, she'd be moving out in a couple of weeks. Gabi knew Darion would worry about her if she was alone. Although Darion had informed Gabi that Johnny was a tad possessive, he adored Gina. He'd been with her in London, and helped out with her mother. Hopefully the fact he wasn't Preston's father had now sunk in, and he was ready to rekindle their relationship.

The doorbell ringing broke the silence, and Gina rushed to answer it. As she greeted them with a hug, Gabi guessed they were relatives of hers. As expected, they hurried over to see Preston, praising him and stating how cute, but small he was. Half an hour passed of guests arriving. When the living room was full, and steady conversations were flowing everywhere, Gabi observed the scene before her. Darion was now holding Preston, whilst Gina was excitedly opening gifts.

Picking up a slice of sponge cake covered in blue icing, she took a bite. As Gina gushed over another gift, and showed it to Darion, Gabi couldn't help but feel like the odd one out at a party. It was as if she were looking in on someone else's life. She wondered if she'd always feel insecure and a tiny bit envious when it came to this aspect of Darion's life. Would he even notice if she wasn't there? Would it always be like that? After all, next would come the christening, Preston's birthdays, Christmases, and every other celebration that occurred.

Before she could feel sorry for herself, the doorbell rang. Neither Gina nor Darion noticed. Gabi went to answer it, and came face to face with Darion's mom and dad. Her shoulders dropped. They weren't exactly the friendliest of people.

"Hi," she greeted them, manufacturing a grin.

"Hmmm…" his dad mumbled, passing her.

"Hi, Gabi." His mom smiled tightly, and Gabi was surprised she had remembered her name.

"Gabi!" Dion appeared and pulled her into a brief hug. "How are you?"

"I'm okay, thanks. How about you?"

Dropping several presents on the counter, she informed her she was fine. Odelia waved at Gabi shyly. She looked adorable in a little pink dress, matching bows in her plaits, and white knee-high socks.

"Hello, Odelia." She bent down and took hold of her hand. "Do you remember me?"

She giggled with a little nod.

"Jane," Darion called out, rising to his feet.

Odelia raced toward him, hooking her arms around his legs. Darion crouched to the floor, and introduced her to Preston. Odelia jumped up and down, squealing in excitement. Darion instructed her to sit on the sofa, and then he placed the baby on her lap, positioning a cushion for support under her arm. Odelia, wide-eyed and in awe, began stroking Preston's head.

"Watch her with him, G," he said, before approaching his parents. "Mom, Dad." He nodded at them. "I wasn't sure whether you'd come."

"We almost didn't," his mom responded drily. "It's not so easy getting a day off when you don't own the company."

Gabi watched as Darion rubbed at the stubble on his jaw, clearly uncomfortable at his mother's dig.

"I don't own that type of bar anymore," he informed her quietly. "It's a normal bar. You should both come. I think you'd like it."

"I'll definitely come," Dion said, before pulling him into a tight embrace. "As much as I'd love to stay and chat, I need to go and cuddle this baby of yours."

"So...I see you're not with Preston's mother," his dad said. "What happened there?"

They weren't suited, but they had the guts to go their separate ways, unlike you pair, Gabi wanted to say. Whitney and Luca had remained together for the sake of Darion and Dion, but they didn't make one another happy. Whitney worked two stressful jobs, hating what her life had become, and Luca was always getting drunk in bars, and gallivanting with other women, making up for lost time.

"We weren't right together," Darion told them. "We decided it'd be best to give Preston a good childhood, rather than stay together, and make it miserable."

Gabi was immensely proud of Darion for putting that out there. He usually kept silent about the emotional baggage and bad stuff, not placing the blame on them. It wasn't because he feared their reaction, but more about not wanting to upset them. No matter how badly they treated him, he always wanted them to be happy.

"Your childhood would have been happier if your dad had gotten off his arse and made an effort," his mother remarked.

"Here we go." Luca sighed heavily.

"Let's not dwell on the past," Darion said, and offered them a drink. "Today is for Preston. And believe it or not, I'm glad you're here."

When they both had a drink in their hands, they pushed themselves through the crowd, and joined Gina. The ice-queen's heart must have melted, for Gabi spotted the merriment in Whitney's eyes.

"Sorry if I've neglected you a little today," Darion said softly, sliding his hands around her waist. Goosebumps prickled along her skin, and she suddenly wished they were alone. When his groin pressed against her, her temperature rose. She hooked her arms around his neck, and met his stare.

It drifted to his full lips, his most compelling feature other than his eyes.

"It's fine," she lied, not wanting to appear needy, or selfish at feeling a little left out.

"I can't wait until everyone leaves so I can have my wicked way with you." He winked, a slow smirk surfacing. His hands landed on her buttocks and he pulled her into him.

"I can't wait until we've got this whole place to ourselves again." She tiptoed and planted a kiss on his mouth. His tongue parted her lips and he deepened the kiss. It became firm and possessive, and he pinned her against the counter. Her moans were muffled, and a heavy, hot pressure settled in her pelvic region. Her nipples strained against the fabric of her dress. She wanted him urgently. He was hardening with arousal, his erection skimming between her legs. Feeling self-conscious that people were watching, Gabi reluctantly tore herself away.

Darion slowly wiped his mouth with the back of his hand. His irises were glowing with passion. Straightening his posture, he picked up his drink. "I'm glad Gina will be only a walking distance away."

"Do you think Johnny will show up?"

They turned to watch Gina. She must have been thinking the same for she was focused on the door. The disappointment was apparent, even through her forced smile, when she looked back at the baby.

"I have no idea."

Lexi, Marnie, Tiana, Wendy, Lennie, Travis, and Darion's aunt however, attended. After Gabi had exchanged pleasantries with them all, she took the rest of her cake and crossed the room. She settled in front of the window, not wanting to get in the way. The whole room applauded and cooed when Gina dressed Preston into a gifted outfit. He was wearing a white t-shirt with blue dungarees over the top. The front was emblazoned with the words, *'Daddy's Boy.'* Him and Gina exchanged a glance, both appearing as if they'd burst with pride.

"He's the double of you, Darion," someone gushed.

"No. He's definitely got Gina's features."

"He'll be breaking hearts when he's older."

The happiness she'd had with Darion a moment ago slipped away. Gabi shoved another slice of cake into her mouth, hoping the sugar rush would lift her spirits. Had she been foolish in believing everything could work out? Her mobile bleeped in her pocket, and she placed her bowl on the side. She clicked onto her inbox. As she read it, her stomach rolled and bile rose in her throat. She took in the words again, ensuring she was reading it right. She was.

Unknown number: Still playing happy families? You'll always be second best. In fact, make that third. Gina will replace you. Don't fool yourself, Gabi. Come home.

She spun around and peered out of the window. Was Lawrence following her again? How had he gotten her number? Lawrence only wanted what he couldn't have, like it was some sort of competition to take her away from Darion. He couldn't have cared about her. He hadn't shown her love for a long time during the last months of their relationship. He was miserable and so he wanted to ensure she was too.

She clenched her lids shut for a second, and then blinked back the tears. Why couldn't he leave her alone? The spiteful digs were torturing her. How could she move on and adapt to Darion's life, have a future with him when Lawrence was always in the background telling her it wouldn't last?

She contemplated responding to him, but knowing he wasn't worth it, she stuffed the mobile into her pocket. Specks of rain began hitting the window. Dark clouds loomed ominously overhead. Then it began pouring down, drenching everything in sight. Gabi watched as a bolt of lightning shot through the sky. She remained rooted to the spot, taking in the depressing weather.

After a few minutes passed, she told herself not to let Lawrence win. Like Eva, he was poison. She couldn't allow him to ruin her happiness. She needed to file harassment charges for certain, or worse, confide in Darion. She knew how protective he could be over her, and hoped for Lawrence's sake it was the last she heard from him.

Arranging her features into one of glee, she rejoined the party. Gina was about to open the gift she had bought for Preston. She hoped it was something she would cherish forever. It was a photo album to store his first of everything: his hospital band, a lock of hair, when he grew and eventually lost a tooth, his first birthday photographs, and so on. And now a photograph of his first and only baby shower.

When one of the guests held up a camera,

everyone huddled together. Gabi was standing at the back, blocked by a tall man. Clasping her hands together, she looked down at her fingers. She saw the faint white line of where she'd once worn the engagement ring from Lawrence. How unpredictable life could be. In one particular moment, when you thought you had everything mapped out, it changed. Circumstances changed. People changed. As she took in Darion's stunning smile, she hoped this time nothing would change. As the light from the camera began flashing, she realised it already had. She wasn't in the picture, and soon, she bet she'd be cut out of it completely, just as she'd feared.

Chapter Thirty-Eight

Gabi rolled over, stretching out her legs. She immediately felt for Darion. A feeling of emptiness made her stomach ache when she found he wasn't there. Sitting up, she grabbed a band from the side and tied her hair up. The clock displayed it was early morning. The sun was yet to show.

A few hours into the baby shower, Gabi had snuck off to watch a movie in bed. The guests had stayed longer than she'd anticipated. There was only so much she could talk about with Dion, Darion's parents, Lexi, Marnie, and Gina until she became knackered. Darion had promised he'd join her as soon as he could. He obviously hadn't. Whatever happened to having his wicked way with her? Not that she particularly cared about that. She would have preferred a cuddle, anything to be reminded he hadn't forgotten about her.

The apartment was silent and the only sound was the rain pelting on the window. She didn't need to see the doom and gloom of the sky, for she could feel it. The weather reflected her mood.

Making her way to the living room, she stepped over burst balloons, and took in the mess of plates and empty cups scattered on the counter. She cursed quietly when she stepped onto a balled up piece of wrapping paper. The room looked like a bomb had hit it.

The sound of gentle snores made her creep further into the dark room. She could make out figures on a blanket on the floor. She wished she didn't see Darion and Gina sprawled out across the floor, sleeping together. When she opened the curtain a little and allowed the light of the moon to gently sweep in, she viewed the scene before her. She almost melted on the spot.

Darion was lying on his back, his legs covered in a sheet and his top half completely bare. A small, naked Preston was sleeping on his chest. Darion's features weren't scrunched up from a bad dream, as she'd seen many times. He appeared relaxed, and his lips lifted slightly at the corners, as if he were smiling. It was the most stunning thing she had ever seen.

She was about to leave the room when Preston blinked his eyes open. Instead she froze to the spot, not wanting to disturb him. When he moved his arms and legs, and his gaze met hers, she expected him to cry. Her breath held tight inside her. He gurgled and the tiniest grin crossed his face. Gabi's shoulders relaxed and she slowly crouched down. She was desperate to reach out and take hold of his hand. His big, curious eyes remained on her.

"Hey," Darion's croaky voice made her jump.

"Oh." She clasped her chest. "I didn't realise you were awake."

"I only planned to get him to sleep, and then I was gonna put him in his basket," he explained the reason for leaving her alone, his expression one of guilt.

"It's okay."

"Come here." He lifted the sheet up.

Gabi crawled beneath it. Together they watched Preston in silence. When Darion's lips pressed against her temple, she rested her head on his chest too. He hooked his arm around her tightly, and for the first time, she really felt like she was part of his family. Maybe she had been wrong. Maybe she would be there for Preston's first of everything too.

***

Sunday afternoon Gabi, Darion, Gina, and Preston were at a restaurant having breakfast when Gina's mobile rang. She answered the unidentified number warily. When she finished the call, she squealed in delight.

"Guess what?"

Darion shrugged a shoulder.

Gina tapped his arm playfully, narrowing her eyes at him for being no fun. "They finished the bathroom early, and I can move into the new apartment."

"That's great news, G."

"I can collect the keys anytime."

Darion rubbed his forehead and sighed. "Are you

sure you'll be okay living on your own? You know you're welcome to stay at my apartment. I just thought you'd prefer your own space."

"I need my own space, Darion. And I'll be fine." She peered into the pram to check Preston was okay. Satisfied he was, she continued, "I'm only around the corner."

Darion pushed his empty plate away. "Promise me you'll call me if you need anything."

"I will."

"So, when do you want to move?"

Gina laughed. "I'm excited, Daz. I wouldn't mind getting the keys today. The place is fully furnished too."

"If you want to move some of your stuff, then I'll help you do it."

"Gabi." Gina grabbed hold of her hand. "Will you do me a small favour?"

"Sure," she responded, hoping it was something she could handle.

"Will you watch Preston for a few hours?"

"Um…" She smiled, swelling with confidence, ecstatic Gina trusted her to look after Preston. "I'd love to."

An hour later Gina and Darion were going back and forth from Darion's apartment, to Gina's new apartment, moving her belongings. Gabi was sat before the television, cartoons playing, and entertaining Preston. He cried at first, probably unsure of who she was. After she'd fed and changed him, he began to accept her. He lay across her lap, moving his limbs frantically, and mumbling incoherently. She bowed her head and kissed him tenderly on the forehead. She lingered longer than necessary, inhaling his sweet, fresh baby smell. She stroked his tiny palm, and allowed him to wrap his fingers around her thumb. He was Darion all over. His eyes were the exact same, his lips had the fullness of Darion's, and his hair was dark. She could just imagine how cute he'd looked when it grew down his neck, and was styled the same. Preston may not be her baby, but she strongly cared for him. It was impossible not to.

***

Darion

Darion set down the last piece of furniture and sighed in relief. Straightening his aching spine, he took in the apartment. It was big enough for Gina and Preston. It was modern and clean, and he was glad it was situated on a quiet road. As Gina unpacked some of her belongings to make the place appear homely, he slid onto a stool at the breakfast bar. He'd be lying if he said he wouldn't miss waking up and being able to see Preston. He'd even miss the mess of baby toys, a constant reminder of his son. He shook his head on a soft chuckle. He decided he'd decorate his spare room into a nursery for when Preston stayed over.

Gina reappeared, happier than he'd seen her in a long while. He knew she was pleased to have her independence back. Without warning, she threw her arms around his neck, her way of thanking him. Darion lifted his arms and held her. The fruity shampoo scent was back, and so was her unique fashion style. She towered over him in black platforms that matched her low-cut jeans and vest.

When her body began shuddering, he guessed she was laughing. Only when he felt wetness on his shoulder did he pull back. Tears were streaming down her face, taking her mascara with them.

"What's wrong, Gina?" he asked, massaging circles into her back to soothe her.

"I'm happy to be here," she snivelled. "But I never thought I'd be a single mom, Daz."

Guilt surged through him. "I never expected it to be this way, either. But we'll both be okay," he promised.

"I can't believe Johnny didn't come to the baby shower." She wiped her face. "I really liked him."

"I know you did. It's his loss, believe me."

Inhaling air, she shook her head. "You wouldn't believe how fucking frustrated I am." She laughed, lightening the mood.

Darion chuckled, and took out his cigarettes. He offered her one, which she accepted. "Go to The Black Door. Stock up on some goodies." He winked.

"I might have to stock up."

Darion put the cigarette between his lips, lit it, and took a long, greedy drag. Blowing out smoke, his whole body relaxed. He passed Gina the lighter.

"If I wasn't feeling so motherly and prudish all of a sudden, I'd have given the playrooms a last go."

"Nothing has to change because you have Preston," he told her. "Look at how many people enjoy the club that are married, in a relationship, or have children."

She groaned. "I know. But it just doesn't feel right anymore." She twisted her mouth. "Each to their own and all, but I can't do it."

He nodded in agreement. "I know what you mean."

"I don't even think I miss it anymore." She took a puff of her cigarette, and then held it between her perfectly manicured fingers. "I think I'd rather go for a relaxing spa day or something." She burst into hysterics. "Fucking hell, Daz. I've changed."

"Nothing wrong with that."

"How are things with you and Gabi?"

"I've booked a surprise holiday for her."

"Oooh. Where?"

"Bora Bora."

"Get you, Mr. Fancy." She pushed his arm playfully. "Will you be staying in one of those stunning bungalows over the sea?"

He nodded. "It's the full fucking works." He grinned. "When she sees it, she's never gonna wanna leave."

"Am I seeing more of a romantic side to Mr. Milano?"

"I don't wanna make the same mistakes I made with Eva." He took another drag of the cigarette before strolling toward the sink and stubbing it out. "I was cold when I was with her. I was completely shut off. I couldn't enjoy the relationship properly."

"She's a heartless cow. If she'd have ended up with you, I couldn't have given it my blessing." She made her way toward the sink, and doused her cigarette. "Imagine Eva playing the wicked stepmom." She giggled.

"It took me a long while to realise it, but I had a lucky escape."

"You sure did."

Darion jammed his hands into his jeans pockets, and leant against the counter. His mind drifted to Bora Bora. The wooden bungalow standing on stilts over the clear, cerulean sea made him smile. The photographs had displayed a huge king-size bed, and a claw-foot bath overlooking the water. Part of the floor in the living room was glass so the fish swimming below could be seen. The long stretch of white, sandy beach looked like paradise. He couldn't wait to be there.

He just had one thing to clear with Gabi first. He hoped he didn't scare her away. There had been more than enough changes throughout their time together to last them a lifetime.

Chapter Thirty-Nine

Gabi

Gabi was sprawled across the sofa reading a book when Darion returned. He had taken Preston to his new home. There was nothing left in sight of Gina or Preston's belongings. The apartment was peaceful but again resembled a bachelor's pad. Gabi made a mental note again to decorate the place with photographs and add her feminine touch.

When the door slammed after him, she put her book down, and quickly sat up. She was surprised to see him standing there, his pupils flashing dangerously. Gabi willed the fluttery feeling in her belly to dissipate. His jaw was twitching as if he was fighting to stay in control. Gabi pushed herself to her feet, anticipation charging through her. Was he mad? Had she done something wrong?

"Is everything okay?" she asked once she was before him.

He didn't respond. Instead he smashed his mouth against hers, his tongue diving in and exploring greedily. He lifted Gabi into his arms. He continued to kiss her frantically, moaning into her mouth, his hands fondling her body. He carried her into the bedroom and dropped her onto the bed.

"Take your clothes off," he ordered, his tone hoarse.

Gabi did as commanded, her excitement rising. She watched in silence as he whipped his shirt off, and removed his jeans and boxers. When she was also completely naked, he tilted his head to the side, taking in every inch of her body. His tongue skimmed along his top lip, and his expression was one of pure animalistic hunger.

"You look fucking amazing, Gabi," he murmured. "Play with yourself, darlin'."

"You too," she instructed, also finding it a turn on to see him pleasure himself.

Towering over her, darkness clouding his eyes, Darion gripped his cock. He stroked his hand up and down the length. His arm, abdomen, and thigh muscles protruded with each movement. Low grunts of arousal left his mouth as he continued to pump his now hardening erection. His chest rose and fell as he began to pant.

"Open your legs."

She parted them a little.

"Wider."

Gabi was reluctant at first, but when desire surged through her body, she was unable to resist relieving herself of the sexual frustration any longer. Her hand slid down between her legs, and she massaged her clit gently. A strangled moan left her throat as she circled the area repeatedly.

Darion grunted, and his features contorted in pleasure as he continued to tug at himself. She couldn't get enough of his perfect physique, of the dirty, mischievous glint in his pupils. They both teased their own bodies until the only sound in the room was their sharp, ragged breathing. When Gabi's lower muscles tightened and contracted, she lay back on the bed. She squirmed, urgent to allow the building orgasm to tear through her.

"Don't come."

She stopped what she was doing. Crying out in frustration, a torturous, needy ache replaced the sweet sensations she had started to feel. Before she could question him, he grabbed her by the ankles and yanked her down the bed. When she was lying close to the edge, he bent her legs so they were against her chest, her knees facing the ceiling. She felt exposed and vulnerable being on display for him.

Rummaging under the bed, Darion retrieved the pink box of kinky stuff. Anticipation charged through her when he selected silk restraints. She waited patiently for his next move. She hoped they would *always* have a sizzling sex life, and desire one another forever. He wrapped the long restraints around each of her wrists, securing her to the bedposts. He then fastened short, tight restraints around her ankles and hooked them to the other bedposts. She was unable to close or straighten her legs. She wasn't sure she liked being helpless, although she trusted him.

She would allow him to do as he pleased. She was partly curious and excited. Putting a finger in his mouth, Darion drenched it with saliva. Then it met her sex, and her muscles throbbed, moistened with arousal. The restraints tightened as her limbs jerked involuntarily. Darion bit his lip, gauging her reaction. He plunged in slowly, causing her to pant. Her body begged for him to go deeper, to stop teasing her with the tip. Darion circled his finger, and then slid in further.

"Oh, yes…" she murmured, wriggling.

"Do you want more?" he whispered.

She nodded. He slipped his finger in as far as it would go, and she groaned. As he thrust in and out of her at a leisurely pace, a hot flush rushed up her chest and into her face. She wanted more, needed more. Instead Darion stopped.

She pleaded with him to continue.

"Patience, Miss Woods."

Anticipation charged through her as he picked up a bottle of lubricant. Spreading it around his fingers and thumb, he put the bottle down, and remained kneeling on the floor. He smothered her sex with the cool liquid, and she realised it was a stimulating lubricant. Her clit instantly swelled and tingled as he soaked her with it.

She jerked with rising passion when his fingers skimmed lightly over her clit. Tendrils of pleasure shot through her, and she made a cry of delight. He pushed into her with two dominant fingers, and her contracting muscles gripped him. She couldn't believe how sensitive the gel made her. The tension in her over-stimulated body began to increase as he parted her sex wider. His thumb circled her clit as his fingers pounded in and out of her.

"Ah..." She whimpered with pleasure and frustration, craving the release from the throbbing, hot tension. She was unsure of how long she could delay the building orgasm that burned down below, and deep inside.

"More?" he asked her with a wicked grin on his face.

She laughed softly at the way he enjoyed tantalising and teasing her. When the tip of his cock met her clit, her knees weakened, and her head fell back. He rubbed it up and down, making her whole body quiver.

"Oh..." she cried, arching her back off the bed slightly.

He slowly eased inside her. She gasped sharply. He pushed in deeper, and deeper, until she could take no more. The size of him was both pleasurable and painful. Darion plunged in and out, his features set in concentration. When his free hand skilfully massaged her clit at the same time, she gave a loud, despairing cry.

She was unsure of how long she could quell the shards of ecstasy that wanted to engulf her. The rhythm got faster and faster. *Fuck!* Her moans came out weak sounding.

She briefly noticed Darion pick up another bottle. Setting it over her breasts, he squirted chocolate over them. Gabi winced at the coldness of the liquid. Leaning over her, he began to lick and suck at her hardened nipples, lapping it up. He closed his teeth around the tender, tight bud, and pulled.

"Ow." She winced.

His laugh was muffled against her breast. Thrusting in deeper, he continued to suck and release her breasts. When the suction grew hard, he began to wear down her defences.

"Don't stop," she begged.

When her breasts were clean of the chocolate, he withdrew. She expected him to keep her hanging, make her plead for contact, but he didn't. He swiftly removed the leg restraints, and lifted her legs over his shoulders. He knocked the air out of her lungs when he entered her deeply. Her insides were burning and aching, whilst her clit was tingling and throbbing from the gel.

"I'm so close…" she murmured, her muscles tightening and weakening.

Darion's penetrations became frantic. He grunted, and moved in and out of her mercilessly and relentlessly. His face was dark with hunger, as if he were possessed. He bit and nibbled her tender skin, and then he grabbed hold of her shoulders for support. He hammered into her faster than ever. Gabi moaned and sobbed, as the pressure became too much. Her thighs were shaking from the endless thrusting.

"Yes…" he growled, showing no signs of slowing.

Gabi could take no more. Her skin was soaked in sweat, and as delightful spasms engulfed her, she screamed out, and shook from the most intense orgasm she'd ever had. She thought the pleasure would never end. Darion followed close, throwing his head back, and spilling into her. Low, feral grunts came from him. He plunged in a few final times, until the wonderful, but exhausting sensations started to ease.

When he tore himself off her, Gabi lay in silence, regaining her composure and strength. She was thankful when Darion freed her stiff arms. He rolled her over so she was face-down on the bed. Every muscle softened under his firm hands, as he started to massage her. She hummed quietly as he soothed the aches in her shoulders, and back. He was hovering over her body, his knees at either side.

"Does it feel good?" he asked.

"Yes..." she murmured. Her lids started to get heavy as sleepiness crept in.

Darion continued to work her with his strong, skilful hands. He stopped only when her mobile bleeped. Gabi didn't have the energy to move. She felt Darion stiffen, probably curious as to who was texting her so late. She had a feeling of who it may be. When she made no attempt to reach her mobile, Darion asked her if she wanted it. His tone was a little sharp, as if he were suspicious.

"Sure," she responded, rolling over when he climbed off her. Taking the mobile from his outstretched hand, she tapped the screen. When she noticed it was from Samuel, she instantly regretted allowing her features to show her relief. Now she definitely would have looked guilty about hiding something from Darion.

"Who is it?" he asked, propping a pillow up.

"Samuel," she responded, typing a response to him. "He must be out drinking with his friends. He wants to meet me before he leaves again."

"Were you expecting someone else?"

Gabi opened her mouth, about to lie. When Darion seemed to be able to look right through her, she told him about Lawrence's calls.

He sat upright, his face flushed with rage. Clenching his teeth, his stare was murderous. "Why didn't you tell me this before?"

"It's nothing I can't handle."

"You shouldn't have to handle it alone," he snapped. "He's threatening you, interfering with your life, and upsetting you." He jumped to his feet, searching the floor for his clothes. "He's disrespecting not only you, but me...*again*." He was obviously referring to Lawrence kissing her when she'd been drunk. Frantically pulling his t-shirt over his head, Gabi tried to grab his hand.

"Please. Just leave it."

"Does he still live at your old place?"

"No," she lied.

Darion grabbed her by the chin, turning her to face him so he could read her expression. "Don't lie to me, Gabi."

She scrambled to her feet. "You never told me about Eva's snide remarks," she yelled, now equally as annoyed. "She almost ruined us."

When Darion was in his jeans, he strode to the living room. Gabi raced after him. She reached for his arm, but he pulled away as if she had burnt him. An angry vein was throbbing in his temple and he looked about ready to explode.

"I'm begging you, Darion," she shouted, "just leave it. I'll call the police tomorrow. He'll never contact me again."

"You're right about that," he said, his icy tone threatening. "He won't."

Gabi spotted his bunch of keys on the counter. She snatched them up and held them behind her back.

"Don't play games." He stepped toward her. "Give me the keys."

"I can't let you do it." She knew everything Lawrence had ever done was flashing in Darion's mind, adding to his anger: the time he had mistreated her, hit her, cheated on her, tried to seduce her behind Darion's back, followed her, stalked her. Darion's ego had taken a bashing one too many times.

Holding out his hand, he took another step toward her. Gabi moved backwards. When he lunged forward, feeling behind her back, she scurried toward the sofa. Darion blew out air in frustration. She tried to sidestep him when he rushed forward, but she was too late. He tackled her to the floor.

"No…" She squirmed, keeping her hands firmly behind her back, tightening her hold on the keys.

Darion tried to wrench them from her grasp. His entire body weight was crushing her, but she refused to surrender. As much as she disliked Lawrence, and knew he deserved whatever crap came his way, she didn't want it to be at the hands of Darion. Knowing Lawrence, he'd file assault charges. They didn't need any more drama or problems.

"Give. Me. The. Keys."

She turned her head, to which their lips hovered precariously close to one another. As he wrestled with her, their bodies colliding, he heightened her desire. The fight was slipping out of her, as the need to have him again became unbearable. She could feel the hard ridge of his arousal. A wicked gleam flashed in his eyes, as if he was feeling the same. He lowered his head and captured her mouth with his. This kiss was impatient and abrasive.

Every nerve ending in her body tingled, when his hands skimmed down her hips. She thrust them upwards, needing further contact. Her hands instinctively grabbed his ass, as she rubbed against him. His cock brushed against her, making her throb and quiver. Then he stopped.

His mouth lifted into a smirk. "Thanks for the keys." He jingled them in front of her face.

With all of the force she could muster, Gabi rolled over, pushing him onto his back, and straddled him.

"I need to go," he reminded her sternly.

Ignoring him, she shuffled down and unzipped his jeans, releasing his erection. Taking it into her mouth, he grunted, his thighs stiffening. She took him deep in her throat, and stole a glance at him. His head rolled back, his eyelids clenching shut. She licked the tip, using slow circles, which caused him to writhe fervently. She wrapped her fingers around his shaft and slid her hand up and down. There was no way she was letting Darion get to Lawrence. If she had to play dirty, then so be it.

"Ah…" Darion's groan was rough sounding. His hands fisted at his sides.

She bobbed her head up and down, tightening her lips around his length. She loved the sounds of appreciation that came from him. She sucked harder, and stroked with her hand.

"Gabi…" he panted, his features screwed up. "Don't stop."

He pushed her head down further. He rocked his hips upwards, groaning every time he entered her warm, wet mouth. She flicked her tongue over the tip again, before taking him deeper.

"Fuuuuck…"

His legs went stiff. His grip got tighter on her head. He pounded into her a few more times, before shuddering, and filling her mouth with hot spurts. He grunted loudly, over and over. When there was nothing left, and he was fully satisfied, his body went lax. He stayed on the floor for several minutes. Gabi wiped her mouth and joined him.

"Good distraction technique."

"Desperate times call for desperate measures."

His brows pinched together in consternation. "Why are you protecting Lawrence?"

"I'm protecting you, not Lawrence." She planted a gentle kiss on his lips. "We need to leave everyone else in the past, and focus on us. Eva and Lawrence have already caused enough trouble."

"I agree." He traced his finger along her bottom lip. "If you don't inform the police, I won't be responsible for my actions."

"*If* Lawrence contacts me again," she began, "then I'll call them."

He sat up, before standing. "Let's go back to bed."

She took hold of his outstretched hand. She had never needed sleep more.

Chapter Forty

Gabi neatened the pile of papers on her desk, and swivelled round on her chair. Peering out of the window, the sun warmed her face, and the clear, blue sky made her grin. Rising to her feet, she scanned the street below. People appeared happy and were strolling leisurely, instead of racing around. It was as if they too, were also appreciating the weather. She hoped it was still sunny when the weekend came. Turning back to her desk, she picked up her cup. She needed a coffee refill. Before she made her exit, Mallory entered.

"Hey, sweetie."

"Hi, Mal. I'm about to make a drink. Want one?"

"Sure."

Mallory followed her into the kitchen. Gabi added a coffee capsule to the machine and placed her cup under it. It vibrated noisily when she pressed the power button. As it boiled the water, she gave Mallory her full attention.

"How are you?"

"Tired." She yawned. "We decorated the living

room over the weekend."

"Ooh nice. What colour?"

"Silver and black."

"I bet it looks stunning." Gabi removed her cup when the machine stopped, and added a new capsule. "I remember when I used to redecorate the house every year." She laughed.

"You decorated regularly out of boredom." Mallory's brow rose. "Ours actually needed it. It's been a few years."

"Did I tell you Lawrence has been pestering me again?" Gabi set Mallory's cup under the machine.

"No."

"It's like he wants me to be as miserable as he is." She handed Mallory her coffee. "I told Darion, and I had to literally beg him not to do anything stupid."

"Why?" Mallory blew over her hot drink. "You should have let Darion smack him one."

She shook her head. "I can't. Even though Lawrence probably does deserve it, a part of me will always feel sorry for him, no matter what."

"You're too nice for your own good, Gab."

She downed some of her drink. As she watched Mallory over the rim of her cup, she saw a mischievous grin cross her face. Putting the cup down, she narrowed her eyes. "Why do you look like the-cat-that-got-the-cream?"

Mallory laughed lightly.

"Spill."

"I'm pregnant."

"Oh my god!" Gabi squealed, and then clamped a hand over her mouth, hoping the whole office didn't hear. "Mal." She stepped forward, and pulled her into a hug. "Congratulations. I'm so happy for you."

"I didn't think it would happen so soon."

"I bet Steve is over the moon."

"He is."

"When did you find out?"

"This morning."

"Have you told Suzie?"

"Not yet. You're the first person I've told. I need to call my mom and dad too."

"Wow." Gabi was stunned.

"I know." Mallory giggled. "Look at us! Suzie hasn't got too long left, I'm pregnant, and you've got a stepson. I certainly didn't expect this."

"Looks like our nights partying at Sasha's and going on shopping sprees will be replaced for nursery visits and walks in the park." Gabi beamed before lifting her cup again.

"Everything okay between you and Gina?"

She nodded. "We're a lot closer."

"And Preston?"

"He's adorable. Darion will be having him three nights a week."

"Is he bonding with him better now?"

Gabi nodded. She drained the last of her drink, and left her cup in the sink. "Do you fancy doing something with Suzie over the weekend?"

"Sure."

Gabi gave Mallory a little wave, and retreated to her office. She kicked off her grey Manalo Blahniks and dropped onto her chair. Her cheeks strained from grinning. She was pleased for Mallory and

Suzie. They were all starting a new chapter in their lives: motherhood. Preston may not be her child, but she loved him as if he were. She couldn't wait until she got pregnant one day. Darion had ditched the condoms, and she prayed they'd have a huge, loving family. She wanted to show Darion how happy childhood should be.

Speak of the devil, she thought, when her mobile buzzed on her desk.

"Hello."

"Gabi…" the low, husky tone she loved hearing, that sounded provocative, filled the line.

"What are you up to?" she asked.

"I'm at Retox sorting some paperwork out." She heard loud blowing, and knew he was smoking. "Am I seeing you tonight?"

"If you want. I've got dance class first though."

"I'll come to your place then."

"Great."

"Guess what?" She giggled. "Mallory's pregnant," she announced before he could speak.

"Another pregnancy? Is there something in the water?" he joked.

"I hope so," she teased.

"Tell her I said congratulations."

"I will."

There was a moment of silence before Darion asked, "Do you remember that surprise I told you about?"

She stiffened, instantly expecting the worst. "Yes…" she said slowly.

"Pack your bags. And your passport."

"Are we going away?" She sat up in interest,

eager to hear more. *Please let it be somewhere hot, with sandy beaches, clear sea, and where we can go exploring.*

"We are."

"Where?" She shook her head at his short answers, the teasing torturous.

"If I told you then it wouldn't be a surprise."

"Darion," she sulked like a petulant child. "Give me a clue at least. Tell me I need to pack bikinis."

"No bikinis."

She slouched, feeling herself deflate.

"You'll be naked the entire time," his voice sounded wickedly devilish.

"So it's somewhere hot then." She paused. "When are we going? How long for?"

"Next week, for a week."

It was short notice. Good job she was close with her boss, Phil, and knew it wouldn't be difficult to get the time off.

"See you later…darlin'."

"Bye."

She put her mobile down, on the verge of bursting with excitement. The day was getting better and better. It was also productive. The hours flew by, and she managed to get everything ticked off on her 'to-do' list. She'd even had ten minutes spare to clear her email inbox.

After work, she strolled to The Royal Dance Academy. She was on cloud nine and believed nothing could ruin her mood. When she had changed into leggings, a crop top, and trainers, she joined her friends in class. The tutor arrived at the same time and greeted them. Gabi needed to kick off some of her pent-up energy. As soon as a hip-hop song began, she jumped up and down, working her muscles, whilst stealing glances at the bright sun. A whole week with Darion, no distractions, no drama, just pure unadulterated pleasure filled her with joy. She couldn't wait.

***

Darion

Darion took another drag of his cigar, and dropped it into the ashtray. When he picked up his glass of whisky, he noticed his hands were trembling. *Fuck!* The ice cubes jingled in the glass as he downed some of the cool liquid. He wasn't sure if he was coming down with something, but he felt hot under the collar. Finishing his drink, he unfastened two buttons on his shirt.

He'd spent the whole day at the office completing paperwork. He'd also held a staff meeting to ensure everything was running smoothly. It was. All of his employees seemed content. He'd then called his old employees, namely Lexi. He promised to pop into The Black Door and visit them all. He missed seeing them daily, but was glad they were only down the road.

Pushing himself up, he headed to the sink. Turning on the tap, he cupped cold water into his hands, and splashed his face. His stomach churned, and a feeling of nausea washed over him. He had to grip the side to stop his weak legs from giving way. *What the fuck's wrong with me?* he scolded himself.

His brain was swirling with worrying thoughts: his parents, Eva, Lawrence, his neglectful childhood, his crazy past. Straightening, he raked his hands through his hair. *Get a grip, Darion.*

Picking up his jacket and keys, he sauntered toward the bar area. Addilyn, Raina, and Derek were busy serving customers. The place was packed, and the music boomed. As he wove through the crowd, he received looks of admiration from both men and women.

"Daz." An old client from The Black Door patted him on the back. "The bar is amazing. You still know how to throw a fucking party." He threw his head back with a laugh. "I was here on Saturday night."

"I missed it," Darion said. "I'll come to the next one." He'd partied enough to last him a lifetime, although he supposed Gabi would probably fancy a good night out soon. They could get merry in the bar like they used to do. Maybe she could even give him a private lap-dance in the VIP booth, like she'd done before. He tugged at his shirt, the thought turning him on. There were so many fun, memorable times he'd had with her, and he couldn't wait to experience more.

He was finally settled and at a happy place. Before, he used to have feelings of doubt, and worried he was missing out on things. Casual sex, different women, the playrooms, they all seemed like a million miles away. He couldn't ever imagine trading Gabi and Preston for that lifestyle again. He'd been insecure with trust issues, and scared of his emotions, and now he felt free. Almost, anyway.

Loving his girlfriend and son came naturally to him, although it was sometimes still difficult to express.

"Addy. I'm off," he said, leaning over the bar slightly, to be heard over the rock tune.

"Okay." She waved. "I'll see you on Saturday." She winked.

"You sure will."

"Bye, Daz," Raina rushed over, as she always did, flicking back her hair flirtatiously.

"See ya, darlin'."

He nodded his head at Derek, and stepped out into the cool night air. Rolling his sleeves up, he casually strolled toward The Black Door. When he was standing under the violet glow cast on the street, he half smiled. Peering up at the window, he could make out the bar staff serving customers, and swaying to the music. He chuckled to himself, remembering his wild ways. The club had certainly made him the man he was. In a way, it had cured him. An insecure, broken young man had been lavished with attention, adored, and transformed into the mostly confident, ambitious man he was today. It was human to experience insecurities here and there, and it was expected, given his past. But as he glanced behind him, and could just about see Retox up the street, a queue eagerly waiting outside the door, he was overwhelmed with pride. His Audi, Jeep, and Yamaha R1 were lined up outside it. He owned his own apartment, and was paying for Gina's home. He had money in the bank and he was more than comfortable. No matter how many people had tried to drag him down, and take everything away from him, he had succeeded. He would *never* give anyone the power to make him doubt himself ever again.

As long as Gabi continued to look at him with love, and like he was the only man on earth to be desired, he'd be fulfilled. He also couldn't wait until the day when Preston was proud of him.

Jamming his hands into the pockets of his jeans, he entered the club. The atmosphere was as lively as ever. He tilted his head to see Wendy was spinning on the pole. Lexi was on the stage, half-naked, and teasing the crowd. Her red curls flew out behind her. Her lips were the same colour, blowing kisses to the front row.

He settled onto his old stool at the corner of the bar. Jasmine sashayed over, and instantly began pouring him a glass of whisky.

"How are you, Daz?" She thrust out her chest as she handed him his drink.

"Good. You?"

"Never better. It's nice to see you."

"You too."

"Daz!" Marnie sprinted over, looking pleasantly surprised. "I didn't know you were visiting." She flung her arms around his neck.

"Thought I'd see how my girls were." He winked playfully.

"How's Gabi, Gina, and Preston?"

"They're good." He tipped his glass and finished his drink in several gulps. "Tiana upstairs?"

"Yeah."

"What about Lennie and Trav?"

"They're around somewhere."

"Okay." He pushed himself up. "I'll be upstairs.

Join me with Lex and Wendy when you're done."

"Sure."

Darion wasn't shocked to see the upstairs was just as busy. Carl was standing in the centre of the room, surrounded by beautiful women. As soon as he noticed Darion, he lifted his hand. Darion grinned at the crowd, recognising most of them. When he was before Carl, he shook his hand firmly.

"Daz, long time, no see."

"Sure is." He nodded at the women in acknowledgement. "The club's doing well."

"Oh it is. I love it here." Carl laughed loudly. "I'm like a kid in a candy shop," he said quietly into his ear. "Anyway." He clapped his hands together. "I'll meet you in the booth, and send some champagne over. I hear some celebrations are in order?"

"You could say that."

Still grinning, Darion settled in a booth, reserved for VIPs. Tiana appeared from the ladies' room and chatted with him for a short while. When a bartender placed a bucket of champagne and glasses before him, Tiana returned to managing the door. He glanced at his watch. He hadn't realised how late it actually was. He made a promise to himself to have one drink, and then get a taxi to Gabi's place.

When Carl eventually joined him, and filled him in on his experiences of the playrooms, Darion listened with interest. He stated Tara didn't suspect a thing, and his marriage to her was actually stronger than ever. He believed he had the best of both worlds. Darion had known that feeling all too well. But he doubted Carl really loved Tara as strongly as he felt for Gabi, for if he did, he wouldn't want anyone else.

When Lexi, Marnie, Wendy, Lennie, and Travis took a quick break to see him, it was like a little reunion. One thing he was ecstatic about was that he hadn't bumped into Eva.

Chapter Forty-One

Gabi

"Hello, you." Gabi leant against the doorframe and grinned.

"Hey, baby."

Darion entered the apartment and swept her up into a hug. She wrapped her legs and arms tightly around him. As their mouths crashed together, it was as if they hadn't seen one another for days, not hours. She breathed in his sweet, masculine cologne, and threaded her fingers through his smooth hair. She tasted whisky on his tongue, but it didn't deter her from deepening the kiss hungrily. He carried her into the living room, and she felt the cold wood of the table against her back as he lay her down. His lips trailed down her neck, chest, and stomach. Even though she was wearing a silk nightie, her skin tingled at his contact.

As he made his way back up her body at a

leisurely pace, he took her nightie with him. It was slipped over her head, and she was naked. His lips were on hers again. He kissed her with so much passion and hunger, causing her body to strain toward his. They kissed until they were breathless, the pent-up sexual tension erupting.

When Darion tore away, he licked his lips, a naughty gleam appearing in his pupils. His gaze swept over every inch of her. He let out a low, evil chuckle. "I can't get enough of you," he told her.

"I feel the same about you," she responded.

"I visited the club today." He ducked his head before meeting her stare again.

Gabi waited patiently for him to continue.

"I thought maybe I would miss that lifestyle, but I was just running back to what was familiar because everything had changed so much. I really don't miss it at all."

"I'm glad to hear that."

Darion began unbuttoning his shirt. As more of his smooth, tanned chest came into view, Gabi's pulse quickened. When he unhooked it from his broad, muscular shoulders and let it drop to the floor, she inhaled air. He looked sensational. Sometimes she couldn't quite believe he was her boyfriend, knowing he could have any woman he wanted.

He unfastened his jeans and lowered them down his legs. Her mouth went dry at the sight of his long, lean legs, firm thighs, and impressive cock, which stood to attention. He flashed her a slow, devilish grin, that dangerous aura emanating from him.

"Stand up," he ordered her softly.

Gabi shimmied to her feet. Linking her fingers through his, she allowed him to lead her to the window. The curtains were open, displaying the garden and street outside. Positioning her in front of it, he remained standing behind her. Gabi gasped, covering her breasts with her arms when a figure crossed the road.

"Relax," Darion said in a sultry tone, pulling her arms down to her sides.

"What are you doing?" she asked, peeking over her shoulder.

He didn't respond. His hand massaged between her legs. Gabi was relieved the window was at waist-level and nobody could see what he was doing. They would be able to make out the rest of her body, though. Her face and breasts were bathed in the glow of the moonlight. She tried to back away. Darion pushed her closer to the glass. When he nuzzled her neck, continuing to stroke her clit, she realised his game. It was the thrill of getting caught.

"Darion...no way," she argued. "If my neighbours see..."

"Shh..." He nibbled her neck gently.

When he inserted his fingers into her, she placed her palms on the windows to balance herself. He moved in and out of her, eliciting a strangled cry. As he kissed her collarbone and penetrated her, she forgot about fighting him off. Her body shivered with rising passion. He plunged into her deeply before removing his hand.

From his reflection in the window, she noticed

him bend his knees slightly so he was at a perfect level. The tip of his stiff cock brushed against her clit. Shards of pleasure travelled up her body. As he slid in a little, her knees weakened, her body greedy for more.

"Do you want me to stop?" his smooth, alluring voice teased.

"No," she murmured, pushing backwards, taking more of him. *Ah fuck!*

Darion eased further into her. Plunging in and out, he built up a steady rhythm. His warm chest brushed up and down her back with each movement. Desire pulsed between her legs, as he yanked her hips down, and bucked upwards even faster.

"Ah…" Her body was pinned against the cold glass. "Darion…" She squirmed when she spotted a shadow going past. "People can see…"

"They can't, we're in the dark," he reassured her, trailing kisses along her back.

She wasn't sure she believed him. She'd be lying if she said it wasn't a little exciting. The tiny part of someone actually seeing them aroused her, although she hoped they wouldn't.

His length filled her completely. She cried out as the tingling in her stomach became almost unbearable. Darion pounded into her, his raspy grunts filling the air. It was so good and she had to control herself from climaxing.

He mumbled in delight, clearly lost in the sensations also.

"Slow down," she demanded.

He did as instructed. His soft, shallow plunges

were torturous and she clenched her teeth. She prayed she could hold off. Her entire body was burning up, her inner muscles throbbing. Grinding down onto him, his smooth cock made her tremor all over.

"Ohhhh…" she whimpered, hazy with lust, and trying her hardest to watch out for people passing. All she could see was Darion's glowing eyes in the window, and her breasts, which were bouncing slightly.

"Mmmm…" he mumbled, reaching around to fondle them.

Darion swivelled his hips, whilst tweaking her swollen nipples. She felt him twitching inside her. As he rocked into her endlessly, she moaned loudly and despairingly. Her senses were reeling and her control was slipping away. Darion's pounding increased the ache inside her. Legs trembling, she savoured the feel of his thick shaft. She didn't think it could get any better until he slammed in fiercely.

"Ahhh…Darion."

She twisted her head around to kiss him. Their tongues swept together urgently as they explored one another's mouths. It sent her over the edge. She shuddered as an orgasm tore into her, causing her sex to tighten and burn. Delightful vibrations took over her.

A rough groan followed, and Darion bucked upwards, slamming into her, riding out his own climax. Their bodies, slick with sweat, connected as they savoured every last bit of pleasure. Gabi's limbs softened, and she balanced against him for support. She was unable to move or speak.

With gentle, lingering kisses on her shoulder, Darion then backed toward the sofa. He dropped onto it, with her landing on his lap.

"Did you like that, naughty girl?" he whispered into her ear, a ghost of a smile surfacing.

"You know I did."

"I wanna hear you say it…" He tongued her earlobe making her squirm. "Tell me you loved me fucking you in the window."

She giggled.

"Tell me." He bit her ear roughly.

"Ow!" She edged away. Knowing he wouldn't give up, she turned her attention to him. With a serious expression she said in a sultry voice, "I loved you fucking me in the window."

He chuckled. "Good." He grinned wickedly, flashing his perfect, white teeth. "Next time, we'll do it on my balcony."

Gabi's brows shot up. "Do you sit there thinking up locations where we can have sex?"

His tongue traced along his bottom lip. "I do."

She shook her head in amazement.

"We've still got a few surfaces to christen at Retox, and I'm not forgetting the pool table."

Gabi pursed her lips. What the hell would she do with her sexual deviant? *Keep up with him, that's what,* her inner voice said.

"Let's go and shower." She pulled him up with her.

After they had showered, and were lying in bed, Gabi switched off the lamp. She snuggled up to Darion. She assumed he was as exhausted as she was, and would soon nod off. When she peered up at him, she saw he was focused on the ceiling. His jaw was twitching, and she knew he had something on his mind.

"Can't you sleep?"

He shook his head. "I'm gonna watch a movie in the other room." He disentangled himself.

"Is everything okay?" She sat up, concerned.

"Everything's fine, darlin'."

He planted a peck on her forehead and strolled out of the room. With a heavy sigh, Gabi rolled onto her front. All of a sudden she didn't feel so tired anymore.

Chapter Forty-Two

Gabi slipped into her cream Jimmy Choo heels and smoothed down her short, cream dress. Darion had asked her to wear it. He'd always told her it was a favourite of his. It clung to her body, and the tight, strapless bodice dipped low at her cleavage. She almost didn't wear it, but the way he looked at her with desire and admiration made her feel special.

It was early Saturday evening and she was meeting Darion at his favourite restaurant. Yesterday they'd had Preston for the night, whilst Gina partied with Lexi, Marnie, Tiana, and Wendy. The more Gabi got to know Preston, the more she fell in love with him. Darion cherished his time with him, for come Monday, he wouldn't see him for a week. They'd be on a plane to some hot, exotic location, which Darion was yet to reveal.

Gabi took her handbag and keys off the side, and locked the apartment. Once she was in her Mercedes convertible, she switched on the stereo.

When the city faded into the background, and she was amongst nothing but the green, beautiful fields of the countryside, she wound down the window. She allowed the fresh air to play with her blonde curls, and she sang at the top of her voice. Pleasant images invaded her mind of what was to come from their vacation: lying on the sand with a cocktail, frolicking in the water with Darion, hours of nothing but making love, sleeping, and exploring. She couldn't wait. She had a feeling it would be their perfect paradise.

It wasn't long until she pulled up in front of the restaurant. She loved how private it was, hidden in the hills. The sky had darkened a little, and the view of the city's lights dotted below was breathtaking. As she stepped out of the car, she inhaled the fresh air in appreciation. The smell of flowers and the nature surrounding her filled her nostrils. It was so peaceful.

As she sauntered toward the restaurant, she fiddled with her nails, not sure why she was suddenly feeling coy. Being around Darion sometimes brought out that side to her. He was spontaneous and unpredictable, and she never knew what she was in for.

She pushed the door open, and her breath caught in her throat at the sight of the room. Big, modern and open spaced, it was now dimly lit with candles flickering on every table. White roses sat in glass vases before them, and fine, silver cutlery and plates had been laid out. Silver shaped confetti hearts were scattered all over the floor. A white strip of carpet led to the back of the room.

She self-consciously pulled at her dress as heat spread up her chest. Had she interrupted something? Or was a party being held in the morning, and the restaurant wasn't meant to be open? She dug out her mobile and double checked Darion had definitely instructed she meet him there. He had. Taking a few steps forward, she scanned the room. Where was he?

Coming to a standstill, her heart skipped a beat, and her skin prickled with awareness. Darion appeared from the back of the room. His dark hair was slicked back perfectly. His jaw had only the faintest of stubble, and when he flashed her his perfect, wide smile, his green eyes lit up. He was wearing a black suit which clung perfectly to his broad frame, as if it were tailor made for him. Beneath it was a white shirt, and instead of it being unbuttoned as he usually wore them, a silver tie hung in place. She had never seen him look so handsome and sexy at the same time.

Their stares locked, and the raw passion between them hung heavy in the air. Gabi licked her now dry lips. Her heart was slamming erratically in her chest. It seemed like forever until he was before her. She got a whiff of the cologne she loved so much. She breathed it in and sighed in contentment. Darion took hold of her trembling hand.

"Gabi." He held it to his mouth and kissed it softly. "We will always face trials and tribulations in our relationship. Sometimes things won't run smoothly, and we may need to go through hell and back." He squeezed her fingers. "I will never promise you it will be easy, but I will promise you it will be worth it." He gracefully slid down on one knee.

Gabi's mouth dropped, tears threatening to spill.

"You're all I want, Gabriella Woods. Marry me. Now. Right here."

She opened her mouth to speak but words failed to come. Was he being serious? She'd thought as he hadn't brought up his previous proposal that he'd changed his mind, and hadn't wanted to rush things. How wrong she'd been. It explained his recent sleepless nights. He must have been nervous. She noticed a priest appear at the back of the room, standing where the strip of white carpet ended. Her legs were shaking and she became light-headed, shocked, but ecstatic at the same time.

Her response came out in a choked gasp. A heavy ache loomed in her chest and she was unable to stop the tears that poured down her cheeks. She wanted to marry the man she loved with all of her heart. It felt wrong though. The day she had dreamt of since she was a little girl wasn't meant to be like this. Her family and friends weren't present.

As if reading her mind, a slow grin crossed his face. His eyes glinted with mischief. When the lights to the back of the room came on, she stared, stunned, at the people huddled together. She was destroyed instantly. She cried harder than ever before. Her parents were there, her brother Samuel, Mallory, Steve, Suzie, Marcus, Kallie, Darion's parents, his aunt, Dion, Odelia, Lexi, Marnie, Tiana, Lennie, Travis, Carl, Tara, Addilyn, Raina, Reece, Derek, Gina, Preston, and lots of other people, some of whom she didn't recognise.

She remained rooted to the spot, wide-eyed and gawping until Darion cleared his throat. "Darlin', you're leaving me hanging here." He chuckled.

She swallowed. "Are you sure you want to marry me?" she asked. "Be with *only* me forever?"

"I've never been more sure of anything in my life."

Gabi wiped her tears away and let out a laugh. "Then yes. I'll marry you."

Darion's shoulders dropped in relief. He obviously hadn't been sure of her answer. As he slowly slipped the ring on her finger, she saw his hands were shaking slightly too. Feeling the weight of the ring, she took it in. It was a square cut diamond on a white gold band. It was perfect. She stopped admiring it to look at him. He was now standing. His glazed eyes were on the ceiling and she saw his throat dip as he swallowed. He clenched his lids shut for a second, as if her agreeing to marry him was too much for him to take, as if he couldn't quite believe it. His chest expanded on a deep breath. Then the mask of strength appeared on his face again.

"Ready?"

She nodded.

The crowd applauded and cheered. Gabi giggled, and grabbed hold of Darion's hand. "Here Comes The Bride" by Wagner Lohengrin began—the traditional song to get married to almost set her off again. She clamped her lips together to stop herself from sobbing.

Darion's hold on her fingers tightened. As they walked down the white carpet, she could see several teary faces before them. Darion had certainly pulled off the most perfect wedding ever. Their relationship had been the craziest rollercoaster of all, but they had made it. They had survived every obstacle and every shocking confession: him owning a swingers club, her kissing Lawrence, him and Gina having a son together. If they could get through all of that in the space they'd known each other, then there was *nothing* they couldn't get through. Darion had been right. It had been worth it. If she had to relive it all again to get to this day, she'd do it in a heartbeat.

She'd be waking up to his handsome face every day for the rest of her life. She knew she would never get tired of looking at him, kissing him, cuddling him, and being in his company. She loved everything about him, even his past, which had made him the person he was.

She knew Darion Milano would be the best husband and father anyone could ask for. He may be unpredictable at times, a complete mystery, and infuriating as hell, but he was daring, fun, spontaneous, kinky, and most of all, he was loving.

She stole a glance at him to see he was already focused on her. He smiled at her weakly and she noticed his eyes were glistening. For the first time, the mask had slipped, and he had trusted her to see his vulnerable side. He had let her in. Feeling her heart swell, she leant over and pressed her lips against his.

"I love you," she told him.

"I love you more."

After they had said their vows, everyone was

seated at tables. They tucked into delicious food, chatted, and laughed for the next couple of hours. Waitresses went back and forth bringing champagne. Then she noticed the huge five tier white cake, complete with bride and groom figurines on the top. Darion had thought of absolutely everything. The speeches brought a tear to her eye, and then it was Darion's turn.

"You don't have to do this," she told him, knowing how hard he found expressing his feelings verbally, and most of all, publicly.

"I want to," he replied, rising to his feet.

She stared at him, taking in his trembling hands. He was a nervous wreck. She reached out and linked her fingers in his. She couldn't believe he was about to announce how he properly felt about her for the first time, beyond the usual "I love you." When silence loomed over the room, Darion cleared his throat. He turned his body to face her, and stroked a loose tendril from off her face.

"As soon as I met Gabi, I *had* to have her…" he began, his voice shaking with emotion. "I noticed her immediately sitting at the bar. She was so naturally beautiful." He paused for a moment, clamping his lips shut, and tilting his head back.

"Darion," she whispered. "Honestly, I don't need a speech."

Ignoring her, he sucked in air and then continued, "Before I met her, I thought I was living the best life I could possibly have. But then I realised it was the emptiest life. Gabi accepted me despite all of my flaws. She saw the real me that needed saving." He stroked her fingers gently, his watery eyes boring into hers. "She made me want to be a better man. She made me want to love one woman forever. I love you, Gabriella Milano, and I promise you until the day I die, that I always will. I will *never* need anything more."

Gabi wiped away tears, and clapped her hands along with everyone else. When he knelt down and cupped her face in his hands, she saw the love, admiration, and longing in his expression. He brought her head down and kissed her so tenderly her heart skipped a beat. She'd never felt so complete and secure.

She slipped her tongue into his mouth and massaged his with gentle, leisurely licks. His grip tightened on her face, and the kiss became firm, fast, and possessive. Their moans collided, their breathing becoming pants. Neither of them wanted to let go.

Eventually Gabi pulled back, "That speech was lovely."

"Everything I said was true."

She ran her hand through his hair, grinning. Then something caught her eye over his shoulder. She gasped. "Lawrence…"

Chapter Forty-Three

Gabi's stomach churned. What was Lawrence doing at her wedding? How had he even known she was getting married? Clambering to her feet, the blood drained from her face, and she knew she must have looked as white as a ghost. Darion's grin slipped as he caught what she was staring at. A low sadistic laugh left his mouth as if he couldn't believe it. He rolled up the sleeves of his shirt carefully, and cracked his knuckles. She saw a storm brewing behind his now darkened eyes.

Before he could beat her to it, Gabi dipped through the crowd, hoping she'd get to Lawrence first, and warn him. Her neck prickled with awareness and she knew Darion was close behind. She was relieved however that the guests were oblivious to the commotion. When she exited the restaurant, she was faced with an even bigger shock. Holding Lawrence's hand was Wendy!

So he had been using Wendy to get information

on her. She knew he'd cheated on her with Wendy when they'd been together. He'd lied about it for months before finally confessing. He had obviously recently reunited with her. How dare he attend her wedding after all of the hurt he'd caused her?

Lawrence's eyes widened when he saw her, having caught the rage on her face.

"What's he doing here?" she asked Wendy, her tone sharp.

"He's my date," Wendy announced proudly. "Gabi, meet Lawrence.

"I already know him," she spat. "He's my ex-fiancé." She shook her head in disgust. "So you've been using Wendy to find out information about me and Darion to torment me with?"

Stunned, Wendy's brows shot up.

"Get out of here before Darion comes over, or I assure you it won't be pretty," she warned through clenched teeth.

"Are you fucking kidding me?" Darion was beside her in seconds. His face reddened. His expression turned murderous. He stepped closer to Lawrence, towering over him. Gabi waited for Darion to threaten him, but instead his fist smashed into his jaw. Lawrence tumbled from the impact. Darion grabbed him by the collar and forced him to his feet. His arm drew back as if to land another blow to his face. Gabi yanked him away forcefully.

"Stop," she cried out. "He's not worth it."

Lowering his arm, Darion punched Lawrence full blast in the stomach instead. "That's for treating this woman like shit, for cheating on her, belittling her, harassing her, hitting her, and for thinking you'd be welcome to her wedding." He pushed him firmly, causing Lawrence to topple to the ground again. "I suggest you get out of here," he warned, his tone icy. "Now. Or believe me; you won't be getting back up." A sinister smile surfaced and Darion's irises flashed dangerously. He meant every word.

Lawrence, the coward that he was, glanced at Gabi one final time before darting off in the opposite direction. "You married *that*?" he yelled, his voice nothing short of astonishment.

Gabi folded her arms across her chest. She could bet money on it she wouldn't see or hear from Lawrence again.

"Sorry about that, Gabi, but he deserved it."

"This time I think you're right."

"I'm so sorry," Wendy mumbled. "I had no idea he was your ex-fiancé. I slept with him a while ago, and he recently got back in touch." She paused. "He used to casually ask questions about Darion. I just thought he respected him or something. Gabi, I would never have told him anything had I known."

"Did you tell him Gina was pregnant and Darion could have been the father?"

She nodded meekly. "I was the only person Gina had told. As I believed Lawrence didn't know either of them, I didn't think it was a big deal when it came up in conversation." The distress was apparent on her face. "Me and my big mouth."

"It's okay," Gabi soothed. "You weren't to know what his motives were."

Gabi was about to return to the party when another surprise appeared. Her mouth dropped.

"Oh fuck," Darion muttered, shaking his head in disbelief.

Eva sashayed toward them in high platforms, her black hair flying out behind her. Wearing black leather trousers and a low cut white vest, she looked her usual over-the-top self. In her arms was a huge present.

"Before you go mad," she said quickly, glancing at Darion, "I'm not here to cause any trouble. I heard you were getting married and I wanted to congratulate you, and here's a peace offering." She thrust the gift to Gabi. She then studied the room through the open door. "You did a good job, Daz." She nodded in appreciation. Then she turned to Gabi. "You could have made a little more effort on the dress, sweetheart."

"It was a surprise wedding," Gabi said sternly. "Not like you'd know anything about romantic gestures." She smirked. "Which is why I'm here and you're not."

"Don't get your garter in a twist. Take care of him." She winked.

"I have every intention of doing so."

Eva's attention moved to Darion. "You always could pull off a suit."

Darion tilted his head back, looking down his nose at her. "Leave, Eva."

"Don't worry, I'm going. I just spotted a cute blond."

Before Gabi could inform her it was Lawrence, her ex-fiancé she was referring to, Eva strode off. As far as she was concerned, Lawrence and Eva were suited. They could ruin one another's lives for all she cared.

Curiosity got the better of her and she tore open the gift. She wouldn't have been surprised if it was a malicious type of gift to ruin their day. Her brow furrowed in confusion when she held up a painting. She ran her hand over it, admiring the different colours in the waterfall. It looked costly.

"She probably wants us to hang this in our home…like we need a daily remind of her," Gabi spat.

As she took hold of Darion's hand, he grimaced, letting go.

"Are you okay?"

"I'm fine." He snaked his arm around her waist.

Studying him in his suit, his hair now a little dishevelled and his knuckles swollen and bloody, Gabi shook her head in amusement. Bad-boy Darion Milano, as protective over her as ever. *He's so fucking sexy,* she thought, biting back a grin. She couldn't wait to have him all to herself later. She had a surprise in store for him too. She was wearing a red, see-through lace corset, complete with matching underwear and a garter on her thigh. She'd stain her lips with Max Factor's Chili Red shade to complete her racy look. She planned to make it a night to remember.

When they were inside the restaurant again, she noticed the dance floor was busy. Others were still sitting around drinking, eating, and talking. Everyone appeared to be enjoying themselves. Gabi paused when she noticed Gina at a table, surrounded by kids who were scribbling and painting pictures. Preston was on her lap, and beside her was Johnny.

"Hi, Gina."

Gina smiled sheepishly, and her brows rose. She gave Gabi a look as if to say, *I've got him back.* Gabi was thrilled for her. She placed the painting down Eva had given them, and grabbed a crayon.

"Hey, kids, you want to colour this?"

They all screamed in unison and began attacking it with crayons. Straightening her posture, Gabi turned to Darion.

"Are you done?" he asked, an amused expression on his face.

"Yes." She nodded. "I think I am."

"Let's get this first dance over and done with," he said, a hint of playfulness in his tone.

"I thought you didn't dance."

"For you, I'll do anything." He nuzzled her neck before biting her ear roughly.

She yelped.

"You owe me big time, though. And I can think of a lot of ways you can make it up to me." He winked and smoothed down his sleeves. Gabi flushed with pride. He was stunning.

"I Want To Know What Love Is" by Foreigner came from the speakers, and the guests returned to their seats. Darion stared at Gabi intently, the admiration apparent. He held out his hand. Her heart squeezed painfully in her chest at how much he meant to her. Butterflies formed in her stomach and she inhaled deeply. Entwining her fingers with his, she allowed him to lead her to the middle of the dance floor. The lights dimmed, and all attention was on them.

Darion's arms slid around her waist, and he pulled her into his body. His lips were close to hers, his stare intense. They swayed from side to side, Darion guiding her along the floor. Gabi pursed her lips, impressed with his moves. He had obviously been attending lessons. As she listened to the song lyrics, it may as well have been Darion singing it, for every word suited him.

"I can't believe you pulled all of this off. Everything is perfect."

"Are you sure?" he asked.

"It couldn't be better." She ducked her head to examine every little bit of him. "You look so handsome."

"And you look sexy in that dress."

"Did you ask my dad for my hand in marriage?" she joked.

"I did."

"What?" She gasped. "Really?"

He nodded. "I was on the phone to them for about an hour."

"You really do surprise me." She was silent for a moment. "And the holiday you booked? Is that our honeymoon?"

"Yes, Gabi."

She rested her head on his shoulder and squeezed her eyelids shut to trap in the tears. He tightened his hold on her, as if he never wanted to let go. Never in a million years had she expected Darion, a man afraid of commitment, a man who rarely did romance, and ran when times got tough, as did she, to have organised a wedding which was everything she had ever dreamt of.

When the song ended, guests surrounded them, congratulating them, and dancing close by. Her mom and dad were spinning around, giggling, as were Darion's parents, seeming closer than she had ever seen them. Lexi had dragged Samuel to the dance floor, Travis was holding hands with Dion and Odelia. Lennie was downing shots with Wendy. Mallory and Suzie were stuffing their faces with cake, whilst Steve and Marcus were talking. Marnie, Tiana, Tara, Addilyn, and Raina were seated at the bar. Carl, Johnny, Derek, and Reece were outside smoking. Kalli and her family were surrounding the DJ booth requesting songs. Gabi couldn't wait to mingle with them all, and enjoy what would be a long, lovely evening. One she wished would never end.

She turned back to Darion. His palms slid down her spine to her buttocks, causing her body to tingle in pleasure. Then he captured her mouth in a kiss. When it got faster, firmer, she felt the stirrings of lust.

"Let's sneak off somewhere." The smooth tone of his voice was provocative. A naughty glint appeared in his eyes.

"Darion, people will wonder where we are."

"It's all part of the excitement…darlin'." His lips curled upwards. "I want you now."

"Let's try and get through one evening without giving in to temptation." She giggled.

Gina appeared, and placed Preston into his arms. Before Gina could step away, Darion grabbed her by the wrist.

"Family time."

The considerate person that Darion was, and not wanting Gina to feel left out, he ensured he, Gabi, Gina, and Preston danced together, like the unplanned, but perfect little family they were.

Chapter Forty-Four

Darion

"Darion?" His dad tapped him on the shoulder. "Can I have a word?"

Confused, and a little anxious at what his dad wanted, Darion handed Preston to Gabi, and excused himself. He hoped for his dad's sake that he wouldn't say anything to spoil the day. As his dad took him to the side, Darion studied him for a moment. He was wearing a grey suit, and he looked smarter than he'd ever seen him. He was glad he'd made an effort. He hadn't been sure his mom and dad would even attend the wedding, especially it being his second time around. When he had married Eva, they had fled shortly after they'd exchanged vows, and hadn't seemed interested at all. At the time, it had broken his heart. He'd wanted them to be pleased for him on what was meant to be the happiest day of his life.

"Everything okay?" he asked his dad, and cleared his throat. "Have you eaten? Drank?"

He nodded briefly, his gaze flitting around the room. "You did well."

"Thanks."

An awkward silence hung over them for a moment. Luca's head dropped and he scratched his neck, before facing him again. "I…um…never did congratulate you on The Black Door," his tone was croaky, and not confident as Darion had been so used to hearing. "I didn't like what it represented. I guess I just didn't want you to have the life I did, drinking it away and sleeping around." He paused, "And I never did congratulate you on your first wedding. I knew that woman was wrong for you, but there was no point in telling you because at the time, you wouldn't have believed me."

Darion swallowed.

"It's better late than never…but congratulations on the new club. I hear it's doing well."

Darion inhaled as a lump formed in his throat.

"Congratulations on the baby. I don't doubt your abilities to be a good dad. I know you've learnt from my mistakes."

Darion pushed his hair back with his palms, fighting hard to suppress the emotions that were building inside.

"Congratulations on getting married…this time to the right woman." He reached out and clasped hold of Darion's trembling hand. Then he placed his other hand on top. "I'm sorry I was too much of a drunken loser to say it, or realise it before, but I'm real proud of you, son."

He offered him a weak smile and walked away. The burning of tears lingered on his lower lids. He watched his dad say something to his mom, who looked over at him. Her features softened and her lips turned up slightly. It was as if she were telling him she was proud of him too, that she was sorry for everything.

Darion turned his back on the crowd of people. A single teardrop strolled down his cheek. He hastily wiped it away, annoyed he hadn't been able to stop it. He squeezed his eyes shut for a moment to regain his composure. He'd waited forever to feel loved by his parents. They hadn't been proud of the lifestyle he had previously led, and he didn't blame them. But now they were proud, and that was all that mattered. They were also holding their hands up to the fact they'd failed as parents. He only hoped that now they'd start to make things right. It was never too late to change your ways, and Darion, of all people, knew that. Taking a deep breath, he slowly confronted the crowd.

He was faced with the most beautiful woman he had ever seen. It didn't matter that she wasn't obviously sultry, that she didn't have the confidence Gina did, or the experience sexually that Eva had, or the need to keep pushing boundaries like the women in the playrooms. She was already content with what she had. It was as if he alone, and what he offered, was enough. For the first time, he actually believed *he* was enough. For Gabi, for Gina, for Preston. And Gabi was more than enough for him.

He approached her at a leisurely pace. As Gina

took Preston from her and began spinning around, Gabi was left alone. Her hands linked together, and she fiddled with her nails, which he knew she did when she was nervous. She had never looked so pure, so extremely tempting. So this is what it felt like: loving someone so much it hurt, that you couldn't imagine them not being in your life, that every low you experienced was worth it to experience the highs. He was ready to start a new chapter as a father and husband. Who knew? Maybe now he could even sleep without nightmares jolting him awake. He was finally at peace—with the world and himself.

When he was before Gabi, he secured his arms around her, and began moving to the music. He focused on her the whole time. They were unable to stop admiring and grinning at one another. He stroked a blonde strand of hair from her face. Her big, brown eyes were shimmering under the spotlights. Leaning in, he seized her face with his hands. He closed his lids and pressed his lips tenderly against her temple, then across her cheeks, until he found her mouth. It was a soft, sensual kiss and he lingered longer than necessary to express his love. His tongue slipped in and caressed hers, sliding against it. He kissed her until his lips were sore and swollen, and he couldn't breathe. So absorbed in one another, it was as if the crowd had vanished and it were only them in the room.

When he tore away, he saw her face was lit up with happiness.

"I thought you said life isn't like the romance books and movies I fill my head with," she

370

whispered.

His lips curled upwards. "This time it is."

"I love you, Darion." The sincerity was apparent and he believed she always would.

"I love you too, Mrs. Gabriella Milano."

Sometimes when things are falling apart, they may actually be falling into place.

Epilogue

One year later

Gabi kicked the door shut with her foot and placed the bag of baby stuff on the counter. Tightening her hold on the little girl in her arms, she kissed her forehead repeatedly. Earlier Gabi had enjoyed a coffee at a play centre with Gina, Mallory, Suzie, Dion, Kalli, and their children. It was their Saturday afternoon ritual.

Just as she was about to prepare a bottle of milk for Aurora, the door creaked open. Turning around, she smiled at the most handsome man she'd ever seen—her husband. His face lit up in equal appreciation. He strolled toward her, pushing up the sleeves of his crisp, white shirt.

"How are my beautiful girls doing?" He planted a soft, lingering kiss on Gabi's lips, then stroked Aurora's dark hair.

"We're good," Gabi responded. "And how's Daddy?"

"All the better for seeing you."

"Where's Preston?"

"Asleep on the sofa."

Gabi carefully placed Aurora in his arms. She watched as he carried her into the living room, mumbling sweet words in her ear. Her heart swelled. He was brilliant with Aurora and Preston. He'd been in the office at Retox earlier, and she knew he was tired. The long hours never affected his quality time with his babies. He enjoyed every single second. After Gabi made up a bottle, she joined Darion.

"Want me to feed her?"

He shook his head. "I'll do it."

She handed him the bottle with a grin. "How was work?"

"Busy."

Retox was still thriving. Gabi no longer even cared it was near The Black Door, for Eva had left not only the club, but Westhaven. She'd ended up with someone deserving of her cunning ways— Lawrence. Rumour had it when she wasn't up to mischief; she was blowing Lawrence's money on shopping sprees. They deserved each other.

"Are your mom and dad still okay to babysit later?"

Darion nodded. "Odelia will be there too." He placed the bottle in Aurora's open mouth.

Gabi reached over and squeezed his free hand. She was glad he was closer to his parents. Ever since the wedding they'd put in an effort to visit him more, including the bar.

"How's everyone doing at the club?" She referred to Lexi, Wendy, Marnie, Tiana, Lennie, and Travis, who Darion saw a lot of.

"They're great. Carl's keeping them busy."

Gabi peered down at Preston. He was snoring gently, a little smile curling his lips. She clasped her hands to her chest, her heart tightening with love. He was beautiful. She resisted the urge to stroke his cheek, not wanting to wake him.

"I better pack some stuff for tonight."

"Pack light." He winked.

She shook her head in amusement and headed for the bedroom. Once inside, she checked the weather from the window. The sky was clear and the sun was blaring. The colourful flowers in their big back garden were blossoming. They'd moved into a four bedroom house a few months back. It wasn't far from where Gina, Johnny, and Preston lived. She sighed in contentment. So far, married life was bliss.

Rummaging through the wardrobe, she skimmed past sexy outfits: nurse, maid, secretary, army, sailor, police officer. Did Darion have anything specific in mind? She settled on a black silk lingerie set. Tossing it into her bag, she added heels and a bikini for good measure. She didn't know which hotel he'd booked or whether it had a spa. She was actually looking forward to wearing her new bikini. She was still in good shape, a result of dance classes and the gym. Rubbing her toned stomach, she sort of missed her bump. Maybe they'd try for another baby in a year or so.

"Aurora's sleeping," Darion's smooth, provocative tone sent a shiver up her spine minutes later.

He flashed her an inscrutable smile, his eyes glinting wickedly. Slipping his arms around her waist, his mouth claimed hers. Their tongues worked together frantically as they kissed with great passion. Burying her fingers in his hair, Gabi moaned softly, unable to get enough. Darion peeled off her top. He placed firm kisses along her neck, nibbling and sucking. Tension coiled in her stomach, heat spreading up her chest as he worked down her body. Just as he was about to unclasp her bra, a loud cry filled the air.

Gabi laughed at Darion's crestfallen face. "Don't worry, you'll have me all to yourself in a few hours." She scooped her top up and put it back on.

"Very true." Darion smacked her ass, making her yelp. "We're gonna have so much fun." His breath was hot in her ear. He flicked his tongue over it before tugging with his teeth.

"Is that right?" she asked, sliding her hands on his buttocks and pulling him closer.

He nodded. "I've got a surprise for you…darlin'."

She giggled as excitement mounted. Brushing her lips against his, she took hold of his hand. Leading him into the living room, another cry came from Aurora. It was time for cuddles and cartoons. After that, Darion could have his wicked way with her.

Two Saturdays a month, he whisked her away for 'date night.' Sometimes it was romantic, and other times it was to fulfill their kinky fantasies.

She snuggled up to Darion, who had a gurgling Aurora on his lap. Preston's eyes flickered open and she pulled him closer. All four of them focused on *Frozen* on the television. Stealing a glance at Darion, Gabi thought she'd burst with happiness. Even though he was now a perfect father and husband, he was still that kinky man she'd met at The Black Door, the unpredictable, fun man who kept things fresh and exciting. All Gabi had ever wanted was love, passion, marriage, and a family. She had that and so much more. They really did have it all.

And it only seemed like the beginning...

Book Playlist

Def Leppard–Love Bites
Nine Inch Nails–Me I'm Not
Linkin Park–Final Masquerade
Menace Beach–Blue Eye
Black Sabbath-Changes
Deftones–Lucky You
Deftones–Xerces
Kongos–I'm Only Joking
Kosheen–Damage
Marilyn Manson–Tainted Love
Marcy Playground–Sex And Candy
TVA–Sensual
Air–Sexy Boy
Muse–Hysteria
Adelitas Way–Dirty Little Thing
Shakespeare's Sister–Stay
Nirvana–Something In The Way
Hoobastank–The Reason
Tove Lo–Habits
U2–With Or Without You
Foreigner–I Want To Know What Love Is

Acknowledgements

I want to thank the readers. Without you, there would be no point to my writing. Also to the book bloggers who spread the word on this series. It means *so* much. I'm also thankful for the friends I have made along the way in this journey. There are too many to name, but the Facebook chats keep me sane and makes the writing industry a much nicer place. Also to my VIP group, who interact with me on book stuff and general chatter. You're the best. And my beta readers who are complete stars! Your feedback is invaluable. I hope you all stick with me through many more books to come! :D

About the Author

S. Valentine grew up in England. Studying English language and literature, as well as law, she worked in a solicitors' for many years before moving to Spain. She does however still visit the UK, which, in a way, will always be home.

Returning to her lifelong passion of writing books, she's also a weekly columnist for *The Ibizan* newspaper for their lifestyle and fashion section. Her other interests include reading, shopping, enjoying a nice glass of wine, and watching shows such as *Sons Of Anarchy*, *Dexter, Gossip Girl*, and *SATC*. She's a social media addict, and loves connecting with new people.

For more information, please visit: www.s-valentine.wix.com/books. If you join her newsletter, you will be the first to receive sneak peeks of chapters, teasers, news, giveaway prizes, and more!

Facebook:
http://www.facebook.com/SophiaValentineAuthor

Twitter:
http://www.twitter.com/SophiaVAuthor

Goodreads:
http://www.goodreads.com/SophiaValentine

Instagram:
http://www.instagram.com/SophiaValentineAuthor

Pinterest:
http://www.pinterest.com/sophiavwrites

Author's Note

If you liked this book, it would absolutely make my day if you could please leave a review on Amazon. If you send me the link to your review, I will enter you into my monthly prize draws to win other eBooks and prizes! My author page is: www.facebook.com/SophiaValentineAuthor

I'd also be thrilled if you'd recommend my book to your friends.

To receive updates on my upcoming material, free chapters, and teasers before anyone else, including prize draws and competitions, join my newsletter by entering your email at my website: www.s-valentine.wix.com/books.

I love connecting with you readers and hearing your thoughts.